The Price of an Education

About the Author

Enver Carim graduated from Exeter University and received editorial training at Penguin Books. As a journalist he met business, military and political leaders in Africa, Asia, Europe and in eight cities of the United States. His PhD thesis was an empirical critique of a Harvard University theory of people's moral development. He ran the London Marathon to raise money for cancer research. His work has been translated into several languages and one short story made into an animated film by the National Film Board of Canada. He is married with daughters and lives in Greater London.

Reviews of previous books by Enver Carim

'*A Dream Deferred* is particularly convincing on the corrupting effect of power on sexuality.'
–*Times Literary Supplement*

'Carim's style can encompass action, psychology and a certain kind of prophetic analysis with great persuasiveness.'
–*New Statesman*

'An impressively powerful and stylish novel...written as well with sympathy, understandng and even tenderness...'
–*Sunday Express*

'I liked the book for its unsentimental quality and its realism. A formidable novel...One of the outstanding titles of the year.'
–*Sunday Times*

The Golden City 'Takes the reader on a penetrating journey through the shadows of a city unparalleled in any other book except perhaps *The Autobiography of Malcom X.*'
–*Los Angeles Herald-Examiner*

'Bubbles with vital juices in spite of all the searing bitterness.'
–*New York Times Book Review*

AIDS: The Deadly Epidemic 'Arguably the most complete and concise overview yet written...Essential public-affairs reading.'
–*Booklist*, USA

'A passionate book, forceful in its message and persuasive in its arguments.'
–*Nursing Times*

Also by Enver Carim

The Golden City
A Dream Deferred
AIDS: The Deadly Epidemic (with Graham Hancock)
Third World Development, in three volumes (as editor)

The Price of an Education

A Story of Loot and Lust in London Town

Enver Carim

 New Generation **Publishing**

For the kind, industrious and lovely

Ruth Florence

'The sexual urge doesn't leave you, you know. I say it's God's joke. He takes away your hearing, your eyesight and makes your knees go, and yet you still want sex.'
– Anne Reid, television and film star

Chapter 1

Sleeping with a woman more than twice my age who'd come to see my mother turned out to be less of an ordeal than I feared when she propositioned me: I didn't have to shut my eyes, clench my teeth or imagine I was embracing someone else whilst doing the deed. The experience wasn't that grim; it wasn't quite as awful as I'd dreaded. Her wrinkles close up was no big deal. She smelled nice. She gave me food. She gave me a wad of cash each time in an A5 envelope which enabled me to pay steep tuition fees, pay off my debts, pass university exams and become a qualified criminal-law solicitor despite being penniless when I met her.

I went to the snug dwelling in Primrose Hill she referred to as her 'retreat'. She owned several houses in London. The clothes and jewellery she wore signalled instantaneously every time I saw her that this woman was rich. There was nothing ostentatious about her, though, nothing flash; she was dignified, soft-spoken, articulate. I turned up at the times she specified because s*he* was in control; *I* was there to do her bidding. I never risked commenting on her kinky requests. It was my way of affording the price of an education which would otherwise have been out of my reach. Where else could I go for money? Companies didn't seem to be recruiting. Jobs were becoming scarce and there were dozens of experienced applicants for the rare vacancy that did occasionally crop up.

'You have to sell yourself,' the careers advisers at school had taught us. 'In your CV and at the interviews you have demonstrate your strong points. You have to show why employers should choose *you* over anyone else.'

I didn't get many opportunities to try out that

1

advice. But I found by chance in the privacy of a stranger's bedroom that I did have something to sell. In fact, I didn't know I possessed anything marketable until this stranger came to my mother's house and chose *me*, out of the blue. *She* made the offer which in my dire straits I simply couldn't refuse.

Writing these pages has been scary because it reminded me of just how contingent my future was when I was twenty years old. My career with a reputable law firm, my growing income, the drug dealers I've helped to prosecute at the Old Bailey: it all hinged on a fluke, on the sheer chance that I happened to be at home with my mother at a certain time on an otherwise ordinary day.

The story begins one evening in March when winter was changing to spring and people were shedding their overcoats, scarves and gloves, and it ends quite suddenly and calamitously amid the loud music, dancing crowds and colourful floats of the Notting Hill Carnival a few months later. I don't mean to jump the gun, get ahead of myself, but that was when the features of my face were painfully and permanently rearranged. Without warning, as my girlfriend Heidi and I emerged from the Duke of Norfolk pub on Westbourne Grove into the dense crowds on the pavements watching Europe's greatest street party shimmying and bopping by, two muscular guys in T-shirts ripped her from my arm. They shoved her away and started punching me, really hard. I shouted to Heidi to go straight home. These two guys pounded me mercilessly. They hammered my cheeks and temples, my ribs and chest and chin, and smashed my nose so badly in a cascade of blows that for a terrifying time as I staggered about trying to defend myself I couldn't breathe properly. I was gasping for air when two of my teeth flew from my mouth. I kept swallowing the sickening taste of blood. With the sounds of music in my ears – saxophones and trumpets blaring, drums pounding, people blowing whistles – and skimpily clad revellers dancing and snogging around me, my shirt and shoes were red with blood, my ribs burning, my lips split, and I had this horrendous intimation as I went down under the hail of blows that I was about to die.

Who were these guys? I'd never seen them before. What was I supposed to have done to attract this grief? I suppressed a sneaky notion that their angry fists were somehow linked to the wealthy woman who'd been supplying me with cash.

Writing about that period of my life makes me mourn again for the face I lost one summer's day in West London. Despite my counsellor's repeated advice to the contrary, I can't help peering at old photo albums to see what I used to look like. It's an irresistible pull: poring over pictures of my true, natural-born identity. I feel nostalgia for my old visage. I wasn't particularly handsome, certainly no matinee idol, but I was comely enough not to make people gasp audibly when I entered their line of vision. They never used to wince when I came into view. I know from the comments I keep overhearing and the pitiful glances I get that my reputation as a formidable presence in a law court has to do, not so much with my cross-questioning technique or my grasp of legal niceties, as with the serious asymmetry of my countenance. The twisted bridge of my nose, my rearranged eyebrows and skew lips, the blue blotches under the skin of my cheeks which no dermatological intervention has managed to ameliorate: their combined effect makes passers-by stare in the rudest way.

Typing these pages has filled me anew with shame. It has drenched my heart again with bitter remorse for betraying my girlfriend. I betrayed her for money. She was bright and beautiful and loved me unreservedly. I'll never forget the morning she offered me the use of her toothbrush after we'd spent our first night together. I was overjoyed that someone so vivacious and clever was willing to be so intimate with me. Offering her toothbrush was a message loaded with love, pretty much a proposal; it lifted my spirits no end. I accepted and brushed my teeth with the biggest smile ever.

Yet I betrayed her. I betrayed myself too, I suppose. I committed a kind of suicide, slaughtering the best in myself. And why? For the readies to pay my way. I two-timed a gorgeous girl for the lolly I got from a woman more than twice my age, a woman who, it turned out, was older than my mother.

It riles me when people talk about the price of an education as though it's entirely a question of money. There are emotional costs in achieving a university degree which can be more draining than an empty bank account, more debilitating.

According to Plato's account of the trial and death of Socrates, the latter declared that 'the unexamined life is not worth living for a human being'. The unexamined life, Socrates meant, yields no guidance as to how one should behave; such a life is devoid of ethical indicators, and insofar as it generates no feedback it is a life without vision destined to accumulate very little learning.

That is why I decided to sift through a particular set of memories: to see what I might learn from that period of my life.

Whilst he was on trial in Athens for not believing in the city's traditional gods and for corrupting the city's youth, Socrates also stated that virtue wasn't given by money, but that '*from* virtue comes money and every other good of man, public as well as private. This is my teaching, and if this is the doctrine which corrupts the

4

youth, then I am a mischievous person.' A majority of the jurors in the world's first democratic court found him guilty, he was sentenced to death and made to drink a goblet of hemlock.

One cannot help admiring the defendant's steadfast courage in the face of the court's obdurate sentiments and his refusal to attempt to escape before the sentence was carried out; one sees him as a moral hero comforted only by the tenacity of his beliefs.

But was Socrates right? Is it enough to believe something for it to be true? Does money really come from virtue? Can one escape privation, hardship, unemployment simply by being good? Or is that just another erudite-sounding delusion dressed up in the garb of 'philosophy'?

Two-and-a-half thousand years after that court case in ancient Athens when whole economies in the European Union are in tatters and people are scavenging for food on rubbish tips, sleeping rough, their sick children without medicine, and thugs are marching in the streets chanting slogans reminiscent of Mussolini, Hitler and Mosley's British Union of Fascists, it occurs to me that my story might yield a few clues.

My story is about the potency of money and one particular way of getting it in tight financial times. On reflection, and looking at it from *her* point of view, I suppose it's also about sex and how to get some if you are no longer young. I didn't know it then, but demographers were pointing out that Britain's population was ageing rapidly and women were already outnumbering men in nearly every age-group. The same was true, a United Nations report said, of the populations of Europe, the United States, China and Japan.

'Population ageing is unprecedented, without

5

parallel in human history,' the report says, 'and the twenty-first century will witness even more rapid ageing than did the century just past.'

Thanks to improved diets, sanitation, better working conditions and medical science, people were living longer, more healthy and active lives than ever before.

For the first time in history the world is on the brink of having more old people than children. This is going to have tremendous social and economic impacts. Who will earn the money to pay the taxes to afford the longer lasting pensions? Will the National Health Service have to be reorganized repeatedly to cope with more and more elderly patients who already account for 75 per cent of NHS activity?

Who will be whose sex partner when the gender balance is seriously out of sync? Will it be among the dwindling young that women find relief? Is it women's destiny to become sexual predators, stalking perennially for partners to satisfy their needs?

Chapter 2

The woman I think of as my benefactor came in a stretch limousine to our house in Colville Terrace off the Portobello Road in Notting Hill to wine and dine my mother and sign her to a jazz label. I saw the gleaming limo roll by the Duke of Wellington pub on the corner and slow down in front of the green wall of the Ormonde Gallery, a shop diagonally across the street from us that specialized in oriental antiques. The chauffeur must have changed his mind about where to park because the right-hand indicator began to flash; the car then pulled over to our side and drew up at the kerb in front of our house. It was a long vehicle with three doors on either side. Its windows were of tinted glass but I could see across the pavement that the chauffeur was wearing a black hat with a shiny peak.

I stepped back from the curtains and shouted up to my mother who was on her way to the bathroom: 'The car's arrived. She's here already.'

'She's very early, if it *is* her,' my mother called back.

'It's a white limousine. It must be her.'

'Tell her to relax on the couch. Keep her company, Leo – she's important to me. Talk to her so she doesn't get bored.'

'I've never met her. What's she like? What should I talk about?'

'Anything – play it by ear. Just don't antagonize her. This is the break I've been waiting for.'

'How long are you going to be up there? I'm meeting Heidi this evening – I don't want to be late.'

'I'm far from ready – she's so early. I want to look my best, but I won't be long. Be nice, Leo. Stay with her, talk till I come down.'

Our doorbell rang a few moments later. Wondering

how I was going to get a conversation started with someone I knew very little about, someone my mother needed to impress if she was finally to get out of the rut she'd been in for so many years, I opened the door.

A well groomed woman was standing on our porch in a waft of pastel perfume. Her posture and imperious air reminded me – I don't know why, I'm not an opera fan – of the late Maria Callas whom I once saw in a television documentary. Her hair wasn't even like the hair of Ms Callas, dark and pulled back from her forehead; it was quite the opposite, blonde and tumbling. She smiled at me and held my gaze. I smiled too as best I could and stepped back so she could come in.

'My mum's not ready yet,' I said.

'That's all right,' she replied. 'I'm quite early.'

She entered the hall and glanced at the walls covered in framed posters and photographs of showbiz and nightclub scenes. The images included Billie Holiday in her prime, Alicia Keys whose debut album *Songs in a Minor Way* had just appeared, recorded before she was twenty, Diana Krall at a grand piano, and, in tracksuit and trainers, North London's rudegirl superstar Ms Dynamite of *A Little Deeper* fame. Alongside was Alanis Morissette at the time of her debut album *Jagged Little Pill*, and k.d. lang doing her stuff in front of a mic. The woman studied the photo of Katie Melua with guitar at the Shepherd's Bush Empire, glanced at me and, nodding at the picture, said: 'Her debut album sold phenomenally well. It went to number-one in the album charts and then went multi-platinum in Europe and the Far East.' Then she turned from the images and I gestured for her to step from the hall into the living room.

I followed her in and asked: 'Would you like a cup of tea? My mother will be a while yet.'

She looked me up and down, quite openly, not concealing the once-over she was giving me, as though wondering whether I was worth responding to. She looked to be in her late forties or maybe fifties, but I've never been good at judging a woman's age; the make-up and the fact that there's hardly ever any grey hair to be seen don't make it particularly easy. Plus she had this superior air, as though she was accustomed to giving orders and being obeyed. I was annoyed by a sudden sensation of being in a master–servant relationship, an inferior in the presence of a commanding dignitary. The tilt of her head, the way she was checking me out, gave me the feeling that I was in for an ordeal, that I was going to have to endure until my mother came downstairs the kind of snootiness that gets my hackles up.

I don't normally go by first impressions. People's demeanour when you meet them might not reflect what they're really like; they might be under pressure or caught up in unusual circumstances, so it's unwise to jump to conclusions on the basis of your first impression. Even so, I felt there was something standoffish about this woman, something aloof. But my mother had said it was crucial that I be polite to her, so I asked again if she'd like some tea. She didn't bother to reply.

She moved round the table and chairs in the living room and sat down on the couch facing the large framed photo on the opposite wall of a couple sitting with drinks in a jazz joint. She made herself comfortable and surveyed me in silence once more.

I hadn't yet decided where to sit, beside her on the couch or on one of the chairs at the table, when she spoke again.

'Tell me if I'm right,' she said in a warm, buttery voice. 'You aren't quite six foot tall – five eleven, I'd say.'

'In my bare feet, yes, you're right, but in my trainers a bit more.'

'Makes no difference, not to your weight, anyway. Tell me if I'm right,' she said again, pursing her lips as she kept eyeing me in my T-shirt and jeans, 'you weigh…let's see…show me the back of your hand, will you?'

I stepped closer to the couch and pushed my arm down towards her face.

'Clench it into a fist,' she said, 'so I can see the knuckles. Knuckles give a good indication generally of a person's skeleton, their bone structure.'

I clenched my hand into a fist with the knuckles upward and held it steady so she could have a good look.

'Mmm,' she went, nodding her head in thought while gazing at my fist. 'Let's see. You weigh…you weigh…I'm usually right when I've seen the height and bone structure. I'd say…eleven stone six pounds, possibly a pound more.'

'I'm impressed,' I said. 'That's exactly what I weigh – eleven stone six pounds.'

She looked up from my fist and made eye contact.

'Is it a hobby of yours,' I asked, thinking it might get a conversation going, 'figuring out the height and weight of strangers?'

'It's a pastime,' she said with a smile. 'Sussing out how the person's flesh combines with his skeleton into the physique you see before your eyes.'

'What if the person is death warmed up – you know, all skin and bone with no flesh to speak of, no muscle?'

'You simply adjust your calculation accordingly.'

'You'd get lots of practice calculating at a gym, wouldn't you? – watching the members working out, with no loose clothing to complicate things.'

'I suppose you would,' she said. 'But the pastime would then be too deliberate, more like a programme – it wouldn't be fun anymore. In any case, I'm too busy. I don't have time to spend in a gym.'

'I'm sure it's better to have no time than too much time,' I said, recalling my mother's instruction that I be chatty and struggling for something to say.

The woman cast her eyes around the room, looking this way and that, at the exposed bricks of the chimney-breast, the carved Tamil Nadu dancing figures on the mantelpiece, the skin drums in front of the fireplace, the rack of CDs, the baskets trailing plants down the wall-unit with its books, ornaments and family photos, and at the vase of dahlias in the middle of the table.

'Cosy,' she murmured.

Her tone when she said that was affable enough, yet to my ears it also sounded condescending. It might have been that I wasn't used to people coming into our house and commenting on its contents and atmosphere, assessing the value of our habitat. It wasn't for sale, after all. I wasn't, God forbid, an estate agent pointing out the attractions of a property fresh on the market and concealing its shortcomings from a potential customer with euphemisms and florid phrases. My mother and I had lived here for donkey's years and had no plans to move any time soon. Notting Hill suited us just fine. We had good neighbours in the surrounding streets and family elsewhere in the borough.

The woman turned to me again, tilted her head and asked out of the blue: 'Would you like to make some easy money?'

'Yes I would,' I answered immediately, realizing that my first impression had been wrong. She wasn't standoffish. She understood that young people too needed money, had to pay their way in the world. I thought she'd want me to run an errand, deliver a

11

document, perhaps, or go to meet a person arriving at a train station. I was an undergraduate pulling pints at night in the Duke of Wellington pub to make ends meet. I was always short of money in those days, lacking cash, scrabbling around in drawers to salvage coins. It was so inconvenient being skint, so embarrassing and demeaning. The chance to earn some dosh was therefore more than welcome. 'What do I have to do for it?'

'Loosen your belt and drop your jeans.'

'What?'

'Drop your jeans.'

'Are you kidding?'

'Not at all. Drop your jeans and I'll give you fifty pounds.'

'Fifty pounds?'

'Yeah,' she said, looking at me with a calm expression on her face.

'Here in the living room?'

'Right where you're standing.'

'You're joking, aren't you?'

'No way. I never joke about money.'

'What if my mum comes in?'

'That's *your* problem. D'you want the money or not?'

She turned at the waist and reached for the handbag beside her on the couch. She opened the bag, put her hand in and brought out a wad of notes. She peeled one off and put the rest back into the bag.

'This fifty is yours,' she said, waving the note between two fingers, 'if you drop your jeans and underpants so I can see what you've got.'

Chapter 3

I looked into her blue eyes and could see she wasn't joking. There's no knowing how people get their kicks, I thought. I'd heard of a politician who used to have his arms and legs tied tight, a whole orange shoved into his mouth and a stocking pulled down over his head until he was at the point of asphyxiation – all for pleasure.

This woman was obviously a female peeping-tom. Was she a middle-aged nymphomaniac? She was well turned out in a black shoulderless frock, with lipstick and eye-shadow and gold earrings that matched the gold watch on her wrist and the choker round her throat. The gold chimed in with her shiny blonde hair. She was the chief executive officer, according to my mother, of a successful group of companies in the marketing and communications industry that included publishers, advertising agencies and recording studios in several countries and was keen on my mother's voice and style. She'd heard my mother singing at the Jazz Café in Camden Town and at the 606 Club in Chelsea and was sure her reputation was on the brink of taking off. All it needed, she'd said, was some astute management. A white blues singer of my mother's calibre was a rare item, she'd said – and English to boot. The marketing ploys were limitless.

I wanted the money and was suddenly conscious of my heart beating in my chest. It hurt a bit, the way it was thudding. Whether it was pounding because of the danger I sensed of my mother stepping into the room while my dick was on display, or because I was lusting for the loot, I can't remember any more. Too much has happened since that fateful day, too many discreet sessions, too much water passed by all concerned.

What a relationship it grew into: satisfying for her,

relaxing, and, for me, lucrative beyond expectations. It was eye-opening too. I discovered how youth and age can entwine in mutually beneficial ways, how energy and experience are able against the odds to overcome their traditional antipathies. I asked Heidi to let me see her copy of *The Book of Laughter and Forgetting* by Milan Kundera so I could look up a passage she'd once read to me: 'The thought then came to him that beauty is a spark that flashes when, suddenly, across the distance of years, two ages meet. That beauty is an abolition of chronology and a rebellion against time.'

Until that moment in my mother's living room with my mother getting ready upstairs I had believed what everyone seemed to say: that it is testosterone that dictates men's behaviour, that makes them randy, lustfully erect in the presence of female flesh. But I discovered that evening in spring that there is another aphrodisiac which arouses men's passion just as irresistibly: the likelihood or expectation of receiving a large sum of money.

Indeed, I have found out since then that money quite often trumps sex as a form of spiritual gratification. This is mainly because the efficacy and power of money have immeasurably wider applicability in human affairs and social life than endlessly repetitious bonking. In/out, in/out, in/out – on a bed, against a wall, on the backseat of a car or in a field, accompanied perhaps by slurping sounds and hoarse cries of joy. But what grows? What amasses, to spend on a good education, say, or on a house or reliable car? What fruitful legacy accumulates to bequeath to someone else?

If I said now in this memoir of my rapport with a much older woman that she undermined the perception I'd had of my integrity; that she made me a contemptible traitor and introduced into my heart an

14

abiding sense of shame for betraying my girlfriend, then I'd be putting the burden of blame entirely on *her*. I'd be trying to wriggle out of my own culpability. She didn't put a gun to my head, after all. I was under no kind of compulsion. Nor was I sex-starved when she made her pitch. Far from it: my girlfriend Heidi was a goer; she hardly ever said no.

Although this woman made me an offer which in my impecunious state promised to change my life in positive ways pretty much immediately, I ought to have turned her down, surely? I should have scoffed or walked out of the room. That's what an upright man is supposed to have done. That is no doubt why remorse has been eating away at my innards ever since. Like burning acid releasing fumes that keep making me bilious, making me want to bend over and puke, my sense of shame for two-timing my girlfriend ceases only for brief periods; it's a merciless excoriation.

And yet, in what I later learned as a lawyer is called *mitigation*, I ought to put the opposing case. It is so easy now to take the moral high ground, to forget the debilitating effects which being broke over a long period of time had on one's options. Events in one's early life, childhood traumas, later privations and ordeals: who really understands the lesions they leave in one's brain, the power they have to shape one's future, for better or worse?

At one point, moreover, my rapport with this older woman turned out to be painful. As I've said, it left me with two teeth missing, bruises on my body, stitches in my cheeks and eyebrows and little scars permanently visible on my forehead. When people ask, I say it was a car accident. I say my head jerked backwards then hit the shattered windscreen. That doesn't account for my left arm, though, which the guys who beat me up broke in two places; it had to be set in plaster.

15

I learned the hard way, unexpectedly, suddenly, whilst surrounded by loud music and happy people boogie-ing to the beat, that individuals who have huge amounts of money also have ways of protecting it. The methods they use to safeguard their wealth and make it grow have little regard for the health or well-being of opportunists.

'You aren't shy, are you?' the woman said, looking up at me from where she was sitting on the couch with her legs crossed.

'Shy? Me?'

'Yeah, you. Why else are you stalling? Do you have the nous to make easy money? Do you have the sense to swoop when an opportunity presents itself, when you spot a gap in the market?'

'Dropping my jeans in front of strangers isn't the sort of thing my mum taught me to do.'

'So you don't want this money?' she said, waving the note between her fingers. 'I'll put it back in the bag then.'

'No – don't do that,' I tried to smile, torn between my sense of dignity and my knowledge of what I could do with the dosh. 'That's all I have to do – drop my jeans and pants?'

'That's all. Pretend I'm a doctor. Show me what you've got and I'll give you what *I've* got. It's fair exchange under no duress, a business arrangement pure and simple.'

I'd misread her demeanour. I'd misinterpreted her vibes when she ignored my question about a cup of tea and kept checking me out with her head tilted to one side. First impressions don't half muck up your judgement.

My heart was thumping against my ribcage as I undid my belt. It would be over in a matter of seconds, I thought. So why not? Fair exchange is no robbery. I'd be a mug to turn down such easy cash. I owed it to other people also to take this opportunity. I owed money all over the place – not massive sums, but amounts that made me burn with humiliation whenever I saw one of the bods I'd been promising to pay back since God knows when.

'Put the money on the table,' I said as a precaution, then pulled down the zip of my jeans. I just hoped my mother wouldn't be coming downstairs for a while yet.

The woman uncrossed her legs, rose from the couch and I caught a whiff of her perfume as she placed the fifty-note on the table beside the vase of flowers. Then she flopped back down again. The material of her dress looked like it might be silk; it was smooth and lustrous and showed the shape of her thighs. I suddenly noticed the tops of her tits too from where I was standing. Her lightly tanned bare shoulders and arms weren't her only elegant features.

I pushed my jeans and underpants below my knees and stood facing her.

'Your T-shirt's in the way,' she said. 'Pull it up a bit.'

The thought flashed through my mind that the customer is always right and I recalled a pearl of wisdom made plain in the previous century by the automobile manufacturer Henry Ford: 'It's not the employer who pays the wages. Employers only handle the money. It's the customer who pays the wages.' So I obliged; I drew the hem of my T-shirt up to my navel.

The woman stared at my hairy crotch much longer than I thought she would, not saying a word. She just looked and looked. After a while, she leaned forward as if drawn by what her eyes were seeing.

'If I were a doctor,' she said presently without looking up, 'I'd pronounce you in very rude health. You *are* in good health, aren't you? I take it you don't just *look* robust.'

'What d'you mean?'

'You don't have any illness or infection, do you?'

'There's nothing wrong with me,' I replied indignantly. 'I'm in perfect nick. I'm a blood donor. I give blood at least twice a year with no come-back from the labs where they analyse the blood samples. I have a golden heart.'

'Do you, really?'

'It's a badge, to stick in your lapel. I got it from the National Blood Service at the West End Donor Centre not far from Oxford Circus when I gave my tenth donation. I never wear it, though – that would be a touch holier-than-thou. But if there's anything wrong with the blood drops they take from a prick in your thumb each time, before you go and lie on the bed where they connect a tube to a needle inserted into your vein – you'll hear about it soon enough, whether it's lack of iron or whatever. They need your blood badly, to save people's lives, and are grateful for it, but it has to be absolutely clean with no risk whatever to the recipients.'

She looked up and held my gaze. 'You still give blood, do you?'

'Yeah,' I nodded. 'Sometimes three times a year. I'm community-minded. My donor number is PO488799T. The time is coming, though, when ICS will replace transfusions for a few special patients because it's safer and cheaper.'

'What does that mean? What's ICS?'

'A doctor at my last donor session says it's a process called intra-operative cell salvage – it sucks blood out of the site of the operation, washes it clean and transfuses it back into the patient.'

'So the patient doesn't run the risk of infection from diseases in other people's blood?'

'That's right. Their own rare blood type, hard to

come by, is cleaned and recycled.'

'So blood donors won't be needed in future.'

'On the contrary, the demand for blood is actually growing – for people with burns, for instance, people undergoing bone-marrow transplants, the doctor said, premature babies, accidents and emergencies. He said the blood-donor scheme is more crucial than ever. There'll always be demand for blood – divided into its parts and distributed where needed.'

'You give blood three times a year? That's frequent.'

'Not every year, but I'm young. Four hundred and fifty millilitres each time. That's what the blood bag holds – just under a pint – siphoned from my arm as I clench and unclench my fist to keep the flow going. Your name, address, date of birth, blood type, number of donations – it's all on computer accessed by a barcode. So when you turn up in response to the letter they send you specifying the date and location of the next session, you just show the letter with your barcode at the reception desk, or your blood-donor smart card, and they scan you in electronically. But to be sure you *are* the person identified in the barcode, that you didn't just find the letter or the card in the street, they keep asking you what your address is and date of birth, and occasionally your phone number. I'm a member of a very special group,' I said, chuffed that I had a conversation going, that I wasn't letting my mother down. My mother needed this woman's experience and contacts badly.

'Oh yeah? What group is that?'

'Only six per cent of people in Britain give blood. I'm one of them. The National Blood Service is a crucially important institution, the focal point of an altruism that saves lives nearly every hour of every day. Isn't it odd that so many people say they love their country, keep banging on about how patriotic they are,

19

yet so few of them consider giving blood to keep their fellow-citizens ticking over? Parts of *my* blood – red cells, white cells, platelets, plasma – are in people all over London. I give millions of enzymes every time and bundles of haemoglobin.'

'You give me a good feeling,' the woman murmured, turning her eyes down again to my dangly bits. 'You're obviously well monitored.'

'You could say that, I suppose.'

She gazed at my goods a while longer.

Then she reached out and touched my left thigh with the tips of her fingers, ever so lightly. She stroked and pressed the muscle, very gently. I wasn't a virgin. I wasn't a stranger to female flesh. I'd primed and prepared my girlfriend Heidi many times, using my fingers, lips and tongue, slowly, steadily, until she was breathing heavily and had become moist, before getting stuck in to consummate our pleasure. I was cool about copulation, blasé. So laid back was I about getting my end away that I needed lots of foreplay to get a full erection – but those little touches on my thigh that evening in March made my tissues go ballistic, made my flesh unfurl, expand and sway from side to side as it rose and thickened in answer to the clarion call of cocks.

My flesh seemed to know before I did how rousing money was, how potent its promise, and was standing up to show respect.

Chapter 4

The woman stared at my erect organ just inches from her face. She saw its head, fresh and shiny above the puckered foreskin, saw the shaft vibrating, but she couldn't have known that the quivering was caused by financial excitement. She couldn't have guessed that I was in the grip of monetary anticipation, that the promise of cash was quite so rousing. She kept looking, looking. Then she glanced up at me again and smiled a friendly, ingratiating smile with her glistening lipstick and eye-shadow, a smile that had me believing I'd known her for years and not only for a few minutes. It's funny how much a person's smile can say instantaneously, how in no time at all it sends insinuations deep into your heart.

'Turn around, would you?' she said. 'And keep your T-shirt up.'

I looked into her eyes, wondering what her game was, then did her bidding. I turned to my right, on my heels and on the balls of my feet, a few degrees at a time, like a flat-footed version of that Baryshnikov ballet guy moving in slow-mo without tights on and with my jeans and pants bunched around my ankles, pausing momentarily so she could see whatever it was that caught her fancy, then turning a bit more with my T-shirt held up, until I'd revolved the full 360 degrees and was facing her again.

'Nice bum too,' she said, 'not all over the place. What's your name?'

'Leo Allen,' I told her, looking down at the top of her head. I stepped aside, bent over, pulled up my Y-fronts and then my jeans.

'That wasn't so difficult, was it, Leo?'

'No, it wasn't,' I shook my head as I struggled to pull

21

the zip up the length of my stiffy. I wanted to be decent before my mother came downstairs.

'If you want something in this life,' the woman said, her smile changing into a benign expression as she kept eye contact, 'go for it. Go straight for it. Supply and demand – that's the iron law of the land.'

'Thanks for the advice,' I said, adjusting the buckle of my belt dead-centre between the right and left loops.

'My name's Roberta Cullen, but everyone calls me Bobbie. What work d'you do, Leo?'

'I'm a student, an undergraduate,' I said, pulling out a chair from the table, turning it to her and sitting down.

'What are you studying?'

'The law.'

'You going to be a lawyer?'

'That's the general idea – otherwise I'd be studying something else.'

She smiled again and the smile widened into a grin and her gleaming white teeth contrasted with the lush colour of her lipstick. Her lips were full in the natural, alluring way, not in that two-sausages plastic-surgery-disaster way which more and more showbiz women seemed to be inflicting on television viewers. She wasn't hard to look at, actually – almond-shaped eyes, clear skin, strong symmetrical nose, a ready, charming smile – but I wouldn't say she was flawlessly beautiful. My girlfriend Heidi wasn't flawlessly beautiful either. Who is?

I realized later that Bobbie Cullen was attractive in the magnetic sense of the word. I felt that the compelling quality of her person had a lot to do with her outrageous confidence. The fifty pounds she gave me that evening obviously exerted an influence, but there was something else about her, something steely that stayed in my mind and made me perceive what I'd

22

never registered anywhere else before: power in a woman that was definite, power with plenty in reserve, but swathed in a sensuality that made it appear to be of secondary importance.

'I've come to sign your mum to our jazz label,' Bobbie Cullen said, 'and to wine and dine her.'

'I know. She told me.'

'I'm going to make Arlene Allen famous. I've arranged a few warm-up gigs for her before a session at the Hi-Hat Club in Camden Town which we'll record live. That'll form the basis of her first album. Our websites and magazines will publicize her gifts. We'll get blogs going about her singing, her style, devote colour spreads to her background and musical influences. The limo outside,' she said, swinging an arm to the window and pointing, 'is going to take her to a new life.'

'I hope it does. She deserves it. She brought me up alone all these years, single-handed. And everyone knows she's a brilliant singer.'

'She is and all. That's why I'm signing her up. Her voice has a tragic quality that can't be faked,' Bobbie said. She kept eye contact and asked: 'What about you, Leo?'

'Me? I'm no singer. I have my CDs, I go to clubs when I can. My girlfriend and I have tickets for the first gig at the Vortex on Saturday, courtesy of my mum. I'm going to be so proud watching my mother cast her spell in front of the mic. Her voice and the lyrics she writes leave print-marks on your heart. As for myself, there are only three things I want: to live longer than my poor dad did before he got a bullet in his face, to become a lawyer blasting the bastards, and to have a place of our own with my girlfriend.'

'Your mum told me about your dad Leonard, how he died in her arms, how he was suddenly gone from her, gone from the world.'

'The shock when he was murdered killed something in her. She was twenty-five when that junkie shot my dad sixteen years ago, and I had just turned four.'

'So you hardly knew your father?'

'Not very well. But my mum's told me everything about him. He was a newspaper journalist.'

'He was a hack?'

'Yeah. Freelance. He wrote feature articles about professional footballers and boxers and the Tour de France for different newspapers. He went very young with the British squad of athletes to the Olympic Games in Mexico City – one of the sportswriters. That was when two black American sprinters, Tommie Smith and John Carlos, stood on the victors' podium with their heads bowed and a fist raised high in the "black-power" salute as the American flag was unfurled and their national anthem played. My mother told me that Smith had won the gold medal in the 200-metre sprint and Carlos the bronze and that the image of them with a black glove each on the raised fist turned out to be a landmark in their country's civil-rights movement. The silver medallist on the podium was a white man from New Zealand who empathized with their protest.

'We have albums of what my father wrote,' I went on, talking to kill time, talking to keep this woman company until my mother came downstairs. 'We have cuttings of his newspaper pieces. They make me proud, those pieces of his. I hear his tone of voice whenever I read them. I've also seen their wedding and honeymoon photos, many times, and pictures of Leonard holding me when I was small. And we have a shot of his last minutes alive taken by the club photographer – blood streaming from his face as Mum held him in her arms near the bandstand where she'd been singing when that

24

junkie grabbed her dress. My dad had lifted me off his lap and put me down on his seat when he went to my mother's aid. He lost too much blood. His life poured down his face. They piled him into a car and raced him to St Mary's Hospital in Paddington, but he was dead on arrival.'

'Is that why you're keen on the law – to catch killers and put them behind bars?'

'Behind bars? Some killers should be hanged.'

'Really? You think so?'

'When I'm angry – yes, I do. When I think how that murder affected my mother all these years, having to look after me on her own, always short of cash, counting pennies, cancelling her life chances.'

'I take it then you aren't going to be a defence lawyer.'

'No way. I'm going to be attacking. I'm going to go looking for the scum – I've already started. And one day I'll be a lawyer with the Metropolitan Police. The Crown Prosecution Service has about two-thousand prosecutors up and down the country – I'm going to be one of them here in London. And when I have the necessary experience and track record, my professional aim is to be the chief prosecutor at the Old Bailey.'

'You're ambitious, aren't you?' Bobbie said, keeping eye contact all the time.

'What's wrong with ambition?'

'Nothing,' she replied, shaking her head. 'Ambition is admirable, as long as people realize it isn't a daydream.'

I didn't like the way she said that. It sounded as though I wasn't serious about my plans, as though I was some sort of fantasizing wastrel. 'What d'you mean – a daydream?'

'Having a purpose in life is hugely important,' she said. 'It focuses one's mind and gives shape to one's days and years. But it won't be achieved without the required effort, without the price that has to be paid.'

'I'll pay the price, no matter what it is. I'll find a way without having to borrow money and get deeper into debt,' I told her. 'I'm going to become a lawyer regardless. That's the best way to get that bastard who shot my dad – by smashing his support system. The time he spent in jail isn't enough. Without heavy penalties for those involved with Class A drugs – from the barons in overall control down to the intermediaries and street pushers – drugs will devastate society.'

Chapter 5

'You mean you've been keeping your eye on the drug scene because of what happened to your father?' Bobbie Cullen said.

'That's right. I'm getting ready for when I qualify as a lawyer. I've secured a two-year training contract in advance with a firm that specializes in criminal law and will start with them after I've completed the one-year LPC.'

'What's LPC?'

'Legal Practice Course – the ins and outs of performing as a lawyer.'

'You still have three years of studying to do – is that right?'

I nodded. 'It's lousy being broke. I've had to arrange a bank loan to finance some of the costs of my studies so far.'

'You must think it's worth it, putting up with the lean years.'

'I can't wait to get stuck into the drug-dealing scum. The typical salary for newly qualified City lawyers is between forty-thousand and fifty-thousand pounds a year, according to reliable sources. That's probably why the bank agreed to lend me the bare minimum, bit by bit – hand to mouth, it feels like, and interest to pay on it. But I want to know the score *before* I qualify, how the drugs racket works in detail. I'm making contacts wherever I can. At the moment the average age of heroin users in the UK is twenty-six years and falling fast, compared with Holland where the average age is thirty-nine and rising – meaning that fewer young people there are getting hooked. As for cocaine in this country, kids as young as fourteen are now using it, partly because the price of cocaine has fallen sharply, from eighty pounds a gram to around thirty pounds. Kids even take cocaine into schools – they carry "stones" of crack in their pockets.'

'Prices don't fall of their own accord,' Bobbie said, frowning and shaking her head. 'Prices don't have their own volition. There must've been a shift in the supply–demand relationship for the price to fall so steeply.'

'You're right, there was. Bumper harvests of coca in South America, and larger areas under cultivation – that's what brought more of the stuff on to the streets. Without the Customs and Excise cops tracking and stinging smugglers of Class A drugs, London could eventually be smashed by a tidal wave of crime. Dealers today pay about eight-hundred pounds for an ounce of heroin, then divide it into three-hundred wraps to sell at ten quid each – that gives them two-thousand two-hundred profit on a single ounce. They cut the stuff – dilute it – with paracetamol or glucose. They're targeting younger kids now, some only twelve years old. It was for this younger market that they renamed the stuff *brown* to disguise the addictive effects and make out it's just a cool powder to smoke, nothing heavy. The more kids they get hooked on heroin or coke at younger and younger ages, the more regular customers they have. They don't just fill a gap in the market – they *create* the market. The money they make is so big that they'll do anything to protect their turf. Hence all the shootings that have been taking place, and not just in London. Manchester too, Leeds, Bristol, Cardiff, Glasgow, they all have their turf wars – dealers bigging themselves up with their guns. In Dublin too. One day the scale of murder might resemble the slaughters in Mexico.'

'So what's the solution, Leo?'

This question brought me up short. Why was she quizzing me? Was she really interested in the drugs scene, or was she flattering me, making me feel knowledgeable, as though I were a font of information? She was in charge of an international group of companies, so she couldn't be as ignorant as she was making out. I wondered for a moment what lay behind her questions – was she humouring me, cajoling me? – then continued blabbing for my mother's sake.

'The solution is to kill the business,' I said.

'How can that be done, killing an entire industry?'

'By meeting the needs of the customers in regulated clinics – free of charge. As you know, addicts mug people, burgle houses, go on shoplifting sprees, what the police call "fundraising activities", because they need the money to pay for their next fix. That's what drives them on and generates crime. They have no conscience about stealing or lying because their craving is biological – it's in their tissues, in their blood, which neither honesty nor ethics can reach. They steal from their own family and friends. Their metabolism simply can't do without the next dose.'

'What about female addicts?'

'What about them?'

'How do *they* get the money to buy their drugs? They don't mug people or burgle houses, do they?'

More questions everyone knew the answers to. I didn't believe she was interested in muggers and burglars. But what should I do? I couldn't just stop talking and smile at her vacuously like a tongue-tied idiot. My mother had said keep her company, don't do anything to antagonize her. Be nice. My mother was depending on this woman's contacts and influence to help her get established in the music business. I loved my mother too much not to comply.

'You'd be surprised the way some women behave,' I said. 'They're just as determined when it comes to money for their next fix. Forty-three per cent of all women in prison are there for drugs offences, and twenty per cent are in for theft and fraud. But you're right, violence isn't their way, not generally. And only about eight per cent of the women in jail were convicted of robbery. They go in much more for shoplifting or go on the game, become prostitutes.'

'They trade what they have for what they want,' Bobbie said.

'Some of them do, yeah. I've discovered that the Latin phrase is *quid pro quo.*'

'You've studied Latin, have you?' Bobbie asked with a bright smile; the shiny expression on her face looked like approbation.

'Not really,' I shook my head. 'I looked up the phrase in the Oxford English Dictionary. I keep looking things up. There's no way you can avoid Latin words and phrases in the law. When I qualify I want to be as prepared as possible for my life as a lawyer. Soon as it's sensible to do so, I'm going to apply for higher advocacy rights.'

'What are they?'

'They allow a solicitor to present a case at the Central Criminal Court – the Old Bailey.'

Bobbie kept her eyes on mine, nodded slowly and said: 'You *are* serious, aren't you? Becoming a lawyer isn't just a daydream.'

'Certainly not. *Quid pro quo* literally means *something for something*; a favour or advantage given in return for something. Those women hire their bodies out, sell themselves, for the money they need for drugs. Did you read in the papers about those three young women in Hull?'

'Yes, I did. They'd been murdered.'

'Apart from being young, they had two other things in common.'

'Apparently. They were heroin addicts and they

30

were prostitutes. The body of one of them was found in a canal.'

'Brutally done in, possibly by a dealer she hadn't paid,' I said. 'They had to earn about three-hundred quid a day to pay for heroin. Their habit makes them frantic. I feel sure that the supply of hard drugs will only dry up when commercial demand ceases. It's a business after all.'

I didn't say it aloud because it suddenly occurred to me that Bobbie Cullen might be tired of the topic, but I knew that the main demand for cocaine was from rich people in the rich countries, including bankers and share traders in the City of London. They loved to be seen by their friends flaunting their wealth by snorting lines of coke through rolled-up twenty-pound notes. Even senior academics at university snorted cocaine, and celebrated barristers at the Inns of Court. *They* were the market. *Their* demand kept the business on the boil. Fewer people than ever considered using cocaine to be a criminal activity; they regarded it simply as a lifestyle choice. Housewives in country towns; college students, fishermen on the coast; musicians in orchestras, office workers, gardeners, estate agents: snorting coke or smoking it in the form of crack was, to ordinary people, no more than a recreation. Respectable businesspeople sold illegal drugs from their premises as a way of financing their own habit. Police forces across the country had evidence that the value of Britain's drugs economy was in the region of £5 billion a year and that much larger volumes of laundered money were shoring up the legitimate banking system.

Probably because she *was* bored with it, Bobbie Cullen changed the subject at that point. She smoothed the dress on her thighs with the palms of her hands and extended an arm along the back of the couch; that movement put the tops of her shiny tits lopsidedly more

31

on show. She must have known I would notice; I was facing her, our knees were almost touching. What was she up to?

'So, Leo,' she said, 'you're going to be short of cash for at least three more years, before you start earning money. I can't say I envy you. Students get a pittance from the government, don't they?'

'They get induced into debt, that's what they get. It's such a bad beat – arse out. I'm going to be broke for quite a while yet. I'm at KCL's school of law. It's on the Strand campus next to Somerset House on the King's Reach of the Thames.'

'What does KCL stand for?'

'King's College London.'

'Oh. I went to St Anne's College, Oxford.'

'What did you study there?'

'Classics – a few of the Greek and Latin poets, Cicero's *Letters*, and Julius Caesar's *De Bello Gallico*.'

'How long ago was that?' I asked, hinting at her age.

Her almond eyes went lovely narrow when she smiled. 'Ages ago. There were no computers then, you know, no internet or mobile phones, no such thing as downloading data. You had to get your body over to the library. You had to step along the shelves and find the titles you were looking for. You had to look things up yourself and make notes – discover things accidentally, sometimes. It was part of the education process.' She paused, then said: 'Do you get to KCL by car?'

'Don't make me laugh. I can't afford a car. I get to the lectures on the underground. The sooner the upgrading of the tube system actually gets under way after all the years it was allowed to fall into disrepair, the better it'll be for all of us. London Underground is ancient, creaky, over-crowded. It's lousy standing endlessly in a hot motionless carriage stuck in one of the tunnels – people sometimes faint from the heat.

Many of the stations are fire risks. They keep being locked so the lifts and escalators can be checked – no one wants a repeat of the 1987 King's Cross fire.'

'I can't remember when last I used the tube. What's KCL like?'

'It suits me to the ground,' I said, wondering which way this chat was going to go next, how much longer I had to be with this woman. Her continuing presence was like a road-block preventing me from going to see Heidi. The fifty-pound note was on the table; she'd seen my dick; the deal was done. When was my mother going to appear? The sooner she came downstairs, the sooner Bobbie would leave, taking my mother with her in the limousine.

'The campus is near the offices of major law firms,' I added, 'and near the Law Society, the Inns of Court and the Royal Courts of Justice. It isn't too difficult to make useful contacts. Plus KCL's school of law is home to research centres such as the British Institute of Human Rights and the Centre for Crime and Justice Studies which publishes the criminal justice e-bulletin called *Crime Scene*. So I'm keeping abreast of criminal-justice issues,' I went on, saying things off the top of my head to fill the minutes which were threatening to become hours, trying not to look at my watch which I knew would be impolite, if not downright rude.

'Thanks to the wheeling and dealing skills of Professor Arthur Lucas, our Principal, King's merged with the United Medical and Dental Schools of Guy's and St Thomas's Hospitals and the Institute of Psychiatry. The merger made it the largest medical school in the country, at a cost of a hundred-and-seventy million quid. All the faculties are now on three sites within a mile of one another, close to the Royal Festival Hall, National Theatre, and the newly opened Tate Modern art gallery at Bankside. You don't have to walk far for a bit of culture,' I said, holding her gaze and smiling.

'I suppose it's the best way to get to know a place.'

'What is?'

'Walking.'

'It is, yeah – definitely.'

'Keeps you fit too, I can see,' she said, nodding her head at my torso. 'You're clearly in good shape.'

'I suppose I am. I do walk a lot. But it's worth it. The view from the windows of KCL is marvellous – upriver to Big Ben and the Houses of Parliament and downstream towards St Paul's Cathedral and Shakespeare's Globe theatre. It's lovely, especially when the sun is glittering on the water, giving it a golden, silky sheen. KCL's campus is A-one.'

'You love London, I can see that,' Bobbie said, smiling a very friendly smile.

'I certainly do. I'm a Londoner, born and bred. What about you? Where are *you* from, Mizz Cullen?'

'Please call me Bobbie, Leo. I'm from Bristol, originally.'

'Bristol was built on the proceeds of the slave trade. It can't compare with London,' I said to sound interesting, to spin out the chat, wondering what else there was to talk about. I didn't want to be late for my date with Heidi. I didn't have one of those slim little mobile phones that had been coming on the market, so I couldn't alert her.

'This city was founded by foreigners – the Romans,' I went off on another tack. 'They called it Londinium. It was decimated by plague, destroyed by a fire that started in Pudding Lane in 1666, and systematically bombed by the Nazis – it just keeps transforming itself. It's a collection of villages and neighbourhoods which tourists know little about and contains everything any sensible person could want – clubs, pubs, concert halls galore, every kind of entertainment, food from all over the world, bridges, palaces, parks – you name it.'

'It's a bit dirty, though, you have to admit.'

'In places, yes, I suppose it is. And a bit more menacing, perhaps, than it used to be. You sometimes sense the tensions on the tube, the way some individuals glare and others feel the need to avert their eyes. But London has far more positives than negatives, and a population that's cosmopolitan.'

'And spectacular views from the pods of the London Eye bigwheel,' Bobbie said in a way that made me feel she was taking the mickey out of my enthusiasm, poking fun at me. Then she asked: 'Have *you* been on the London Eye yet, Leo?'

'No, I haven't – not yet. It's such a novelty, people are so keen to get a ride on it, you have to book ahead or be willing to queue for ages for tickets when you turn up near Westminster Bridge.'

'*I* could get tickets for two, you know – without queueing.'

'Could you – really?'

She nodded. 'I could, Leo,' she said, smiling that friendly smile again and moving her thighs on the couch in a way that might have made her feel more comfortable but which made *me* feel uneasy. Her thighs were clearly discernible under the silk of her dress; *she* looked to be in physically good condition too. She kept moving her thighs apart, opening and closing them, her knees touching then separating again in a kind of fleshy semaphore signalling code. 'Think about it and let me know,' she said, 'before your mother comes down from getting ready.'

She glanced at the gold watch on her wrist. 'I'm taking her to a string of clubs around London to celebrate. We'll eat, have drinks and sign the contract at one of the tables I've booked.'

Chapter 6

I didn't know what to make of her offer of tickets for two on the London Eye. Going up in one of those pods with *her* was the last thing on my mind. She was my *mother's* associate, not mine. She belonged to an earlier generation, to a cohort of people who seemed to find it easy to break the ice and become friends. I'd only just met her and she was flaunting her thighs and offering to go for a ride overlooking the Thames.

'Because of the reorganization of KCL's campus,' I said to change the subject and struggling not to look at my watch, 'I've been meeting lots more people without having to fork out for travel. Luckily, I don't have to pay rent here either. My father left my mother this house – the life insurance paid off the mortgage when he was murdered. She lets out a room in the basement and on the top floor to students. It's lousy being a burden on my mum, not yet being able to pay my way. I owe her so much. I was born in this house —'

'Really? You've lived in Notting Hill all your life?'

I nodded. 'All twenty years of it. My parents were in this house a few years before I was born. And my father's father, Seymour Allen, has been in this neighbourhood since he was eight years old. He says many of the houses in those days were run down, semi-derelict, with leaking roofs, broken windows, blocked lavatories. They were owned by slum landlords notorious for the way they treated their tenants and extracted the rent from them. They weren't above using bully-boy thugs to get the money from those who fell behind. My grandad told me one of those landlords was called Peter Rachman. The brutal tactics Rachman used to remove sitting tenants from his properties, so he could get higher rents from other people, were exposed by the press. His name became the word for that kind of landlording: Rachmanism.'

'Was your grandad one of his tenants?'

'No. But people had heard about Rachman down the grapevine. That's what motivated my grandad to complete his five-year apprenticeship and become a journeyman cabinet-maker turning out desirable pieces of furniture.'

'Really?' Bobbie said, leaning towards me. 'What sort of furniture?'

'Wardrobes, sideboards, chests of drawers... bureaux. He did a course in French polishing too – was responsible himself for the finish of his pieces, the way they looked – gleaming with a deep gloss. His hand-made pieces were snapped up by specialist shops. My grandad says it was his hands, with saws, planes, chisels and other tools, that helped him save enough money to buy a house in Ledbury Road for cash outright; he didn't have to pay interest on a loan.'

'He sounds like a wise man.'

'I think he *is* wise, even though he finished school when he was fifteen.' I smiled at Bobbie and said: 'I can't believe what houses used to cost in those days. The one *he* bought, in Ledbury Road, with a basement and three floors – he paid twelve-hundred and fifty pounds. As well as the title deeds, he still has the estate agent's leaflet advertising it for sale. But he had to work on it – re-plaster the walls himself, fit new windows, make it liveable.'

'He'd be lucky today to find a house like that in these parts for a *quarter-million*,' Bobbie emphasized. 'He must have seen quite a few changes in his time, having lived in this area so long.'

'He has. He's told me many stories about Notting Hill over the years. He says he wishes there were camcorders in those days. He'd have taken videos of the properties gradually being improved in Notting Dale.'

'Notting *Dale*?'

'That's what this part of the W11 postcode area used to be called. You'd never guess, would you, that this part of London was once quite rural. Large flocks of sheep and goats grazed everywhere. People fleeing the Irish famine came to work as navvies on the railways being built in the 1840s. Of course, by the time my grandad arrived in the district it was totally built-up, fully urban, with a cosmopolitan population. It was gradually becoming a desirable district in its own right, no longer a disgrace compared to other parts of the borough such as Holland Park and, along the Thames further south, Chelsea. But my grandad says the thing he would *not* have wanted to record with a camcorder was the violence that broke out in these parts when he was in his teens.'

'What violence?'

'The race riots – in 1958.'

'He saw it himself, did he – that violence?'

'Yeah. He told me it was the year that one of Shirley Bassey's songs was climbing up the charts – "Kiss me honey, honey, kiss me" and a couple of years before she had a huge hit with "As long as he needs me". My grandad saw a guy step forward from among his friends in Talbot Road, lean back as he raised a milk bottle and hurl it at a window of the house in front of them. A burning length of cloth was sticking out of the bottle and Seymour watched it fly through the air in a rising arc, the flame guttering in the wind. The guy had thrown it with such force, my grandad said, that the window shattered in a shower of glass fragments that fell to the pavement as the flimsy gauze curtain caught fire, then the drapes and, seconds later, the carpet on the living room floor.'

'He witnessed it first-hand?'

I nodded. 'The house was soon ablaze, he told me, with flames roaring in the street.'

'What a nasty thing to see.'

'He saw worse things.'

'Such as?'

'Such as gangs of Teddy boys in long Edwardian-style jackets, stovepipe trousers and chunky boots swarming through the streets in the direction of Powis Square in the evening of Sunday 21st August. He says he remembers that evening well because he was on his way back from a friend's house where he'd had a tooth extracted.'

I felt easier talking to Bobbie about my neighbourhood's history than about the drugs scene. It didn't make me feel uncomfortable with connotations of crime and corruption. And Bobbie's interest seemed to be more than politeness.

'Your grandfather had his tooth extracted by a friend? Was he a dentist, this friend?'

'Naah. He was just a guy who knew things. He sat Seymour down in a sagging armchair with torn upholstery under a naked electric bulb in a room where the only other furniture was a sleeping bag on the floor.' I smiled at Bobbie. 'He's told me this story many times. His friend tied a length of twine around the aching tooth and ordered him to "keep your gob wide open and up". Then, on the agreed count of three, he yanked the molar clean out of the lower gum and out of Seymour's gaping mouth.'

'Ouch!' Bobbie exclaimed.

'That was exactly my response when I first heard about it. Talk about DIY dentistry. But Seymour said it was worth it; he said the troublesome tooth was gone and wouldn't bother him any more. He said he kept tasting the slow seep of blood as he walked home, and bent over and spat the queasy taste into the gutter a couple of times. Kids playing hopscotch on the pavement paused to gaze at him.'

'Then what happened?' Bobbie asked.

I told her what my grandfather had told me. As he approached the corner of Powis Square he saw the group of Teddy boys up ahead. There were more than a dozen of them and they looked menacing. Some had iron bars in their hands, others were brandishing butcher's knives. It chilled Seymour's heart when he noticed the leather belts weighted with metal nuts and bolts which a few of them were swinging. They were out for blood again; he could sense it, he said.

His neighbours had seen gangs of thugs like this one roaming the streets of Notting Hill and Notting Dale. Mobs of about twenty or thirty, fuelled by visceral hatred, had begun attacking people the night before, Saturday 20th August, all over that part of West London. Individuals minding their own business were taunted, my grandfather said, verbally abused and set upon on the pavements and asphalt of Bramley Road, Artesian Road, Latimer Road, Portobello Road near the junction with Colville Terrace and busy Ladbroke Grove. They were beaten senseless, left with welts and gashes on their bodies, their blood discolouring their shirts and dresses and spreading across the paving stones.

Black women were stuck indoors. They were too afraid to go shopping for food and other necessities for fear of being assaulted by groups of thugs roaming the streets with weapons in their hands.

The Teds and their accomplices smashed cafés if that was where they came upon black people listening to their unusual music – rocksteady, bluebeat, not yet ska or reggae – or coming out of a bicycle shop or a pub in All Saints Road.

'Nigger hunting' the mobs called their violent quest.

'I am *so* glad that period of history is past,' Bobbie said. 'It is so shameful.'

'I agree,' I said, and told her more about the Notting Hill I knew – the music clubs, the bars, the world-famous People's Sound reggae shop, the Electric Cinema along Portobello Road, the Tabernacle Arts Centre. At the red-and-gold facades of the Notting Hill Housing Trust bargain stores people bought nearly-new designer clothes at knock-down prices.

When he was in his twenties my grandfather got a job in the kitchen of the Mangrove restaurant in All Saints Road where people came to savour the West Indian cuisine; it had been opened by a man from Trinidad called Frank Crichlow. Seymour prepared the ingredients for each day's menu decided by the chef. He peeled pineapples, sweet potatoes, pumpkin, the soursop used in ice-cream and sorbets; he cut up green bonnet peppers, star apples, pawpaws, passion fruit, pomegranates, avocados, mangoes, naseberries and plantains. He skinned and chopped chickens, salted mackerel, laid out janga, a kind of crayfish, prepared okra, nutmeg, tamarind and cho cho, and helped to make festival, a deep-fried sweet cornbread, and duckunoo pudding made from bananas, coconut and spices and wrapped in green banana leaves. Some of the drinks were made from sorrel. Bammy was a flatcake the chef made from fried cassava.

Seymour also washed the dishes, I told Bobbie Cullen to fill in the time till my mother came downstairs. He scrubbed the ovens and swept the floors. Despite the police raids on suspicion of drug dealing on the premises, which always proved in court to be false allegations, badly disguised racial harassment, Seymour loved being at the Mangrove because it had an edge; it was tinged with danger and attracted rebellious spirits. And the fragrances and bouquets in the kitchen transported him every day to the Caribbean.

The theatre and film star Vanessa Redgrave, the cast of the television series 'The Avengers', the Motown vocal group The Four Tops, Diana Ross and the Supremes: they all came to the Mangrove to enjoy the vibe and the meals conjured up by the chef who oversaw my grandfather's work. One night while Seymour was relieving himself in the men's lavatory, 'the Prince of Soul' Marvin Gaye stepped up beside him and proceeded to relieve himself too. Eating at one of the tables one night was the pianist/powerhouse blues and soul performer Nina Simone. A decade after the riots Notting Hill had become a cultural magnet, a colourful escape from the surrounding uptight blandness.

'Powis Square, just along the street from here,' I told Bobbie, 'has in recent years been dubbed South Africa Square for the duration of Carnival and has been the site of one of Carnival's three main stages.'

Bobbie smoothed down the bodice of her black shoulderless dress with her palms and wriggled about on the couch. I stared at her. Her perfume was wafting through the air. What was she up to? Was this how she got comfortable, by drawing attention to her breasts which were only half-concealed by the cut of her frock?

It embarrassed me, made me feel awkward. Her blonde hair and blue eyes were pretty much the same colour as my mother's; it was like seeing my mother flaunting herself at some gormless git – not a very prepossessing sight. It made me self-conscious. I felt a sudden need to avoid further disconcerting antics. I wanted to get up from the table and look out the window or, even better, leave the room altogether.

But I couldn't. I was stuck there. To leave the room

would be to abandon my mother; I'd be leaving her in the desert. I'd be undermining her golden opportunity to break into the music business in a big way. I'd be failing to accomplish the simplest task: keep this woman company until my mother came downstairs. Talk to her about anything sensible that came into my head. But do *not* antagonize her.

Was that so difficult?

'I've never been to the carnival, I'm sorry to say,' Bobbie said, throwing her right arm along the back of the couch and making eye contact again, 'just seen snatches of it on television over the years. What's it really like?'

'I think it's excellent.'

'In what way?'

'In many ways. Londoners work long hours, some say the longest hours in Europe. They're stressed out all year round and Carnival is a cool way to relax and unwind in a massive street party. When the action is in full swing with the soundsystems piled high everywhere, this house is right in the heart of things. Colville Square, just a few metres from here,' I said, turning and pointing, 'is where the Rampage soundsystem was located on August Bank Holiday last year. They specialize in R'n'B, hip-hop, garage and ragga. And Powis Square echoed to the high decibels of Studio One whose music policy revolves mainly around reggae, soul and garage. To say nothing of the whistles and horns people were blowing all over Notting Hill – that's how they express their joy, in between gyrating their hips and snogging one another. Carnival is tactile, it's a pulling time – the food and drink and samba beats make a strong aphrodisiac. About forty-thousand Mas dancers in competing teams sway along the route of the parade in their magnificent costumes. African masks three metres high, huge glistening butterflies made of

43

painted gauze, delicately adorned sea nymphs bobbing on the foam – the cameos flow by for hours on end.'

'I've heard the music is sometimes too loud.'

'Depending on how close you are to the soundsystems, it can be deafening. You feel the vibrations in your chest as the steel drummers on the floats pound out their rhythms. Away from the procession, there's a big choice. Last year, if you wanted hardhouse and techno, the Sancho Panza soundsystem was the place to be, just off Kensal Road. There were no fewer than four dozen places pumping out music – soca and calypso at the Mangrove on All Saints Road, funk and disco on Southern Row, house and garage on Blenheim Crescent. Notting Hill was again the most musical place in Europe, with stunning costumes, steel bands and smiling revellers dancing everywhere. Last year Carnival took place on Sunday twenty-sixth and Monday twenty-seventh August and was the thirty-seventh Carnival – about a million people turned up on each of the two days.'

'People say it's been gentrified,' Bobbie said and pulled a face. 'What do *you* think, Leo?'

'They have a point. It's more controlled than it used to be. Metal railings now keep the crowds on the pavements and there are mounted police on stand-by in the side streets. Last year, there was a police helicopter flying the length and breadth of the carnival route, keeping watch and feeding info to officers on the ground about potential trouble spots, what they call "pinch points". Plus all the soundsystems have to be switched off at seven p.m.'

'Talking about trouble spots, there always seem to be reports about crime at the carnival – in the papers afterwards.'

'I'm a law student,' I reminded her. 'I hope to join the Metropolitan Police one day, and I live in Notting

Hill. I pay attention to those reports, but they're overstated, really, as they've always been.'

'What d'you mean, Leo – overstated?'

'After a stabbing during Carnival a few years ago, one of the tabloids ran a story that was completely over the top,' I told her, shaking my head. 'It said the carnival was a sordid, sleazy nightmare that had become synonymous with death. Can you believe it? Carnival with its music, dancing and joyfulness synonymous with death! It's the exact opposite.'

'That was printed in a national paper?'

'Yeah,' I nodded. 'It makes you wonder if Prince Charles is unpatriotic, or out of his mind. He said something like: "It's so nice to see so many happy, dancing people with smiles on their faces."'

'God, how time flies,' Bobbie sighed, shaking her head with a distant look in her eyes. 'You turn around and another year has gone by. Is that right – the carnival has been taking place for thirty-seven years?'

'It has,' I replied. 'Teams now take part from Brazil, Bangladesh, the Philippines and God knows where else. The streets become clogged with milling crowds and that attracts pickpockets. Pickpockets love crowds, anywhere in the world. You just have to be sensible – don't walk with your wallet in view. Most of whatever violence takes place usually involves drug dealers trying to do business, or sorting out people who owe them money. It's heavy human traffic, everyone letting their hair down – and it's free. Not much else in London is free.'

'I suppose not,' Bobbie said. 'For everything else you need money.'

'Carnival's vibe is excellent,' I went on, wondering when my mother was going to appear. 'People come to Notting Hill for the same reasons – the rare grooves, to boogie in the open air and enjoy all kinds of exotic food

– jerk chicken, curried goat, fried snapper, Cajun salmon. And at stalls all over the place there are bowls of rum punch for sale. I made a packet last year charging people fifty-pence each to pee in our lavatory.'

'People queued up to use the loo in this house?'

'You got it in one.' I rose from my chair at the table, stepped to the window and pointed. Bobbie got up from the couch and came and stood by my side; we had a clear view of our porch and small front garden. Her chauffeur wearing a black hat and grey suit was leaning against a door of the white limo and smoking a cigarette. Beyond the limo were several cars parked along the opposite kerb; pedestrians were walking by on the pavement past the green wall of the Ormonde Gallery.

'The council's portakabin toilets were parked right there,' I told Bobbie, pointing, 'where those cars are, one for men, one for women, but those mobile loos couldn't cope. They were overwhelmed. Crowds of people on the pavements and in the street were writhing, bent over, pressing their legs together. They'd been drinking beer all day and were dying for a place to relieve themselves. It was clear their bladders were bursting and they were suffering. I waved to them from our porch and called out that they could use *our* lavatory, at fifty-pence a pee. Hordes of them swarmed across the street, rushed through our gate and up the steps here, clutching coins in their palms. It was a stampede of the imminently incontinent.'

'So you've made easy money before. You're an entrepreneur,' Bobbie declared with an approving smile.

'Not really – just desperate for cash, but at least I don't give people the red eye.'

'What d'you mean, Leo – the red eye?'

'It's Jamaican street slang for looking at people's

46

possessions with covetous eyes. It's the look that says I want what you have – your watch, your wallet, your mobile phone – and I'm gonna take them from you, by force if necessary.'

Chapter 7

Struggling to contain my impatience, I wondered how much more time I'd have to spend with this woman before my mother came downstairs from getting herself ready. I'd run out of things to talk about.

The sooner my mother appeared, the sooner she'd be off in the limo. She deserved a treat; I couldn't remember when last she'd been out for a night to enjoy herself. My mother was nowhere near old and was quite good-looking. The more she went out, the more likely she was to meet someone who'd break the spell she seemed to be living under. She seemed to be waiting for something. Waiting. Endlessly. Her memories of Leonard my father were like a cocoon enclosing her, cutting her off from real contact with the world. She went through the motions, went to her job, did the daily chores in a kind of daze that hadn't lifted or dispersed despite all the time that had passed since we lost Leonard.

My mother wasn't fully conscious of, or interested in, what was happening around her. Only her singing made her come alive. Only her gigs in front of a jazz band brought the colour back to her cheeks and made her smile with a joy nothing else seemed able to ignite. But even her singing was tied in to Leonard's death because it was while she was belting out a song in front of an audience who knew the score that the trouble started which led so swiftly to the murder of her man.

'Have you been abroad, Leo?' Bobbie Cullen asked when she was sitting on the couch again and I on one of the chairs.

'Overseas, you mean? No, never.'

'To France even, or Holland?'

'No. It costs money to travel.'

'Not all that much.'

'Not if you're loaded – I suppose not. I'd really love to have been in Munich in September last year, at the Olympiastadion when England beat Germany five–one in the World Cup qualifiers. That's a sacred date, that is, Saturday the first of September 2001. England came from behind, one–nil down, then Owen equalized in the twelfth minute. He went on to score a hat-trick. The goals by Gerrard and Heskey made it an historic margin. At long last we'd beaten Germany, and so decisively, and in their own country too. The position was finally reversed.'

'If you *had* been in Munich,' Bobbie said, her face changing into a frown, 'you might've been caught up with all the England thugs screaming abuse and smashing shop windows. You might've been arrested and sent home in handcuffs.'

'That didn't happen in Munich. You're quite wrong. That trouble took place the year before, in Belgium during Euro 2000 when Alan Shearer's header won the game one–nil. Don't you like football?'

'It's interesting. Sometimes it attains a certain beauty, I grant you, but the fleeting aesthetics can't excuse the rowdy hooligans who seem to be an inseparable part of it.'

'You can't blame the players for the way some of the fans behave.'

'No, you can't, but you *can* force the football authorities to pay for the damage caused and for all the police time and effort involved. Football is a billion-pound business. Uefa ought to be compelled to pay for the mess it makes.'

'*I'm* thinking about nimble dribbling, fast swerving, Beckham's superb passes, great goalkeeping, screamers into the net, and *you're* talking about money. It's not the same thing.'

'It *is* the same thing, Leo. Think of the enormous sums involved. Even a cursory glance at the turnover figures of Premier League clubs, their transfer fees, steep ticket prices, their match-day revenue, TV revenue, sponsorship money and pre-tax profits makes it clear that football is an enormously lucrative business. The players are dispensable, the managers are dispensable – they get fired all the time. All that matters is the money. Every time a football team run on to the pitch, what you see are eleven millionaires, many of them multi-millionaires, pretending they're playing a game when in fact they're running in their shorts straight to the bank. I'm all for people making money, getting ahead in life. Money makes the world go round. The more well-off people there are in the world, the better the world will be. But you shouldn't delude yourself that it's not about money. You shouldn't let football warp your faculties, Leo. You're so sensible in other ways.'

I looked at her and felt abashed. I didn't know what to say. She didn't say anything else either for a long time.

What on earth was my mother doing upstairs? Ironing a dress? Painting her toe-nails? Clipping them? How much longer was she going to be? I didn't want to keep Heidi waiting, wondering where I was.

After a while I noticed Bobbie Cullen's gaze move to the large framed poster-size photograph of a couple on the wall opposite the couch. She studied it with obvious interest.

'The man looks familiar,' she said, glancing at me and motioning with her head. 'That's Charlie Parker, isn't it? But that beautiful white woman with him – who is she?'

'Yes, that's Charlie Parker, the legendary alto saxophonist who blew in the bebop revolution with the trumpeter Dizzy Gillespie in the 1940s. The woman is Chan Richardson, a dancer and ex-model.'

'I thought I recognized him. Cool, so cool Parker was, far out on his own. But Chan Richardson – what was *her* game?'

'She was a hip publicist on the jazz scene who became his common-law wife.'

The couple were seated at a table, both of them relaxed and smiling, chilling out at the Birdland nightspot in Manhattan in the fall of 1950. Parker's bulky frame was leaning forward over the table somewhat, Chan's right arm concealed by his left shoulder. Her dark eyes were shining, her dark hair combed behind her ears. Her smile was vivacious, her mouth partly open, her lower lip noticeably fuller than the upper one as she looked straight ahead at the photographer. She had on dangle earrings and a medallion on a chain round her neck was resting on her bosom. Parker's teeth too were visible, his smile cagey, knowing, his eyes glancing to one side. He was wearing a white collar and dark tie under his jacket; an open beer bottle on the table was parallel with his tie, and the rims of three glasses were just about visible in the foreground.

'It's my mother's favourite photograph,' I told Bobbie. 'A moment of mature happiness in black and white, she calls it, captured forever. She came across the photo in a book about the high life and hard times of Charlie Yardbird Parker called *Bird Lives!* which Leonard once bought her as a birthday gift. She had that particular shot enlarged to poster size.'

My mother considered Charlie Parker to be a beacon of the 20th century, a supremely important musician who succumbed before he was 35 to the demons that had tormented his talent. He died, according to one doctor's diagnosis, 'of everything' – sex, booze, food, late-night jamming sessions, drugs, financial frustration, cumulative racism and fatigue. He burned himself out in a society run by reactionary bigots. Chan Richardson, my mother told me, had been brought up by her mother after her father died in despair following the 1929 financial collapse called the Wall Street Crash. They lived in a brownstone house on West 52nd Street and Chan's mother managed to acquire the hat-check concession at the famous Cotton Club on Lenox Avenue in Harlem. The club featured many of America's greatest musicians, including the big bands of Duke Ellington, Count Basie, Cab Calloway, as well as Louis Armstrong, Nat King Cole, Ella Fitzgerald, but, notoriously, firmly refused admission to black jazz fans under the Jim Crow racial-segregation laws. Dinner at the Cotton Club in those days, my mother told me, was one dollar fifty cents.

Chan used to help her mother there and grew up with live renditions of 'Ornithology' and 'Groovin' High' filling her ears. Her culture heroes turned out to be the leaders of the explosive bebop revolution whom she met regularly – Bird, Gillespie, Bud Powell, Thelonious Monk, Charles Mingus, the young Miles Davis, Errol Garner and Max Roach, innovator extraordinaire who invented the modern polyrhythmic style of drumming. Chan got to know them all. She was a white girl in a black world that was incomparably cool, my mother said. Chan was an effective publicist who sometimes smoothed the way with the police as well, paying fines when the guys got busted, living fast and soaking up the exhilarating sounds as her companions blew in with their horns and 'axes' the biggest single change in the history of jazz.

I turned in my chair after a while and looked over my shoulder towards the door. I listened out for my mother coming down the stairs, dressed up to go on the town in a chauffeur-driven limousine, but I couldn't hear anything. I finally succumbed to the temptation and looked at my watch. It was 18.40. I turned back to face Bobbie Cullen.

Bobbie smiled at me with her blue almond-shaped eyes. 'How would you like to visit Sorrento, Leo,' she asked, 'or sail on a yacht along the magnificent Turquoise Coast?'

'*Turquoise* coast? Where's that?'

'In the Mediterranean, on the southern side of Turkey. The water's gloriously clear and there are coves where the captain casts anchor so we can dive in and have a swim. There's a sunken city whose remains you can see through glass panels in the hull of the yacht. The Romans in ancient times used some of those coves as shipyards where slaves built their fleets. That part of the world is steeped in much deeper history than western Europe. If you'd like to come, Leo, I'd take you to Izmir on the Aegean Coast, where the poet Homer was born in the eighth century BC, although it was called Smyrna then. We could visit Ephesus where Mary, mother of Jesus, was buried, and Truva, near the port of Çannakale, which in olden times was called Troy. That's where the Greeks under Menelaus, Agamemnon and Odysseus built their huge wooden horse, filled it with armed soldiers and presented it as a gift to their enemies after ten exhausting years of the Trojan war.'

'And when the Trojans went to bed that night,' I said, 'the Greeks came out of the wooden horse with their weapons?'

'That's right,' Bobbie nodded. 'As Virgil puts it in the *Aeneid*, "They marched on a city buried in a sleep deepened by wine."'

'The Trojans had no chance.'

'None whatever. They were slaughtered and their

city burned down. The battle-weary Hector spelled it out: "Your walls are captured, and all Troy from her highest tower is falling. Priam and our dear land have had their day.'"

'You know the words by heart?'

'Some of them,' Bobbie said, looking at me in a very friendly way. 'Those times were brutal, Leo. They were all about blood and guts and fickle gods. Neoptolemus, son of Achilles, stabbed Polites dead with a spear in front of his mother and father, Queen Hecuba and King Priam of Troy. Then he grabbed Priam by the hair and dragged the king slipping in his son's blood to the royal altar. In front of the queen and their daughters he pushed his sword into Priam's side right up to the hilt, pulled him bleeding to the door of the palace and then hacked his head off. The poets bear witness to those gory times, and excavations are showing that ancient Troy really did exist.'

'Sounds very interesting.'

'It is, Leo, and so different. You can see the rock tombs from the sea, holes cut into the cliff face of the Taurus mountains with columns and pediments beautifying them, where people of the Lycian civilization used to place their dead.'

'The tombs are still there?'

'Yes,' she nodded again, 'and the bones too, no doubt. You're a thoughtful person, Leo – wouldn't you like to visit places that put our modern lives in perspective, that remind us to make hay while we can before bad times befall us because we too will one day be gone from the face of the earth?'

'I'd love to large it by going there – of course I would,' I replied. 'But it's pie in the sky until I'm qualified.'

'Not necessarily. You could accompany me and stay in five-star hotels every time we left the yacht.'

54

'Could I?'

She kept eye contact and her smile deepened, a kind of conspiratorial smile that made me feel for a moment that I was in cahoots with her.

'It's important to make hay while the sun shines,' she said, talking again about hay. 'There's no way of knowing when life will end – it could happen suddenly. Think of all the people who died in the terrorist attacks on the World Trade Centre last year through no fault of their own. Think of all those who go down with their buildings in earthquakes or get blown away by tornadoes despite their insurance policies and the care with which they look right and left before crossing a street. They were probably all innocent, all peace-loving, but their number was up. We're living in dangerous times, Leo. Terrorists are out to get us. Who thought we'd ever worry about anthrax spores in our mail, or people planting bombs in hotel basements, in restaurants? Who knows what's coming next, and where from?'

I kept eye contact and wondered why she, a total stranger, was talking about such deep things. To die suddenly, to die in your prime, was such a terrible waste, I felt, even though I myself hadn't yet got to anywhere near my prime. Death was the last thing on my mind.

Then Bobbie said: 'Your mother's eyes are violet blue, Leo, more or less the same shade as mine, but yours are dark brown.'

'That's because my dad's eyes were dark brown,' I said. '*His* grandparents were from Jamaica. They took him there once to see the island where their ancestors had lived.'

She nodded: 'And your lovely amber skin – it's their complexions combined, your mum and dad's. It has a tint of golden honey in it, your skin.'

'People in the Caribbean call it "high complexion",'
I told her. 'It's a way of saying someone's the product
of a racially mixed marriage. My hair used to be quite
fair too, my mother says, but for some reason it
darkened as I grew older.' I couldn't help smiling after
I'd said the words, which seemed to imply that I wasn't
young any more.

'You've only ever lived in this house?' Bobbie said.

'Yeah. I love this house. I was brought up here and
now I do a hell of a lot of reading here – law books
mainly, and some history and politics. I read early
every morning for a few hours, and four nights a week
non-stop from seven to one or two a.m. There's so
much to get through and remember – law of contract,
tort, criminal law, principles of the law of evidence,
criminal responsibility, the law of the European Union.
I also scan *The Lawyer Magazine*, *The Law Society
Gazette* and *Criminal Justice Matters* to keep up to date
with changes in the legal profession. Law books are
expensive. They set me back a lot, even at secondhand
prices, but there's too much of a scramble in the
library. I suppose being broke comes with the territory
– it's what being a student means, always short of the
readies.'

'It doesn't have to mean that, you know.'

'It doesn't?'

'That fifty there,' Bobbie said, motioning with her
head to the note by the vase of dahlias on the table, 'put
it in your pocket. It's yours.'

I eyed her and reached for the money. I couldn't
remember if I'd seen a fifty-pound note before. I
looked at the Queen's face which seemed more radiant
than ever, then at a guy called Sir John Houblon on the
other side; I discovered later he was the first governor
of the Bank of England, standing in front of his house
in Threadneedle Street. I folded the note and pushed it

into the right-hand pocket of my jeans.

'You like that money, don't you?' Bobbie said.

'No diggity. It's off the hook,' I agreed happily.

'There's very much more where it came from,' she declared, keeping eye contact. 'You could start repaying your mum for all her support, instead of having to wait years to show your gratitude. You could buy her gifts – you'd have the means to show your appreciation.'

'Would I?'

'Of course you would. We're consenting adults, Leo – you and I. Our agreements are well within the law and made under no duress. We aren't harming anyone.'

I loved her gaze and gazed right back.

'Keep it a secret,' she said, 'and I'll give you a whole lot more. Is it a deal?'

'Very much so,' I grinned.

'Let's shake on it then – a secret.'

She rose from the couch and pushed her right hand out towards me. I rose from the chair by the table and clasped her palm; I felt her flesh squeezing mine back as we looked into each other's eyes. It was strange standing there shaking the hand in secret of my mother's business manager.

'What will I have to do for the extra money?' I asked. 'Drop my jeans again?'

'No,' she said. 'It's easy money, but not *that* easy. You'll have to do more than that. I always look before I leap.'

'What then?'

'You'll have to be my companion, keep me company after hours. Sleep with me when I'm in the mood and have the time. Kiss me thoughtfully here and there.'

'Kiss you? Sleep with you? You mean —'

She must have noticed the flabbergast on my face, the effect of her totally unexpected words. She looked

57

so suave and sophisticated, so wealthy and comfortable in herself that I wondered if perhaps I'd misheard her, but she said: 'Yeah, that's what I mean. Be sensuous, and satisfy me in a big wide bed.'

'Satisfy you? You mean...really?' I searched her face. 'You want me to...give you one?'

'Not just one, necessarily. Not in and out and Bob's your uncle. I loved what I saw when you dropped your pants, the way your flesh swung up when I touched your thigh. You're full of the energy I love.'

'You aren't kidding, are you?' I said, the possibility registering for the first time that money might soon be filling my pockets, not just the fifty-pound note I'd already received. The thought was vitalizing; it sent a surge of energy through me, rousing my flesh to press up against the denim of my jeans. Financial desire, I was discovering, was just as uplifting as sexual desire. Both kinds excited tissues and membranes deep in one's being.

I did something then I'd never done before. I began to wonder what sort of experience sleeping with an older woman, trying to pleasure an older woman, would be. Not *any* older woman, of course, but one rendered immensely charming and delightful by huge supplies of disposable income. I'd only ever been sensuous with girls my own age, and for the last two years and a bit it had been Heidi's insides that I'd enjoyed, hers alone, faithfully, after preparing her from the outside for the pleasures to come.

'I never kid about money,' Bobbie Cullen said. 'Money is the measure of value, and I expect value for money – a high ratio of bangs per buck.'

'Meaning what, exactly?'

'Customer satisfaction,' she replied, looking me straight in the eyes. It suddenly sounded as though she was talking about business, about a commercial

58

transaction. 'After-sales service, customer loyalty,' she said. 'The care that makes people come back for more fulfilment, to feel renewed again.' I was sure I heard a tremor in her voice when she added: 'The longer you can go, the better. You *look* as though you have the requisite stamina, but *do* you? I've found to my cost that looks can be deceptive.'

'This big wide bed – where exactly is it?'

She turned back to the couch and picked up her bag by its straps. She opened it, brought out a card and gave it to me.

'That's the address of one of my houses in London, the one where I unwind,' she said, pointing to the card. 'It's my retreat. I relax there, let my hair down. I'll show my gratitude if you come to that address tomorrow night at ten.'

'No kidding?'

'None whatever. But don't come before ten. I'm meeting television people on Lake Lucerne in Switzerland tomorrow after taking your mother out tonight. What's your favourite fruit?'

'I like all kinds of fruit,' I said, bemused a bit by her zig-zagging chat.

'But what d'you like *best*?' Bobbie prompted. 'Tell me and I'll have a special treat prepared.'

I thought about it for a moment, and said: 'Mangoes. I do love ripe mangoes. I've enjoyed them since I was a kid.'

'Ripe mangoes it'll be then,' she smiled. Then she added: 'There's something else I'll want to see when you turn up. I always look before I leap. Don't forget to bring it.'

'What d'you mean? Bring what?'

'That blood-donor barcode you mentioned earlier.'

Chapter 8

The fifty-pound note didn't burn a hole in my pocket; it didn't stay in my pocket long enough. What it did instead was put me in two horny dilemmas.

I hadn't seen Heidi in five days and had arranged to take her for a bite on the roof terrace of the *Brasserie en Haut* overlooking the bustle of Portobello Market. The food there was French provincial and Italian, reasonably priced and you could have drinks too without feeling a pain in your wallet.

It was about time I did the paying. Heidi was always picking up the tab, always opening her purse when we went out. I felt shit about it, I felt I was an incorrigible scrounger, but she kept insisting that it didn't matter. It made sense for her to cough up, she said, since her parents were loaded and gave her more money than she needed. It was Heidi who paid for the two £30 tickets when we caught the gig at the Barbican Centre where Sonny Rollins blew the house down with his tenor sax. The place was packed full, no standing room either. The audience responded to the sextet on stage with rapturous applause, such was the quality of the music. I loved every minute of the magic those American jazzmen were making, but I suspect that my hands began to sting as I clapped, not just from the resounding pressure of flesh on flesh, but also from a sense of penance for yet again not paying my way. With Heidi by my side, it occurred to me once more that in certain situations money showed itself definitely to be a gendered thing.

Usually, however, it was the *theatre* Heidi bought tickets for because she was heavily into drama. Drama was her passion. She said you couldn't appreciate a play properly if you didn't surrender your imagination to it entirely; suspension of disbelief was crucial.

It was thanks to Heidi that I first went to the Old Vic on the south side of the Thames beyond Waterloo Station. We witnessed a production of *Macbeth* there; it was one of Heidi's favourite plays. She seemed to go into a trance during the opening scene where the witches do their chanting against the background of thunder and lightning: 'When shall we three meet again?/ In thunder, lightning, or in rain?'/ 'When the hurly burly's done,/ When the battle's lost and won.'/ 'That will be ere the set of sun'. And a little later they all three cry out: 'Fair is foul, and foul is fair:/ Hover through the fog and filthy air.' Heidi gripped my forearm so hard I thought she was going to break the bone or start me bleeding with the nails of her fingers. When I tried to draw her attention to the pain she was causing, she silenced me with an exasperated 'Shhh!'

Heidi's mother was German and her father English – her full name was Heidi Hildegard Hathaway – and she was perfectly bilingual. She too was a student, studying comparative literature at University College London on the Bloomsbury campus between Gower Street and Woburn Place. Her parents had met at the Goethe Institute off Exhibition Road on the west side of town where her mother was working whilst immersing herself in the English language and where her father had gone to enquire about the possibility of consulting particular Schiller manuscripts at first hand. There was nothing Eurosceptic about Heidi's family. The way they travelled back and forth from London to Berlin, London to Frankfurt, to Munich, going to concerts and art galleries and switching from English to German when they spoke, sometimes in the same sentence, you'd think the two countries were a single space in their minds and the two languages branches of a common heritage.

When the euro became legal tender on New Year's Day 2002 in twelve member states of the EU, Heidi's parents said it was a wise and inevitable development. It didn't seem to bother them that German marks, French francs, Spanish pesetas and other traditional currencies were about to disappear into history. Those monies were everyday symbols of the divisions that had fragmented Europe in the past, they said. Discussions in the media of the imminent single currency hadn't really penetrated my consciousness; it was a distant, foreign matter. The switch-over, when it did happen, only registered with me in London because it was a prelude to the big positive change in my own finances which began three months later, in March 2002, when Bobbie Cullen came into my life and offered me fifty pounds to show her what I had.

Heidi told me that one of her parents' favourite composers was Handel, a German who'd spent the last forty-odd years of his life in England. He wrote music that is still performed today, Heidi said, especially the oratorio *Messiah* with its stirring 'Hallelujah' chorus, and the *Water Music*, composed in 1717 to entertain the Elector of Hanover who'd become King George I as he made a journey by barge on the Thames from Whitehall to Chelsea. It was Heidi also who told me that Sir Simon Rattle, the celebrated conductor, used to be a jazz drummer in his teens and that his father felt betrayed when he moved full-time into classical music. He became principal conductor of the Berlin Philharmonic Orchestra in 1999.

Heidi's was certainly a cultured background. She knew the slang words for 'cunnilingus' in six languages and would recite love poetry by heart as she lay with her head on the pillow and my head between her thighs, jerking from time to time with the joy my tongue was propelling into her, slurring some of the words in consequence. The words were from Shakespeare's sonnets, from Congreve, from D.H. Lawrence:

'All I ask of a woman is that she shall feel gently towards me when my heart feels kindly towards her.'

Heidi felt gently towards me – no doubt about it. She lived with her parents in an airy, spacious Edwardian house off the Brompton Road behind the Victoria & Albert Museum, not a long walk from South Kensington tube station. That's how I used to get there: on the Circle Line from Notting Hill. Heidi too was an only child. She had her own room and bathroom and the use of her parents' extensive library which lined the walls of the house's three other bedrooms and boasted a gleaming grand piano, furniture with leather upholstery and tables with inlaid surfaces holding brass reading lamps. Heidi told me her parents had chosen to live in that part of London because they felt it was lucky for them: they'd first seen each other in a building in that district near the Natural History Museum.

One of the first things Heidi's father did when he and her mother started going out together was take her to see the Albert Memorial in Kensington Gardens. Queen Victoria had adored her German husband. Theirs had been a pretty erotic relationship, Heidi told me, and their passion had given them nine children – five daughters and four sons – who in turn married into other royal families across Europe; there was, Heidi said, nothing insular about them. When Prince Albert died of typhoid at Windsor Castle in 1861 after 21 years of marriage, the queen went into mourning and sank into a kind of depression for a very long time, but rallied sufficiently to commission the Albert Memorial in memory of her beloved husband. The structure, designed in the Gothic Revival style and located on a grassy knoll now facing the Albert Hall, was opened by Queen Victoria herself in 1872. Heidi told me it became a rendezvous for *her* Anglo-German parents, Ilse and Gregory Hathaway, when *they* became an item.

Her parents were friendly and kind when Heidi introduced me to them. They enquired about my studies, offered to lend me books, invited me to have meals with them, which I thoroughly enjoyed on several occasions. Their chat at table was sprinkled with phrases such as *es ist schade, es macht nichts, wie spät ist es? Wecken Sie mich bitte um Sieben Uhr.* They were away from home a lot of the time, travelling in Europe, happy to be constantly in each other's company.

I did what I could to make up for having so little money. When Heidi said she wanted to renovate and redecorate her room, I pulled up the old carpet and removed all the metal grips. I tied a hankie round the back of my head to protect my nostrils from the dust and renewed the wooden look of the floorboards in her room with an electric sander, sealing it in with a coat of varnish. I put on overalls and a baseball cap and painted the ceiling and the walls of her room in her preferred colours – undercoat and two topcoats all round. Heidi removed the paintings from the alcoves and I fitted bookshelves into them. I also scraped layers of gunge from around the fireplace and restored the lustre of the black marble mantelpiece with a lot of elbow grease.

'It's all so clean and fresh,' Heidi said when the work was done. 'You've made it new, Leo. Thank you so much.'

'It's my pleasure. I'll do anything for you, Heidi. You know that, don't you?'

'Yes, I do.'

She'd stepped out of the bathroom and had a towel wrapped round her shapely body, her damp fair hair hanging in clumps. She kissed me long and lovingly and when she was dressed took me down to the living room and made tea which we drank whilst watching television. Heidi was keen on *Frasier* and *The Simpsons*; they made her laugh out loud and come out with witty comments, slapping my thigh sometimes when a scene struck her as particularly hilarious.

She'd say something in German once in a while, and though she always translated it because she was too polite to leave me wondering what was on her mind, I would realize anew each time that there were parts of her that were out of my reach. The German side of her periodically put a distance between us. It was the kind of gap that hadn't bothered her English father or German mother one bit and it made me feel parochial. It had to do with slightly different ways of perceiving and saying things, which in my case came across as blurred, as though I'd seen them through frosted glass. It was a gap which Heidi herself wasn't conscious of at all, so willingly did she offer her other gap to me, the one between her thighs covered in a mat of hair which she made more accessible for penetration by lifting her legs and draping them over my shoulders.

Heidi was well balanced, out-going and very game in bed.

How the hell was I going to tell her about the fifty quid?

That was my first dilemma.

If I didn't tell her that an executive woman in her forties or fifties had given me money for showing her my cock and had promised me lots more money to sleep with her the very next night, I'd be living a lie. I'd be withholding material information from my beloved. The gap between us would become a ditch full of reeking rubbish. I'd be a liar and feel like a traitor and pine for my honest self again. But if I did tell her about the deal I'd done with that communications high-flyer who was more than twice my age, who was, possibly, *older than my mother* – if I did tell her I'd given my word and shaken hands to seal the deal, I would lose Heidi right away. I knew that for a fact. And my word as far as Heidi was concerned would thereafter be worthless.

Tears would well up in her eyes. She'd go pale from pain and shock. That would be the effect, not only of the betrayal itself but also of the realization that I'd been *capable* of betraying her all along. Heidi's feelings weren't coarse. Her emotions seemed to be just as educated as her intellect. That was one of the best things about being with her: one felt the allure in her company of a sophisticated sensibility that was nevertheless rooted in the rigours of the real world. The better I got to know Heidi, the more things I found in her to love. I had a dream in my heart that was going to be the crowning glory of my life: having children with her and bringing them up internationally after we'd gone travelling and made love in cities across the world. Heidi was never arsey about money, never bolshie.

'The view from here is great,' she said as we sat at our table on the roof terrace of the *Brasserie en Haut* overlooking the bustle of Portobello Market.

'I knew you'd like it,' I replied.

All the other tables were taken as well. The place was crowded and the waiters had to twist and turn between the backs of the chairs, doing a boogie as they balanced the plates and brought the food to the diners who turned and smiled at them appreciatively.

The lights in the street below, the goods in the illuminated windows – furniture, clothing, jewellery, tapestries – the pedestrians on the crowded pavements checking out the merchandise for sale on the stalls, the occasional cry of a trader drawing attention to the quality of his produce much in the way that London's costermongers had been touting their wares for centuries – the hubbub of Portobello Market rose up to where we were seated and mingled with the smell of steaming bourguignon and platefuls of pasta and filled me with guilt and a chastising sense that this was not the setting in which to break bad news.

I had a vision suddenly right there in the crowded restaurant of Bobbie Cullen as a toothless hag in a frayed dressing-gown bent over a zimmer frame as she shuffled forward in slippers too loose for her feet. I saw myself in her bedroom lifting the duvet like an impatient lover and flinging it aside to reveal – ye gods! – a shrunken body barely distinguishable from the pale white sheet and barely moving with each shallow breath. Her face was fallen in, torso full of hollows, the pelvic bone plain to see pressing against her dry brittle skin, the place where her pussy should have been a calcified crater with three or four threads of colourless cotton, the remains of her pubic hair. Her arms and legs too were frail and puckered, the leftovers of flesh hanging like flags at half-mast in memory, it seemed to me in my guilt, of a youthfulness that had long since passed away. The vision was the exact opposite of the beautiful, warm-blooded person sitting opposite me at the table.

'Are you all right, Leo?' Heidi asked, watching me closely, her fingers toying with the napkin.

'Yeah. I'm fine.'

'You don't look fine.'

'What d'you mean?'

'You look different.'

'Different? In what way?'

'I don't know – worried, uncomfortable.'

'Why should I be uncomfortable?'

'How should *I* know? That's why I'm asking – are

67

you okay?'

'Of course I'm okay,' I smiled, resting my arms on the check tablecloth. 'Can't you see?'

'It isn't the money, is it?'

'What money?' How on earth could she know about the money I wondered in alarm. I tried to keep the smile on my face and tried also at the same time not to appear too studied, even though I knew as a law student that the face an individual presented to the world was very probably just a face in another sense of the word – a façade, a front, a mask behind which anything on earth could be going on. God: when you're guilty the whole theory and dynamics of blameworthiness botches your serenity and bowls over your best efforts to appear blasé. You understand from the inside better than many qualified lawyers what *tort* is all about: injurious, harmful deeds that don't involve a breach of contract but for which a civil action can be brought.

'The money to pay for our meals tonight,' Heidi said. 'Are you sure you have enough?'

'Of course I have enough,' I said, sighing in relief, sighing thankfully, then adding: 'Otherwise I wouldn't have asked you out. And on Saturday it's the Vortex in Stoke Newington – remember?'

'I remember,' she nodded and smiled in her lovely way. 'I'm looking forward to hearing your mother sing. I've always liked her voice, but I've never heard her sing.'

'You're in for a treat. There might be other gigs after that one.'

'I can't wait for Saturday, Leo. But for the mo, if you need help with the bill —'

'I don't need any help, Heidi,' I cut in. 'This isn't the Ritz Hotel or the Savoy. It's a place that gives value for money and it has an excellent view of the goings-on down there,' motioning with my head to the street.

'Why are you so touchy, then?'

'What d'you mean – touchy?'

'You know, uptight. Your face is twitching as if you've got a nervous disorder.'

'Since when have you been a doctor?'

'I'm not a doctor, Leo. What's with you?'

'I'm sick and tired, that's what.'

'Sick of what, exactly?'

'Sick of needing your help. Sick of not having enough money. Sick of you paying for everything and standing by with your fat bank account in case I stumble and can't scrape together the readies to pay my way.'

Her eyes dimmed and a shadow darkened her countenance. Her eyes were brown with just a tinge of green; I loved looking at them. She regarded me in silence for a long while. I hated myself for upsetting her. I hated myself for putting her on the receiving end of anything other than kindness, love and friendship. Most of all, I hated the way I'd just sounded – whining about a disability I could find no one to blame for, bleating like a wimp because the gods had dealt me a dud hand and left me without the loot to start life on the right side of the tracks.

Being broke tempted me sorely to believe that money was the root of all evil. It tempted me to believe that money drained the natural beauty from any relationship and left it anaemic and skeletal, like the algebra of high finance plotted on a graph. Yet I knew in my heart it wasn't money as such that was the problem. Money, I knew, was the root of good things too. Money enabled medical researchers to make new discoveries in effective treatment. Money enabled orphans to be housed, fed and clothed. It encouraged farmers to grow food and was the invention that made life in cities possible at all. Money had enabled Heidi and me to go to concerts and theatres and have our spirits cleansed by superb music and the cathartic experience of tragedy. Money had empowered us to feel more deeply alive. That was the glorious property of money: its capacity to liberate by lifting away the obstacles that block one's potential and prevent it from blossoming forth.

'Leo,' Heidi said, reaching her hand across the table and touching mine. 'Leo, look at me.'

I looked into her eyes; they locked on mine.

'Are you blaming me, Leo, because my parents are rich?'

'Of course I'm not. It's not a question of blame.'

'What's money got to do with love, with our feelings for each other? What's money got to do with the way we kiss and cuddle?'

'Is this a cross-examination? We're in a restaurant, not a courtroom.'

'You've got me worried, Leo. You've never been like this before.'

'I've never faced up to the facts before.'

'What facts?'

'That I can't take you to the kind of places you prefer. That I can barely take you anywhere and am reducing you as a result.'

'Reducing me? What are you talking about?'

'Shrinking your life, narrowing your horizons, holding you back from the things you want to do.'

'It's *you* I want to do things with, Leo. I love what you do,' she said. She lowered her voice and held my gaze, her eyes now sultry: 'I love your lust. I can't think of a better way to wait until you're qualified and practising as a lawyer. We'll be graduates then, both of us – me doing translation and interpreting work for big firms when I leave UCL, you coming down on the drug dealers with a vengeance. So please don't go on like

70

this, Leo. I don't like it.' Her eyes became thoughtful, and she added: 'This isn't some kind of last supper, is it? Is that why you brought me here – to tell me?'

'Of course it isn't,' I tried to smile. 'I didn't mean to be morbid, Heidi. I'm sorry, darling.'

'Well then,' her face brightened. 'Let's drop the subject. It's not worth quarrelling about. It reminds me of the opening couplet of Alexander Pope's "Rape of the Lock": *What dire offence from amorous causes springs,/What mighty contests rise from trivial things.* Love and money don't mix, Leo. Money is just a means to an end.'

'Whose end?'

'Anyone's.'

'What about *my* end?'

'What d'you mean?'

'What about my desire to show you a really good time and pay for it from my own pocket?'

'You *are* showing me a good time, Leo. It's *you* I like being with. That's why I like it here. Come on, let's enjoy ourselves,' she said, turning her head and looking at the people at the other tables tucking into their food.

By the time a waiter brought the dishes we'd ordered on our way up to the terrace and we began to eat, I knew I couldn't do it. I couldn't tell Heidi about the fifty pounds Bobbie Cullen had given me. There was just no way the information would leave my relationship with Heidi intact.

The trouble was, there was no way either for me to enjoy being broke.

That was the other dilemma. There was no way I could pretend that being continually penniless was a spiritually uplifting experience. Being dependent on others all the time, cadging and hustling for a handout – 'Buddy, can you spare a dime?' as the Yanks used to say in the Great Depression – had had exactly the opposite effect. It had pierced my self-esteem and caused a steady slow-bleed of self-respect. It had torn my integrity so that I was beginning to feel like a pauper walking about in shreds.

That, in the end, was the appeal of making my own money: that I would feel whole at last, all of a piece, healed by the balm of inner satisfaction; and that I would be able to make up for those times when my mother wept secretly because she couldn't afford some of the things she'd wanted me to have. That was what I wanted more than anything else: to make my mother happy, to vindicate her lone struggle, to feel the pride that comes from being erect, standing on one's own two feet, the self-sufficiency fuelled by an income accruing from one's own exertions, one's own capabilities.

Many months later, as part of my recommended reading at college, I came upon *The Ethics of Ambiguity* by Simone de Beauvoir. This title was published in France in 1947, two years before her much more famous and seminal treatise *The Second Sex*, and in its concluding section she writes: 'One does not exist without doing something. So that he may assert his will, man is obliged to stir up in the world the outrage he does not want.'

Chapter 9

I didn't know what to wear.

I didn't know the etiquette. I hadn't been to a stranger's house before with the intention of getting into bed with her, so I was at a loss how I should be dressed when I rang her doorbell. If I turned up looking too casual, it occurred to me, I might send the wrong signal; the woman might think I was unduly offhand. She might feel slighted. She might think I didn't value the encounter, didn't want more money and therefore wasn't bothered about my appearance.

My kit might then be out of keeping also with the decor. The card Bobbie Cullen had given me showed that the house was in the Primrose Hill district, a part of London where there were dwellings of a superior quality. I looked up the street name in my copy of the *A to Z* and found that it was just north of Regent's Park about a quarter-mile from the perimeter of London Zoo. It wouldn't be right, I felt, to pitch up looking scruffy in an expensively appointed house where I might, just conceivably, have to greet other individuals and make small talk before they left and I proceeded to the business at hand. The impression I'd got – not my first, woefully wrong, impression – was that if Bobbie Cullen was one thing, it was *busy*. She was always meeting people. She probably entertained business contacts at her houses, threw cocktail parties and had caterers coming and going with cool bites to eat.

On the other hand, if I went over the top and arrived wearing suit, collar and tie and with my shoes shining like mirrors, my body language would be garbled. I'd be presenting myself in a guise too different from what it was when Bobbie made her proposition; I might then come across as a different sort of person. I couldn't take that chance because I wasn't sure what exactly it was about me that she'd found sufficiently attractive to invite me to her 'retreat'.

I stood in my boxer shorts in front of my open wardrobe, indecisive.

It wasn't as though I had loads of clothes to choose from. I had a dark-blue suit to go to court in when I wanted to study the proceedings. I had a blazer, a zip jacket with hood for when it rained, and a trench coat. I had four shirts with cuffs and collars, none of them white, about six T-shirts, three pairs of jeans, a couple of fleeces and a woolly jumper for winter. My black Timberland shoes were gleaming at the bottom of the wardrobe. I preferred to spend my money on law books and, when possible, on taking Heidi out for a drink. I believed in my heart that if I passed all my exams with high grades over the coming years and had case histories and legal precedents at my fingertips, and, through contacts with more undercover agents, developed a grasp of the workings of the drugs trade internationally, I would make an impact in my chosen field and have a much better wardrobe in due course.

I wasn't in a hurry for smart clobber. It wasn't a priority with me. During my gap year between school and starting university, I'd got six months unpaid experience with the Metropolitan Police; they knew from colleagues who'd given evidence in the case that my father was shot dead by a junkie and that I was highly motivated to smash the drugs business.

I 'shadowed' officers as they went about their work, sitting with them in squad cars and hearing how they analysed situations and decided on a course of action. Much of the other six months I spent in the holds of ships moored to wharves and piers along the Thames between Erith in Kent and the Flood Barrier on the Woolwich reach of the river, and in rusting warehouses and lock-up garages on the waterfront, observing and lending a hand as Customs & Excise agents and Drugs Squad officers with sniffer dogs uncovered caches of cocaine and heroin. I didn't need smart clothes to get that experience; jeans and trainers were enough. And though I didn't get paid either and had to bring my own sandwiches, I knew that what I was learning would jump-start my career one day.

Clothes weren't a fetish with me. I didn't go around judging people by what they wore. Although I knew that clothes spoke a powerful language to everyone with eyes to see, a visual communication system whose messages came across in the vocabulary of colour, cut, texture and fit, and that clothes were erotic to the extent that they showed the human body to best effect, I also knew that clothes could be false. They could tell lies. Clothes could pull the wool over people's eyes. Anyone, not only organized-crime hitmen, could step into a boutique and buy garments to make a particular impression. All the bible-thumping and heresy-hunting bishops and cardinals in their cassocks who'd been shown in recent years to be paedophiles, child abusers, and nuns in their habits and headgear who'd been exposed as sadists revelling in the mistreatment of children in their care – the evidence was overwhelming that clothing was frequently used as an eye-blind, as camouflage, as a way for people to send out false messages about themselves.

I was a law student. I couldn't help being aware of the high-ranking church officials facing serious charges in court; the news was plastered all over the media. Priests and bishops had been in courtrooms all over the world facing the music for abusing and sexually assaulting young boys in their care and, sometimes, lonely women seeking emotional succour. Honest Catholic people answerable to their God must have been hugely embarrassed by the fines the Roman Catholic Church has had to pay in so many dioceses, including the Boston Archdiocese under Cardinal Bernard Law, the Archdiocese of Portland, the Diocese of Tucson, of San Diego, and of Fairbanks in Alaska, following hundreds of lawsuits against bishops and priests. The fines have added up to about a billion dollars so far – all because, under cover of their pious kit, their sacred vestments, ravening clerics have been stalking and pouncing on the vulnerable in their congregations like beasts of prey, for years and years on end. And they've been systematically protected by their superiors from law enforcement agencies.

Catholic students studying law with me at King's told me over lunch in the canteen, not just once, how deeply ashamed they felt. They felt they'd been betrayed, repeatedly, as though they were living in a recurring nightmare. A pretty woman with dark hair and dark eyebrows told me she was deranged, not just bewildered; she said she was, in her head, a psychiatric case going round and round in a way that made the sacrament a fraudulent transaction, the bread and wine not the body and blood of Christ but false-nutritious fast food fed to perennial fools to fuel their gullibility. With people in the canteen stepping by carrying their food on trays and others eating at tables near us, she said with pain and tears in her eyes that she was on the brink of abandoning her belief in the Church as the guardian of her soul.

Things became so bad in the worldwide congregation, there were so many psychologically damaged people thanks to the predators in perfidious togs, that their victims set up a website to contact and support one another; it was called SNAP – Survivors Network of those Abused by Priests. It's a support group whose activities have had an unfortunate side-effect, one can't help thinking, in that it has cast suspicion and made the mud stick also on Catholics whose own behaviour has been entirely blameless – insofar as anyone can claim to be entirely untainted by wrongdoing.

Heidi once told me that Shakespeare said something like 'the apparel oft proclaims the man'. But, in the light of recent experience, it seems obvious that the 'apparel' can be an eye-blind disguising darker motives.

I found it interesting how certain famous couturiers had a seedy look about them despite the cost of the clothing they wore; how their outfits always failed to conceal a certain grubbiness that put a patina of pigswill even on their most expensive threads.

Image had clearly become more important than substance to many people. Image was what the advertising industry made its millions from. And politicians understood very well that the impressions they sought to create, the virtual realities conjured up by their spin doctors, need not be rooted in any of the world's underlying truths. So many individuals were willingly gullible; so many were dying to inhabit make-believe-land.

Which was why there were many other things I could do right away with a ready supply of cash than spend it on clothes. Pay back the people I owed, for a start. Pay my fees in cash – avoid interest charges. Eat nutritious food regularly without burdening my mum.

I was dithering in nothing but my shorts in front of the wardrobe with its door wide open when my mother Arlene stepped into the room. Her blonde hair, which had been piled elegantly on her head when she went out last night, was now hanging down to her shoulders. The eye-shadow she'd put on was still noticeable. She was wearing a FloralArt T-shirt tucked into old jeans without a belt. She was forty-one and looked younger, her high-boned beauty coming vivaciously alive whenever she smiled, even though a paleness had crept into her skin in recent years from the steady anxiety of having to make ends meet from her too-infrequent gigs.

My mother was in an unusual bind. She was caught in a web of tensions that kept threatening to undermine the best moments of her life. She loved nothing better than to sing in front of a jazz band songs she'd written herself, but every time she stepped to the mic a silent terror took hold of her heart. Each gig still had frightening associations; it made her fidget uneasily. The memory flashed before her eyes of a gaunt junkie with lank, dishevelled hair at the foot of the stage grabbing the hem of her dress sixteen years ago.

The band was swinging and she was belting out the lyrics and the junkie, by way of bigging himself up, kept pulling the hem of her dress, jerking her dangerously towards the edge of the stage. Arlene looked down at Leonard sitting in the front row with me on his lap and he understood immediately. Leonard put me down, rose quickly, darted to the junkie and swung him around, away from the stage.

'What d'you think you're doing?' Leonard hissed into the guy's pallid face.

'I'm doing my thing,' he replied with a grin.

'Go do it somewhere else,' Leonard told him. 'Leave my wife alone.'

'Your wife? *Your* wife? Who the fuck are *you*?' the guy shouted at the top of his voice. 'Who the fuck are *you* to tell *me* what to do?'

The band stopped playing. The full-house audience, willing witnesses later, held their breath, and from her vantage-point on the stage Arlene saw the guy pull open his jacket with one hand, draw a pistol from his waistband with the other, and, not pausing one second to think about what he was doing, fire point-blank into Leonard's face. A jet of blood spurted up to where Arlene was standing, soiling her dress with her husband's gore.

Although the culprit was white, the deed was described by the police as a 'respect' killing. My father hadn't shown enough respect for a drug dealer who was harassing his wife.

Sixteen years later, that horrible moment, so sudden, so utterly unexpected, played itself out before Arlene's eyes each time she stood in front of a band. It was as though she expected another murder to be committed as she sang. But she forced herself each time not to succumb to the fear, not to let it paralyse her. She resisted with all her might. She remembered how happy she and Leonard had been together, how they'd taken their baby boy in a push-chair when they went out shopping. She knew she'd be letting Leonard down if she allowed the memory of that moment to kill her ambition as well, to let a greasy-haired guy bombed out on heroin blow her talent away and destroy everything she and Leonard had been planning.

During the daytime Arlene worked in the flower shop opposite Queensway tube station, an outlet that was part of the FloralArt chain. She knew her chrysanthemums from her gardenias and African marigolds, and was a dab hand at laying blossoms together into beautiful bouquets wrapped in cellophane and tied with ribbons, but the money she made there wasn't very good. When a storm damaged the roof of our house and rainwater came pelting through the gaping hole, seeping through the ceiling and making big wet bubbles appear in the wallpaper, and the electrical wiring crackled as the lights kept going off and coming on of their own accord, Arlene resisted the bank's suggestion that she put the house on the market

and move into smaller, cheaper dwellings, such as a
two-room maisonette.

Chapter 10

The house meant too much to Arlene to sell; apart from me, it was her most intimate link with Leonard. What she did instead was raise a loan with the house as security and then had the roof repaired and the wiring replaced; paying off that loan became a strain. She and I stripped the walls down with metal scrapers and re-papered them with rolls we bought at a car-boot sale on Kensal Rise.

My mother smiled at me as I stood in front of the wardrobe, a warm, happy smile that made her look more lovely than she'd been in a long time, and kissed me lightly on the forehead.

'I'm so excited, Leo,' she said in her low-key voice. 'Things are starting to happen for me at last.'

'You had a good time, then, last night.'

'I certainly did.'

'Where'd Mizz Cullen take you?'

'We had drinks at her club off Soho Square, then went for supper at a splendid French restaurant overlooking the Thames in Richmond.'

'Richmond – in Surrey?'

'Yes,' my mother replied, nodding. She kissed me on the cheek, turned away and stepped to my bed. She picked up my copy of *The Big Issue*, glanced at the cover and put it on the quilt as she lay down to relax. She rested her head on the pillow below the shelves with my framed photos of Courtney Pine and the Jazz Warriors blowing at a festival gig, and the gifted dead-and-gone trumpeter Chet Baker. Alongside them was a shot I particularly liked, of the Fugees hiphop trio – Wyclef Jean, Pras Michel and Lauren Hill – a nineties' group whose debut album *Blunted on Reality* was released in 1994; their second one, *The Score*, out in

81

1996, went platinum, not just once, but times 15. It won two Grammy awards.

'It was marvellous, Leo,' my mother said. 'The best restaurant I've been to – no question. We could see through the huge windows the trees along the banks and people in boats with lights on moving through the water. All the waiters spoke with French accents. The meal took more than two hours – I can't remember all the courses, a different wine with each – I could easily have become pixellated. Then Robin, the chauffeur, drove us back to London, first to Jazz at PizzaExpress in Dean Street where we caught one set of the Stan Tracey Trio, truly superb stuff, then to the snug basement of the 606 Club in Chelsea where Bobby Wellins was blowing, and then to the Palm Court Lounge of the Waldorf Meridien Hotel for a blast of Brazilian music. At the Blue Note afterwards in Parkfield Street, Islington we had helpings of drum 'n' bass, breakbeat and Afro-rhythms. Bobbie *had* said she was going to take me on the town, but she wasn't finished yet. We spent the rest of the night in the relaxed ambience of the Kaftan Bar in Wardour Street.'

'What's she like?' I asked, sitting down at the foot of the bed.

'Bobbie Cullen?'

'Yeah.'

'I'm tempted to say she's my guardian angel. She's straightforward. She gets to the point, but she's friendly with it. She enjoys a laugh and loves good music. I'm sure she buys her clothes in Bond Street or Paris – the very best. The Hermès Birkin bag she had with her last night, would you believe it, Leo? – she said it cost ten-thousand pounds.'

'The handbag she had when she came here yesterday?'

'Yes. It's a funny old world, isn't it? Ten-thousand

pounds for one bag. On the way from the 606 Club she asked the driver to pull over on Chelsea Embankment and park for a while in front of the gardens of the Royal Hospital.'

'Why'd she do that?'

'That's what *I* wondered. We were directly across the river from Battersea Park and I could see the lights of Chelsea Bridge. It's like a snug cocoon in that limo with its thick pile carpet, TV and cocktail bar – so quiet and secluded. The mobile phone lay neatly in the palm of a beautifully sculpted bronze hand. The back seat where we were sitting is really a leather-upholstered sofa in the shape of a horseshoe. That's when Bobbie got some weed out of her bag, rolled a fat joint with Rizla papers and asked me to sing something from the jazz repertoire. There we were: two blondes smoking good-quality weed in a chauffeur-driven limo, and she wanted to hear me sing unaccompanied.'

'Which number did she want, Mum?'

'She didn't specify. Any song I liked, she said.'

'And did you?'

'I did, with great pleasure,' Arlene smiled again. 'I sang to her, there in that cool vehicle, as if she *were* my guardian angel saving me from endless penny-pinching. The lights strung out along Chelsea Bridge reminded me of a birthday cake with burning candles and I felt that she and I were celebrating something important.'

'What did you sing to her, Mum?'

'Instead of one of my own songs, I sang a number immortalized by Billie Holiday: *You go to my head*.'

'How does it go again? I haven't head it for a long while.'

My mother beamed, took a breath and sang the words of that number to me as she lay with her head on my pillow: '*You go to my head,/You linger like a haunting refrain/And I find you spinning round in my brain/Like the bubbles in a glass of champagne.* She really liked it, Leo. I could see, the way she looked at me. And when I signed the recording contract —'

'You signed the contract – did you really, Mum? – while amped up on wine and weed?'

'Of course I did. Everything was cool – why would I go aggro? The mood was right. She counter-signed it, then brought out her cheque-book and wrote a cheque for twenty-five thousand quid.'

'Made out to you?'

'Of course, Leo. Who d'you think?'

'Did she post-date the cheque?'

'Don't be silly. She wrote yesterday's date. She said she couldn't let me go away empty-handed. Larger sums would be forthcoming at the times specified in the contract.'

'Then I think your life *has* changed.'

'So do I, my darling. That's why I'm so excited. I deposited the cheque in the bank this morning. Think about it, Leo: on the strength of one song she gave me a twenty-five grand advance. She took a puff from the joint, passed it to me and, while I was taking a few drags and blowing smoke rings, she wrote out the cheque and signed it. What a woman – she trusts her judgement. She goes by gut-feeling.'

'You've always liked people like that.'

'I have, but Bobbie Cullen is the best. I won't let her down. I won't do anything to spoil our relationship. I only wish your father Leonard was alive to see that his faith in me wasn't misplaced. He'd be so happy for me, Leo.'

'I'm happy for you too, Mum. Heidi and I are looking forward to the gig at the Vortex on Saturday night.'

'She's a lovely girl, that Heidi. Take good care of her, Leo. Bobbie says she's going to get me more exposure, more gigs, and a set we'll record live at the Hi-Hat in summer.'

'I feel so proud – my mother the recording star.'

'We'll see – when the Hi-Hat gig comes round.'

'It's an awesome club – only the best perform there.'

'I just hope nothing happens to spoil things.'

'What could happen? You're well away, Mum.'

'Bobbie's not a bullshitter. She knows what she wants and pays good money for it. I gathered from what she said that she doesn't put up with shoddy goods or second-rate service. We were together for about eight hours last night, enough time for me to pick up her vibes, and I've got a feeling about her. Despite her friendliness and laughter, which are genuine, she's a business person through and through and jealous of what she's built up. Hers is a reversed position. *She's* in control of her world – she won't let men rock her boat just because they've been in the business longer than she has. I don't know what it is, Leo,' my mother said, pausing, glancing at me afresh, her eyes pensive, 'I can't put my finger on it – but I feel there's a sadness in Bobbie Cullen, an old sorrow, perhaps. She isn't ageist either. She told me she's fifty-two but still keeps in touch with the clubbing scene; she does that so she can spot gaps in the market as the scene changes. She said dance culture is a multi-million-pound business, but that it's going through changes. She says the number of clubs has fallen by nearly one-and-a-half million over the past year, and that the average per capita spend – is that right?'

'What?''

'Average per capita spend. I'm sure that's what she said.'

'Sounds like how much each person spends.'

'Well, Bobbie says it's fallen too, from eleven pounds twenty-one pence to ten pounds eighty-three.

Fewer people go to clubs, she says, but the ones who do still go, go more frequently. Regular clubbers are mainly in the fifteen to twenty-four years age-group.'

'So what's changing? They've always been the biggest group of clubbers.'

'The competition to the clubs – that's what's changing. It's not just clubs competing with other clubs, Bobbie says. It's bars that play club-type music and don't charge admission – *they're* pulling the punters away. One in ten nightclubs have closed over the past three years, she says. The rest are trying to innovate.'

'Why's she so interested in dance culture?'

'It's the money, stupid,' my mother replied in mock derision. 'Bobbie's an entrepreneur. She's always seeking new ways to create wealth, and dance is a huge, multi-million-pound market. She keeps an eye on *Mixmag* and has checked out Cream, the superclub in Liverpool. She's on first-name terms with managers at the Ministry of Sound club in Elephant and Castle and with one of the owners of the club called Fabric in Charterhouse Street. She says Fabric had the first Bodysonic dance-floor in Europe, a concept borrowed from Hong Kong and Japan. It's a soundsystem that catches the low-frequency sounds in music, usually the bass line, and turns them into physical vibrations. The dancers *feel* the sound pulsating through their bodies – they feel they're *inside* the music. With three underground storeys and unisex toilets, Fabric takes about two-thousand clubbers at a time, each paying fifteen quid to get in, which means thirty grand on the door. That kind of money,' my mother said, nodding and pulling a face, 'is the real reason why club doormen look so tough, intimidating – to give any potential robbers pause for thought. People with money always have ways to protect their money. And the bars rake in about fifty grand a night, Bobbie says. So the per capita spend *there* is much higher.'

Chapter 11

'Bobbie Cullen sounds as though she's on the ball,' I said.

'She *is*, Leo,' my mother emphasized. 'She's in the moment. She has her fingers on the pulse.'

'She told me she was going to Switzerland – when she was here last night.'

'That's right, to a meeting with Swiss media executives on a ferry-boat on Lake Lucerne. She flew there a few hours after bringing me home.'

'She must've had a sleep first, surely?'

'I suppose she must've. She said she was going to make a pitch for the contract to produce television programmes for them.'

'What sort of programmes?'

'About London's vibrant scenes, she said – music, fashion, the Tate Modern that opened two years ago.'

'Wow.'

'That's what *I* thought. She's full of energy, Leo. In the time I was with her she must've sent four or five texts from the limo as we moved through the streets of London. She's so cool. She'd smile at me, ask me to excuse her for a minute, then take the mobile from the bronze hand holding it. She'd flick the phone open, key in her message, read it back in the display and then send it.'

'She obviously has the latest gear.'

'She says she'll use it until it becomes obsolete in a year or so and a better gadget replaces it. Meanwhile, she accesses info on the web with it – share prices, latest news, whatever. She thinks of that phone as a handy business tool.'

'Sounds as if she's ahead of the game.'

'That's what *I* thought,' my mother said approvingly.

'She'd send her text, smile at me on the seat nearby, say "Business that couldn't wait", and start chatting with me again. I like her a lot, Leo. There's something inspiring about her. She's polite, but she won't take crap. In a strange way, she reminds me of Leonard.'

'Leonard? Bobbie Cullen reminds you of my dad?'

'Yes,' my mother said. 'Gentle on the outside, sensual even, but tough within. The difference is that she's impatient – in the nicest way. She's fifty-two years old and hates wasting time, you get the feeling. She wants to fill her life before it's too late.'

'Fill her life with what?'

My mother sat up on the bed, raised her shoulders in a shrug and pushed her lips into a pout. 'With the pleasures of success, I suppose – of being in control. With the choices that money brings. Who knows? Perhaps she's trying to make up for something, replace an earlier loss.'

I began to feel scared.

I began to have second thoughts about going to Primrose Hill.

I began to wonder if I'd cope. How would I perform in bed with an impresario who signs cheques for twenty-five grand on the strength of nothing more substantial than the rendition of a song, who won't let men rock her boat, who refuses to accept shoddy goods or second-rate service?

I didn't mean to put a spell on my own prick, but for the first time in my life I wondered if I'd be able to get an erection in the presence of such a personage.

Would my cock rise to the occasion? My fear stemmed also from an insinuation of incest, from the thought of penetrating a woman who reminded my mother of my father and inspired her to boot.

I was a law student at King's College London and my mind was suddenly flooded by L.W. King's translation of the *Code of Laws* of Hammurabi, the 'righteous king' of ancient Babylon located in Mesopotamia in what today is called Iraq. Those people invented astronomy, architecture, *cuneiform* writing, facial make-up and they developed agriculture by building dams and irrigation channels. It was they who divided each day into hours, each hour into sixty minutes and each minute into sixty seconds. They were practical as well as conceptual. As well as backgammon, a board game still played in countries all over the world, they bequeathed to us another enduring achievement: the quadratic equation of Babylonian mathematics. Hammurabi was the sixth king of the first Babylonian dynasty founded 4,000 years ago. In deference to his chief god Marduk, he famously demanded that punishment fit the crime. His judgements, nearly 300 of them carved into stone tablets, are his enduring memorial and humanity's first written rules of conduct.

128. If a man take a woman to wife, but have no intercourse with her, this woman is no wife to him.

129. If a man's wife be surprised [*in flagrante delicto*] with another man, both shall be tied and thrown into the water [drowned], but the husband may pardon his wife and the king his slaves.

142. If a woman quarrel with her husband, and say: 'You are not congenial to me,' the reasons for her prejudice must be presented. If she is guiltless, and there is no fault on her part, but he leaves and neglects her, then no guilt attaches to this woman, and she shall take her dowry and go back to her father's house.

155. If a man betroth a girl to his son, and his son have

intercourse with her, but he (the father) afterward defile her, and be surprised, then he shall be bound and cast into the water [drowned].

157. If anyone be guilty of incest with his mother after his father, both shall be burned.

And I ransacked in my mind the edicts of Moses set out in Leviticus in the *Old Testament*, another code to guide human behaviour. *Thou shalt not have carnal knowledge of thy mother. Thou shalt not have carnal knowledge of thy mother's mother, or of thy mother's sister.*

I checked if there was any ruling against carnal knowledge of thy mother's business manager, thy mother's chief executive officer or someone with thy father's personality profile: gentle on the outside, sensual even, but tough within.

'Are you all right, Leo?' Arlene asked, leaning forward to where I was sitting on the bed and regarding me closely.

'I'm fine.'

'You don't look fine.'

'What d'you mean I don't look fine? I feel great.'

'Is anything bothering you, Leo?'

'On the contrary, something's making me very happy,' I said in an effort to conceal my fear.

'And what is that?'

'What you've just told me. Your twenty-five grand cheque, the gig at the Vortex on Saturday, the live recording at the Hi-Hat Club in summer – only months away. Any mother's son would be chuffed the way things are changing.'

'Your father would be so proud of you, Leo. You're a bright, clever young man. *I'm* already proud of you, but when I see you in court one day doing your stuff –

God: how proud I'll be then.'

'We'll both be proud – me of you and you of me.'

'You being sarkie or something?'

'Not at all. I just wonder sometimes why money – possession of money – should play such a crucial part in people's lives. If you hadn't worked your butt off all these years I wouldn't even be in college today. But that wouldn't mean I wasn't able, would it?'

'Evidently not. It's a hard truth to swallow, I know, but the world doesn't owe anyone an income. You've got to go out there, Leo, and make the world over in your own image. You've got to bend things to your liking. Who came rushing forward to help us when Leonard was murdered? Did the bank help? Did the building society help? Did the fucken Tory government help? All they did was blame single mums for the country's problems. Vomitrocious they were, toe-rags for eighteen years.'

'Only Lester's mother Josie kept coming round to see how you were – that's what you've told me, many times. She used to bring pots of food, knowing you were too listless, too sorrow-struck, even to feed yourself or your baby boy. Isn't that true? Josie was the difference between life and death.'

'She was and all. I've never been able to repay her.'

'She didn't stand by you for payment, did she? She was your friend and behaved like a friend.'

'It doesn't bear thinking about what would've happened if Josie hadn't kept coming round – washing you, changing your clothes, taking you and Lester to a kids' show at the cinema,' Arlene said. She sagged back on to the pillow and gazed pensively at the ceiling. 'We met by chance, you know. Thank God for accidental events. Josie and I were in the same maternity ward of the Princess Louise Hospital in North Ken, and gave birth to our sons on the same day. You arrived in the world twenty minutes before Lester. And right there as we held our babies in bed Leonard suggested that he be Lester's godfather and that Lester's dad, Ozzie Maddox, the optician, be *your* godfather.'

'Why are you telling me this again?'

'Because I feel that my life is about to change and I'm looking back over the years to remember my friends, the people who stood by me.'

'How are you going to acknowledge them?'

'By throwing a hell of a party, for starters – with live music. It'll be a celebration of their solidarity, of their kindness and the love that's made our neighbourhood an extension of our family.'

'Our extended family,' I found myself replying, 'the butcher, the baker, some neighbours from Jamaica.'

'Come here, Leo,' my mother said. 'Give me a hug, you lovely boy.'

I rose from the bed and turned to her, she got up and put her arms around my bare chest; our cheeks touched as we embraced. I caught a whiff of last night's perfume. I was reminded again as she pressed me to her breast of what I'd always known: that without my mother I'd have been nothing. I wouldn't now be healthy and strong. I wouldn't be able to read or write. I wouldn't have got to know so many parts of London, all the places she took me to, first in a push-chair, then walking along the pavements with her holding my hand, then on tube trains and red double-decker buses. I was one of the kids at school who had no father. She read to me in bed most evenings and used to race me on open spaces to see who could run faster – then smile and lift me up and kiss me on both cheeks as we caught our breath.

We went to car-boot sales to replace household items that had broken down and I noticed how my mother argued and haggled. We visited street markets where the prices of fruit and veg were more manageable. We had picnics on open land when it was bright and sunny, sometimes near the Serpentine lake in Hyde Park, sometimes on a wooded hill of Hampstead Heath. We fed the pigeons in Trafalgar Square and the ducks in St James's Park. We shuddered together in the Chamber of Horrors at Madame Tussaud's. We marvelled at the expanse of stars and the endless universe with our heads tilted back on the seats of the Planetarium.

My mother took me with her wherever she went, regardless of the purpose of the journey, and I got to know more and more parts of my home town. I became a Londoner through her. I discovered the Hackney Empire through her – she sang there one night when I was twelve, when Bernie Grant, MP for Tottenham, was still alive and going strong. Bernie Grant died in April 2000 after being a thorn in the side of the Tory governments of the 1980s and 1990s. He was born in Guyana and was one of the first three black MPs in the House of Commons. He was a firebrand but also a good listener, according to my mother who'd met him twice. An inspiration to black Britons, he never stopped campaigning for racial justice, which was probably why more than five-thousand people went to his funeral.

It was my mother who took me to Tower Bridge to see it break in the middle and rise up to let through tall ships coming up the Thames. She took me to Brick Lane, where the tempting smells of curry came from kitchens, where Asian women in saris worked at sewing machines in sweatshops and got their sons to form vigilante groups because, my mother explained, the police weren't protecting them from racist firebombs. The only person my mother trusted enough to leave me with when it was absolutely necessary was

Josie Maddox, and it was in Josie Maddox's Victorian house in Powis Square that her son Lester and I became best friends.

'What are you doing now?' my mother asked, moving me away from her and looking into my eyes.

'I was about to go to the bathroom.'

'You going out afterwards?'

'Yeah, I am.'

'Anywhere in particular?'

'Not really – but I might be back late, so don't wait up for me.'

'If you see Heidi, say hello from me.'

'Will do,' I replied, smiling as best I could and walking out of the room on to the landing.

I could feel the heat in my head and wondered if she too had noticed the deception. I felt lousy about lying to my mother and had a premonition that I was going to regret it. Against my better judgement, however, I didn't want to change my mind and come clean; I wanted to take her advice and have a go at bending the world to my benefit. Plus I'd already given Bobbie Cullen my word; I didn't want *her* to think me unreliable. Most of all, I didn't want to pass up this rare opportunity to make easy money on a big wide bed.

I was feeling jumpy about doing a good job, but I was also game. I wondered how Bobbie would compare with Heidi, how pleasuring a woman of fifty-two would feed back into my libido, what benefits it would bring, whether some of her life experience would seep into my tissues and deepen my sensibility in any way. I wondered how Bobbie would resemble Heidi when it came to the nitty-gritty of the sexual act, even though the one was more than thirty years older than the other. How would the pleasures of lying with Bobbie, of fondling her, differ from the glorious sensations of ministering to Heidi's needs? Which positions would she prefer? Would she be as mobile as Heidi who, like me, was also twenty, as in control of her inner muscles, as fragrant and flexible?

Bobbie had said I should embrace her lovingly, kiss her here and there. She said she loved the look of my flesh when it rose suddenly and stayed erect, but wondered if I had the stamina to keep going for a long time. She'd get a good answer from Heidi.

Jeez! It suddenly dawned on me that Bobbie and Heidi were going to be in the same place, the Vortex jazz club, at the same time, when we all went to enjoy my mother's singing on Saturday night.

They musn't get too close to each other. Absolutely not.

I suddenly realized I had to make damn sure they didn't become more than superficially acquainted. If they became friendly and Bobbie started dropping intimate hints about me, I'd be in trouble. I'd be on the spot if Bobbie mentioned the scars down my chest which I got when a Drugs Squad officer and I walked with torches into a dark booby-trapped warehouse and were badly scraped by a falling phalanx of sharp nails. I had to have an anti-tetanus injection; so did the officer; we had to rest completely until the dressings and bandages stopped seeping blood. It was weeks before I stopped dwelling on the thought that I could have been dead; I could have been impaled near derelict docks along the Thames. I would find it hard to explain to Heidi how a businesswoman I'd only met once knew about scars on my body that were usually concealed by my clothes.

That's the trouble with knowing, and in one case, loving, perceptive, intelligent women: they are perceptive, intelligent.

No doubt about it: I had to keep the two of them apart, without appearing to do so. There was no need at all for them to get to know each other. I would introduce Bobbie Cullen as my mother's business manager and then steer Heidi away quickly. Bobbie was much older than Heidi and me, so it wouldn't look suspicious if we preferred to hang out with a younger crowd at the club. That joint was always bumping with cool people who appreciated talent. It was one of my favourite places in London.

As for tonight, everything would depend on Bobbie's attitude, I decided. The whole atmosphere would hinge on how she regarded me. Her demeanour and tone of voice would be crucial to the money I hoped to make. I knew for a fact that I wouldn't earn a penny if she behaved like a chief executive in bed, ordering me around. I wouldn't be able to function properly, let alone satisfy her, if she treated me like a subordinate with menial duties: do this, do that, fetch the papers, make the tea. My raunch would seize up, my stiff flesh collapse. The earthy links between my brain and my pelvis would snap. I'd lose my sexual power, and with it my chance of making a good sum of money. I'd be a young guy with an old body for the duration, shrivelled in shame. She'd kill my cock stone dead if she turned out to be bossy between the sheets.

I lingered momentarily on the landing, unsure of what to expect, and then, throwing caution to the wind, and in preparation for Primrose Hill, went into the bathroom and had a shit, a shave and a shampoo.

Chapter 12

It was a clear night in spring that first time I found my way to Bobbie's retreat, with enough of a cold breeze to make me glad I'd put on two T-shirts under my zip jacket. There hadn't been a lot of traffic about when I'd walked from the tube station to where the house was located, just the occasional car passing by with side-lights on. A man was being led by a yapping dog on a leash as he held a mobile phone to his ear with his other hand. Across the road, a woman and a young girl were strolling hand-in-hand in the opposite direction.

I turned into Bobbie Cullen's street and saw that it was a cul de sac. Checking the number of the dwelling to my left, a two-storied house with shuttered windows upstairs and down and a porch-light above the door, I counted the houses and figured that Bobbie's place was the last one, beyond which an expanse of grass sloped up to a wooded hill. In the sulphurous glow of a street-lamp which I could hear hissing I noticed a small white van parked in front of the garden wall of the farthest house.

I stopped in the shadow of one of the trees, leaned against its trunk and looked at my watch: 9:51. Bobbie had told me not to come before ten. It was best to obey that order strictly, I thought; I didn't want the rendezvous to start on a bum note, with her asking if I was deaf or couldn't remember the time she'd specified. I was wondering whether I should walk back for a while the way I'd just come, to kill time, when the front door of the last house opened and a man stepped out. The oblong of yellow light changed to black again when the door closed.

I looked into the gardens on either side of the street to see if anyone might be watching me, but there was no one else in sight. The man walked around to the driver's side of the van, opened the door and got in. The engine started almost immediately, and the tail-lights and front lights came on. The van was small enough to make the U-turn in one go, and as it went slowly by I saw the lettering in green paint on the side: *Anadol Mezes: Shish Köfte, Böbrek Izgara, Ezmeli Kebab, Salmon, Trout, Calamari* and a central London phone number.

It occurred to me with mixed feelings that if that *was* the house where I'd been invited to make easy money, then other people might be there too. They could be foreigners, going by the strange words on the side of that van. Perhaps they'd been to Switzerland too as part of Bobbie's entourage and were too knackered from all the travelling to go out for a meal and had phoned for food to be delivered instead. Which probably meant that they'd be in the house for some time still: the food had only recently been brought.

I began to wonder how long it would take them to eat the food. That depended in part, I knew, on how many of them there were and how much they talked while scoffing. Did they use knives and forks, or was the nosh the kind you shaped into patties with your fingers and put straight into your mouth? Perhaps they belched to demonstrate their appreciation, which could take time: marshalling the pressures in your stomach wasn't easy: digestion was a natural process yielding gases as a side-effect, not something one could command at will.

I kept leaning against the tree, looking up through its branches to the moon which seemed to have a bluish mist over its surface, and looking at my watch which Heidi had given me two Christmases previously. A pang of guilt shot through my chest when I realized that I was timing my entry to another woman's house with a timepiece I'd received as a gift from my girlfriend.

How naff was that? How gross? My heart began to feel heavy, ponderous with a premature remorse for a deed I hadn't even done yet. In the gloom of that tree a bilious sensation made me feel shitty. A sense of shame seeped down in me, immersing my self-image, my notion of my unsullied character, in a brackish fluid. Some part of me was already starting to drown.

A sickening intimation said I was going to pay for betraying Heidi.

Then, as though rising to the surface and filling my lungs with fresh air, I remembered why I was going to Bobbie Cullen's house. I was going there to become self-sufficient. I was going there to make my own money which I could spend on Heidi, spend on my mother, spend in ways which would prove my independence and integrity. Waiting in that house, I was convinced, was a big boost to my maturity; maturity without a long, endless, snail-like lapse of time.

At 10:14 it occurred to me that Bobbie Cullen's limousine was nowhere to be seen. I'd seen that vehicle in front of *our* house yesterday; it was too long and wide to fit comfortably into a domestic garage. Bobbie had probably told her chauffeur when to turn up the following morning. And there were no other cars parked in front of her house. So it was possible that there were no other people *in* the house either.

What should I do? Wait outside while she was waiting for me inside? Which meant keeping her waiting. That wouldn't be cool, nor would it be right to waste the night leaning against this tree when I could be earning my fee on a big wide bed as Bobbie had said.

Move your arse, bro: don't be slow. Your time has come to coin it, no need to purloin it, a rapping cadence coursed suggestively through my head, due perhaps to the hiphop tracks I'd been listening to in recent months. It's yours on a plate, mate, fate is at last on your side, no need to hide your longing and desire. Crawl out of the mire – go and light her fire.

I pressed the doorbell and heard it ring inside. As I waited on the porch with palpitating heart a collage of images flitted across the front of my mind. Old memories came alive, of me, six years old, seated at a table with other children in sunlight while we scooped up with spoons mounds of rice soaked in freshly squeezed mango juice. It was so tasty, delicious. We'd stopped chattering and were gobbling, little yellow runnels of mango juice trickling from our lips down to our chins. I was wondering why that image, so poignant and nostalgic, was seizing me on the porch of a house I'd not been to before, when the door opened inwards and I saw Bobbie Cullen's smiling face.

'Hello, Leo,' she said, moving her arm back in a welcoming motion. 'Do come in.'

I stepped into the wainscotted hall and the first thing I noticed was a large painting of a bunch of bananas in the centre of red squiggly sunbeams on an off-white background. It was simple, eye-catching and, as you looked at it, curiously calming. Below that modern painting was an antique piece of furniture, a mahogany or oak chair wide enough for two with what looked like suede upholstery the colour of papaya. Bobbie later told me it was a 17th-century love seat designed to accommodate a lady's skirts; it was not, she smiled as she explained, meant for amorous pursuits, despite its name.

I looked down at the bare floorboards and patterned rugs and again an image of my childhood filled my mind: my fingers sticky with mango juice, my lips and chin flecked with mango pulp, my white vest smeared with the same happy stuff.

'I take it you found this place easily,' Bobbie said.

'I did,' I replied, nodding, 'thanks to the card you gave me.'

She was wearing a loose, shiny, black robe with wide sleeves and a sash tied round the waist; down the left side of the robe, from her breast to way below her knee, was a swirly dragon in gold, its long fiery tongue a bright red fork, the same colour as her sash. I could see she had nothing on underneath. I could see hers was a handfullish body, not bony, not bulky, *voluptuous* might be the word for her sensual shape. Her feet were in gold slippers, her violet-blue eyes clear, her blonde hair somehow less formally done than when I saw her for the first time yesterday.

'I brought the letter with my blood-donor barcode you said I should bring.' I put my hand into the inside pocket of my zip jacket and brought out the white envelope with the two-hearts logo on it. I opened the envelope, drew the letter out partially and proferred it to her. It occurred to me that she was some kind of employer and I was showing her a reference.

'Come,' she said. 'Let's sit on the love seat while I read it.'

We sat there under the oil painting and she took the letter from my hand. She looked at the National Blood Service logo of two overlapping hearts in the top right-hand corner, one red, the other hollow, at my name and address and the date. I could see the text from my position beside her. 'Dear Mr Allen,' it said, 'Your donation is needed more than ever before. The gift of blood offers new life and new hope to ever-increasing numbers and your single donation can often benefit at least three people. Every medical advance brings new challenges, and it is only through

102

the commitment of donors like yourself that we can ensure a regular and safe supply of blood to meet patient needs. The next blood donation session in your area is at,' and the community hall and its full address was printed in capital letters, along with the full date and the times of the session in the afternoon and the one in the evening.

'Please let me know if the venue or the session times are not convenient for you,' the letter continued. 'The demand for blood and blood products is forecast to continue rising and we urgently need new donors. Please ask your friends or colleagues to give blood. Bring them along with you or call the helpline number below.'

The letter was signed by the Head of Donor Communications. Below the signature was the message in bold capitals which I could see over Bobbie's shoulder: 'PLEASE BRING THIS LETTER WITH YOU TO THE SESSION. THE BARCODE WILL HELP US PROCESS YOUR REGISTRATION MORE SPEEDILY.' Below that, ranged left, was my ID donor number and barcode.

'Thank you for bringing this, Leo. I did want to see it,' Bobbie said. She folded the letter, slid it back into the envelope and returned it to me. There was a look of approbation when she made eye contact, a kind of thumbs-up glance. I wasn't sure why: because the letter proved I was perfectly healthy, didn't have a contagious disease? Or because it showed that I was community minded? 'I too have an envelope for you,' she added, 'a brown one. You *are* staying the night, aren't you?'

'The whole night? Would you like me to?'

'Yes, I would.'

'Then I will,' I said. 'I saw a man drive a van away from here,' I tacked on, trying not to get too excited by what might be in the brown envelope. 'Had he delivered food by any chance?'

'Yes, he had,' she smiled. 'Would you care for a bite now, a bowl of ripe mangoes and ice-cream, perhaps, or some Turkish *mezes* – or would you rather have your bath first?'

'I'm going to have a bath, am I? I've just had a shower.' My words sounded like a kid complaining about too much hygiene.

'It doesn't matter,' she replied. 'You said your favourite fruit was mango, didn't you?'

'I did.'

'Then follow me, Leo,' she said, rising from the seat and motioning with her head. 'I'll show you around – it'll help you relax.'

I realized as she led me through it that the house was a bungalow; it had no upstairs. The two bedrooms, large sitting room, kitchen and bathroom were all on the same level, surrounded outside by well tended gardens. Each room was decorated in a rich colour that contrasted with the furnishings, the pictures, an ornate candlestick, and stone, glass and copper vases full of clusters of red and white roses, tulips and carnations, deep pink azaleas. There were fragrant hyacinths in an earthenware pot. My mother would appreciate the abundance of flowers here, I thought; she too was surrounded by lovely blooms in the FloralArt shop where she worked putting bouquets together and selling them. Nothing in any of the rooms particularly matched anything else, yet there was no sense of jumble. Bobbie seemed to prefer uncluttered spaces with a relaxing aura which nevertheless weren't minimalist. I thought the house was cool.

'I use this place to unwind,' she said as she led me around. 'It's my London retreat, my therapeutic pad.'

As we approached the bathroom the images in my

mind of my childhood grew steadily stronger, until Bobbie opened the door. A waft of pure pleasure hit me then. I saw the bath-tub and folded towels and into my nostrils slid a concentrated sensation of mango memory, bringing fully alive secret places in my heart I'd long forgotten ever existed.

'I could've got orange-and-cinammon, or apples-and-aloe,' Bobbie said, 'but when I asked what your favourite was, you definitely told me that it was mango.'

I hardly knew this woman. I'd just had a shower. But a feeling pretty close to the adoration of the magi almost overcame me as we stood on the tiled floor. On the ledge of the window, below the silver slatted blinds, were onyx tubs and jars containing lotions, creams, aromatic ointments and cleansing balms, but the bath gel that had frothed up the steaming water and sent rising a memory-jogging vapour was so heavy with mango fragrance that it filled the bathroom and drifted like a pastel breeze out into all the spaces of the house, wisping even through the front door's letter-flap and making me recall bits of my sixth birthday treat as I waited on the porch.

'So, Leo,' Bobbie said, 'it's up to you. Do you want to get in first, or shall I? It's definitely big enough for both of us.'

'We're going to bathe together?'

'It's best to be clean and fresh, don't you agree? We barely know each other. I'll soap your back and you can do mine, then we'll shower the foam away,' she motioned to the wide glass cubicle in the opposite corner. The toilet bowl and the bidet were alongside it.

I remembered what she'd said yesterday when we were waiting for my mother to come downstairs; she'd said it twice: 'I always look before I leap.' Bathing must be a way of taking precautions, I thought.

'It's too hot in here to be wearing that top,' she said.

It's not a top, it's a zip jacket, I wanted to say; *top* sounded so girly. But I couldn't argue: the room *was* hot. The large mirror on the wall was misted with steam, and the decorative tiles on all sides were opaque; sliding down here and there were little beads of moisture.

I took off my jacket, but when I turned to step away and leave it on the chair I'd seen outside the bathroom Bobbie blocked my way. She reached for my belt, undid the buckle and pulled down the zip of my jeans in one fast move.

I dropped the jacket, lifted my arms and had my T-shirts over my head and on the floor in no time at all; likewise my boxer shorts, trainers and socks.

Bobbie looked at my chest and midriff, made eye contact, smiled and said: 'You certainly are in good condition. Your torso looks sculpted,' she added, reaching out and running the fingers of one hand across the muscles of my abdomen.

'I exercise regularly,' I told her. 'Do sit-ups and press-ups every morning at the foot of my bed.'

But even as I was speaking and feeling her fingers on my flesh, a mix of emotions passed through me. I was excited by being one bit closer to getting a load of money, but I experienced also a fleeting sensation of fear, of being possessed by someone I didn't know who might have power over me. Then I remembered the brown envelope Bobbie had mentioned, and the money that might be in it; she *had* said she'd make it worth my while – and something funny happened.

I started getting what Heidi and I called a 'turnover'. My cock lurched, did a kind of bob. This was, with me, the earliest stage of an erection, of a stiffy, the first awakening, the shrugging off of penile torpor. Heidi had told me that the German slang for an erection was

106

Ständer, as in *Ich hab 'nen Ständer* – I have a cock-stand, a boner.

And Bobbie hadn't even taken off her robe.

Was it the money which I hoped/guessed was in the brown envelope that was rousing me, or the pure childhood happiness which the smell of mango had resurrected, initiating at the same time the resurrection of my rod?

Whatever the precise cause, the effect reached more deeply than the galvanic skin reaction which lie detectors in police stations were designed to pick up; it galvanized my gonads and sent such a charge through my dick that it reared its head suddenly like a startled stallion's.

Bobbie's eyes were rapt; she didn't miss the commotion below.

She moved her hand down and coiled her fingers around my rising flesh, not roughly, not imperiously, but in an affable way, like shaking hands with a new friend. I could feel her palm filling up as I grew thicker and harder.

'I'll lead you in, shall I?' she said, making me think of a tethered horse being led to the water, but she said it with a smile and kicked off her slippers. 'Then we can lie in the water facing each other.'

'Whatever you say, Bobbie,' I smiled back. 'It's your call.'

She let go of my tool which proceeded immediately to point to the ceiling, loosened her sash and shrugged out of the shiny black robe.

Her skin wasn't as pale as I'd expected for someone her age; it was lightly tanned all over. Nor did the tan look as though it was from an electric lamp or from a chemist's bottle. I recalled her saying during our chat the previous evening that she'd gone sailing on her yacht along the Turquoise Coast on the southern side of

Turkey; maybe she lay on the deck for hours on end with sunblock on her skin. And she'd said the captain sometimes cast anchor in one of the coves where the ancient Romans used to get slaves to build their ships; she dived into those waters for a swim. It could be that she swam a lot.

I saw that the nipples of her amplish breasts were on the way to being engorged; she was in process of having two little erections of her own. She was quite curvy. I saw no hollows or loose skin, or the brittle dryness I'd dreaded in someone her age. Her flesh actually looked well toned. Who knows? Perhaps she'd bought one of the videos of Jane Fonda doing aerobic exercises on a treadmill in a gym when she was fifty years old. Hanoi Jane, they called her at one time, my mother had explained, because of her solidarity with the inhabitants of that city while it was under heavy aerial bombardment during the Vietnam war. Her exercise video used to be advertised in the media, my mother said; I'd seen one of the ads in an old magazine while waiting in a dental surgery to have my teeth checked.

Between Bobbie's thighs was a triangular bush of hair that was so thick and so dark compared to the hair on her head that I wondered for a second whether she had it oiled and coiffed by a specialist hairdresser.

We made eye contact again in that large steamy bathroom and she touched me with a few tactical strokes. Then she turned away to get into the bath and I turned too. She lifted her right leg over the side and stepped into the hot frothy fragrant water, and I did the same almost in unison. When she swung her other leg over I followed suit, preparing for our pre-coital ablutions in a kind of formation dance.

'It isn't too hot for you, is it, Leo?' she asked.

The water *was* hot, very, but no longer *that* hot.

'We'll get used to it in a little while,' I said, lifting a foot up to cool it for a bit, then the other.

We stood facing each other, our naked bodies damp from the vapour, like Adam and Eve in a modernized primal swamp anticipating our first-ever sinfulness and disobedience. The only snake in sight, however, was mine, and it wasn't coiled in swelled-up self-importance, but stiff and straight and beginning to salivate.

'Give me a kiss then, while our legs adapt to the hot water,' Bobbie said without smiling, an intense look in her eyes.

I don't know what she saw in *my* eyes as we moved closer. My back was to the taps between which I'd seen a packet of 3-in-1 cleansing wipes – eye make-up removers – and a tube, standing vertically on its cap, containing 'Micro-dermabrasion Exfoliator'. Lying beside the tube with less beauteous/scientific import were two pink cotton flannels, folded over, one on top of the other.

I have to start earning my money, I thought, start doing breadwinner work; that's what this is about. I dropped my right hand and rummaged my fingers in her pubic bush, pressing gently and stroking; she shut her eyes and moved her head from side to side. Then she took hold of my hands, drew them round her waist and placed them on the cheeks of her shapely arse, giving me a long kiss which she suddenly made into a French one with her darting tongue.

'Mmm,' she went in a drawn-out sigh. Whether the sigh was from my hands on her butt or from the feel of my hardness against the flesh of her belly-button, I do not know.

I'd never dreamt that expectation of money would let loose such erotic sensations. I'd never imagined that I would one day be standing up to my calves in hot water with the most enormous erection pressed against a warm, scented cache of cash. I was a law student, not a student of literature. Literature was Heidi's patch. So I had to take her word for it when she told me that Philip Pirrip's great expectations of a fortune in the novel of that name by Charles Dickens changed his prospects out of recognition. Pip, as he was known, was a poor orphan from a humble village, Heidi said; he went to London, met new people there, had a smart suit of clothes made, learned how to be a gentleman and changed his accent and the words he used when speaking. I wondered whether he walked around London with a massive erection all day long while waiting for his fortune to come through.

Bobbie placed her hands on mine, removed them from her arse, stepped back and squatted. I saw between her raised knees the dark hair below becoming wet and bubbly from the gel-foamed water.

I squatted too, facing her, got used to the hot water on my bum and my submerged balls which were on the way to becoming my poached goolies, then stretched my legs alongside hers till I was up to my neck in soft luxury.

She smiled at me and said: 'Isn't this civilized?'

'It certainly is,' I'd just replied when, with a sweeping move of her hand, she splashed some of the mango-water into my face. The taste of it brought back another flash of memory. I splashed her back, but not much, not vengefully; I knew I was the junior partner here. The low-key splashing fun went on for a minute or so.

One of Bobbie's knees then appeared above the surface with tiny bubbles on it; it went down as she straightened her leg and pushed her foot slowly, sensuously along my inner thighs. Her foot touched the shaft of my semi-floating cock with a slippery

110

sensation; I felt the toes wriggling in a kind of soapy, footloose foreplay. She pushed a bit more, gently, and I felt the pressure of her heel against my pelvic bone, my tackle squashed against my belly. She released her foot, then moved it backwards and forwards again along my inner thighs.

'What are you doing?' I asked, keeping eye contact.

'Getting to know you. D'you mind?'

'Of course not. That's why I'm here.'

'I wondered if you really would come.'

'Did you?'

She nodded and the foam lapped over her chin. 'I thought you might have said yes out of politeness.'

'My mother did bring me up to be polite, but I came for the money we agreed.'

'I know,' she said. 'We all have our priorities.'

'What's *your* priority, Bobbie?'

'Soap my back nicely, will you, Leo? – with one of those flannels,' she nodded to indicate the pink cloths behind my head. 'I'll do your back if you like. Then, when we're in bed and you've made me feel the way I hope you can, I might tell you.'

Chapter 13

I wouldn't describe Bobbie Cullen's sexual proclivities as kinky or perverse, but when we'd dried each other with the towels in the bathroom and had gone into the kitchen she did bring from the fridge a bowl of mango and ice-cream which she suggested I eat whilst sitting at the kitchen table stark naked. She sat down on the other side, her gown hanging open showing her breasts. She had a bowlful too, but the flavour of *her* scoop of ice-cream was vanilla. Mine was chocolate.

'How'd you know I prefer chocolate?' I asked.

'I guessed from our conversation yesterday,' she said.

'What an unexpected treat.'

'I told you I'd have something special prepared, didn't I?'

'Yes, you did. Did it come in that van I saw outside?'

She nodded, and, as she savoured her mouthful and smiled, a bit of ice-cream leaked from her lips; it made her look very young and sensuous. 'All of this did,' she said, pressing the back of her hand to her mouth and waving her spoon at the array of dishes laid out on trays on the wide table between us.

I looked at the plates with different kinds of food on them. Their savoury bouquets and racy aromas hung in the air, making me realize suddenly that I hadn't had a bite to eat since well before my shave and shower earlier that evening. I was quite peckish. The various colours and shapes of the unusual titbits and delicacies were eye-catching, even though I had no idea what they were.

I looked up and asked Bobbie: 'What is this stuff?'

'Each dish is called a *meze*,' she said, 'a Turkish

appetizer. What the French call *hors d'oeuvres*, I suppose. Have you tried any of it before?'

'No, I haven't,' I shook my head. 'I haven't been to Turkey.'

'You don't have to go to Turkey for excellent *mezes*. They're available here in London. Each one is designed with fresh ingredients to arouse your appetite before the proper meal.'

The way she said the words 'proper meal' had an erotic connotation. And the way she looked at me across the table, her full tits in full view above the plates, her nipples like periscopes spying the spread, I knew she meant that our session in bed was going to be the main course.

I finished my bowl of mango and licked the last bit of ice-cream off the spoon, then pointed at one of the dishes at random: 'What's that?'

'*Börek*,' she said, and, when she saw how blankly I was looking at her, added: 'They're pies of flaky pastry stuffed with meat, others with potato and, sometimes, cheese.'

'Sounds good.'

'Go on – help yourself,' she coaxed me with another encouraging smile. 'I ordered it all for you. Pick up whatever takes your fancy and tuck in – build your strength.'

'What's that?' I pointed at another dish.

'*Gozleme*,' I think she said. 'It's fried aubergine with yoghurt – very tasty, with onion, coriander and a touch of garlic.'

'And that?' I enquired, indicating another dish, my appetite getting worked up by her answers almost as much as by the actual goodies.

She said something that sounded like '*Patijan dolmas* – eggplant stuffed with tomatoes, onions, cumin and a hint of garlic. When cold, they're called *imam*

113

bayildi. Those dolmas are so satisfying, Leo, that centuries ago an imam fainted from pleasure after trying some. They're suffused with subtle flavours.'

I stopped asking questions and started eating. Bobbie helped herself too. The bites *were* appetizing, uncontrollably more-ish; I kept reaching out and trying something different. For some of it I had to use a knife and fork; for the rest my fingers sufficed. There was a pile of paper napkins with the company's logo printed on them, *Anadol Mezes*; I dabbed my hand whenever juice or gravy trickled down to my palm.

Bobbie continually picked up a different dish and proffered it to me. For the burnt green peppers stuffed with spiced rice I used the knife and fork and a tang of lemon juice buzzed my taste-buds. Bobbie said lamb *köftes* were named according to their ingredients and shape and the method used to cook them. She pointed and said the plump oval ones dipped in egg and then fried were called 'ladies' thighs' – *kadin budu*: talk about food having a come-hither name.

At that table that night, starkers and continuously under the scrutiny of the two alert nipples of a much older woman who smiled a lot and whose damp hair was hanging down to her shoulders, I was enjoying an eating experience and hearing the names of way-out treats that had been completely beyond my ken. In a very delicious way, I was out of my depth – even before I started on the Turkish sweets called *baklava*, *helva* and the *kadayif* pastries. I thought it wiser not to have any of the wine which Bobbie said was called *raki*. I didn't want to risk blowing the whole gig by falling asleep on the job with her arms around me. I opted instead to wash everything down with two cups of the thick, dark coffee.

I needed the energy that food gave me. The honey in

the *baklava* stood me in good stead, the sugar in the pastries. Although Bobbie turned out to be unexpectedly passionate, she needed lots of foreplay. She was so tight when we started, so hard to get into, to enter properly, chafing a bit, that I wondered how long it was, how many months perhaps, since she'd been intimate with anyone.

Yet when at last I did gain entry, thanks to nipple-sucking and the Open Sesame! of my pressing fingers in her hairy crotch, and position-changing and angle-adjusting on the bed and had been thrusting a while and grinding moistly in there, she shouted: 'Deeper, Leo! Deeper!'

Her voice startled me. It sounded like an order, such an imperious tone. Was it her bossiness coming out, I wondered, her chief-executive lung-power. Was this her idea of romantic chat? I looked at her face looking up at me, the pillow pristine white under her head, her violet-blue eyes pulsing a muffled, hitherto-censored message of lustful longing that was so clamorous in its poignant soundlessness that it seemed somehow also to be nostalgic. What had I let myself in for, I wondered. She'd looked so sedate and unflappable, calm and in control, yet here she was shouting like some impatient minx. Was it so long since she'd last fucked that she'd forgotten her bed manners? She suddenly seemed a much more complex, hard-to-discern person than I'd taken her to be when I took her fifty pounds.

My single mother had brought me up to be polite, so I didn't ask Bobbie when last she'd bedded anyone. I didn't want to pry; that wasn't why she was paying me. As things turned out, 'Deeper!' was the first of a series of specific requests she would make in our get-togethers, but this initial one did sound very much like a command with which I ought not to argue. She was, after all, the leader of our duet, the paymaster. Money, I was learning, does have a defining influence in relationships; the customer has the clout.

'You want it deeper? Really?' I asked. 'I wouldn't want to be blamed.'

'Blamed? For what?'

'The consequences of your request.'

'You silly boy. I wouldn't blame you.'

I was a law student, not a student of literature like Heidi. I hadn't written this memoir then; I had no idea how much of what one remembered was supposed to go into a memoir. I didn't know what experiences this rapport was going to bring. At college I'd only written essays. What are the rules of memoir-writing? was a question that only arose much later when I sat down to record that period of my life. With nothing else to guide me, I decided that the safest thing was to be true to what actually happened; I should stay with the core of the experience, the essence of this bipartisanship.

'Very well,' I said to her, taking the opportunity to practise an authoritative courtroom tone, 'then I shall commence,' and proceeded to pound her with a sequence of deep, discrete, staccato thrusts which Heidi had joyously dubbed jackhammer jolts when I first tried them out on her.

'Oh! Oh! Oh!' Bobbie cried after each plunge, and, when I eased off the in-depth uppercuts and resumed a more quotidian pressure, she opened her dewy eyes – 'Oh God, Leo' – and held my gaze. I saw there a look which I took to be a mix of rhapsody and awe, glistening too with slivers of something like melancholy. 'Silly *me*,' she said. 'The last thing *you* are is silly. Not at all.'

'You like it?'

'Yes, Leo, I do. Keep going.'

I fondled her and scratched her back as our breaths mingled. And when we'd been at it a while longer her

116

innards softened perceptibly, as though recalling more sensuous times. Her breathing grew heavier and, gradually, hoarse. She began to heave and to thrash her head from side to side and her tongue darted out to wet her parched lips.

'Yes,' she shouted again, very loud. 'Yes, I love it, Leo! Keep going, Leo. Please.'

I don't know if she thought I was deaf. My ears were pretty close to her mouth. It might have helped if I'd brought along a mute, the kind that Wynton Marsalis and other trumpeters stick in the bell of their horns when blowing low-key stuff.

I kept going. Faster. Her money might be measured out according to the speed and stamina I managed to maintain. She opened her eyes and smiled at me and her look was so congenial, so brimful with benevolence, so very *loving*, I was tempted to think, that an intimation came to me as I was thrusting vigorously that what I was doing might be more valuable to her than an expensive hairdo, or a designer dress, or a handbag that cost countless bucks. What was it worth to her, I wondered. More than the price of removing laughter lines? The cost of cheek implants? The bill for a course of Botox injections? More than what an anti-ageing concoction commands? How much in legal tender would the look in her eyes translate to?

'God. The sensations are *so* good,' she said. 'I'd forgotten the feeling. It's on its own – *sans pareil*, as the French say.'

'What's on its own?'

'This female feeling, inside. There's nothing like it – no way,' she replied, thrusting her pelvis up to meet mine coming down. She joined the rhythm. She met my efforts midway with hers, oscillating more and more rapidly until it felt as though she was quaking of her own accord, a tectonic free-for-all, rocking me on her

117

belly as her body rumbled towards a climax amid the sensual sibilance emphasized by the sticky liquid leaking out of her. Some source deep in her tissues was hurling forth a glutinous cascade.

I had to hold tight to stay on that undulating landscape.

'Aaaah! Ooooh! Hmmm! Hah! Hah!' she articulated in her zealously hoarse language which I found I actually understood. It was a tumbling sequence of guttural morphemes and cooing sounds, throaty, braying, birdlike, as our pelvises pounded in a rising crescendo that made her hair fly across her face and her arms jerk up and fall, her tits and torso judder and her pussy tank up with juice as she ejaculated again so strongly that my plumbline prick was suddenly convinced it was a dipstick deep in lubrication.

The earthquake was over. Only her heart still pounding. It felt safe to dismount. I withdrew from her sticky sheath and lay by her side. I can't say truthfully that I felt satisfied; *I* hadn't come. This was, strictly speaking, *work*, not pleasure. The purpose of the exercise was *her* pleasure, not mine. But it sure is nice work, if you can get it, especially now as I write about it eight years later in these credit-crunch, employment-scarce, public-spending-cut times.

Bobbie dozed in silence for a while, then fell asleep. I could tell she was in slumberland by the steady way her breasts rose and fell and by her regular, audible breathing. Her lips pouted and pulled to one side. A little tic made the skin of her cheek quiver. She was nice to look at as she slept. Her experienced, mature face, framed by damp clumps of blonde wavy hair, wasn't totally unlike my mother's face; my mother too had blonde hair and blue eyes. And the way Bobbie's nostrils opened and closed slightly with each gentle exhalation of breath was also the way Heidi's nostrils pulsed when I kissed her sleeping mouth.

I'm not sure how much time passed in that bed before Bobbie's voice roused me from my daydream which had drifted into a doze. She was facing the ceiling and saying in a quiet voice, almost to herself: 'It's unique. It's incomparable.'

'What's incomparable?' I asked.

'The way I'm feeling now.'

'How *are* you feeling, Bobbie?'

'Supple, beautiful. So womanly.'

She turned her head on the pillow and smiled at me, a smile that had far too many messages in it for me to decipher, but all of them converging into a superbly benign vibe.

I wouldn't say that she was greedy. Ravenous, perhaps, famished from a sexual drought that had gone on for who knows how long. Nor do I wish to belittle her friendly heart by comparing her behaviour now as I write this memoir with the behaviour of avaricious bankers and MPs claiming huge 'expenses' for moat clearing, for the cost of putting up mock-tudor beams, the cost of pay-per-view porn and what not, but she too wanted more.

Her next orgasm during that first get-together came, while her legs were draped over my shoulders, in such a voluminous gush that I felt her juice slide viscous along my vibrating erection and fill my pubic hair with even more stickiness. And after that release of joy she fell asleep again, smiling and burbling a bit.

To be fair, she *had* said she wanted value for money. She never joked about money, she'd said. Yet when at length she opened her eyes after that second sleep there was a look in them that seemed to resemble, I don't know, shyness, bashful reserve? And the extent of her wanting was revealed by what she then said: 'Would you like to take me from behind, Leo?'

119

That took *me* by surprise. It was the last thing I'd expected. I'd thought she'd be satisfied by now, sated. My mother had said Bobbie was fifty-two. Surely someone her age couldn't be so voracious?

Was she a middle-aged nymphomaniac?

Before I'd had time to think about her question and reply, to wonder about the peculiarities of her lust, what deserts it had crawled across on all fours, the rigours it had been through, or how this particular rapport was developing, she grabbed the duvet and tossed it off our bodies. She turned over on her side, pushed out her arse and wriggled it invitingly. I felt her hot curvy flesh burning against me, and, bloody hell! desire welled up again. It was of a kind I hadn't anticipated. Her hunger was charging *me* up, like jump-leads boosting another car's battery.

This was *not* on the agenda. I wanted more of this creature exotic in her wealth, whose copious joy was trickling down *my* legs and who was beckoning me with her butt to enter again her cache of cash.

So I did.

Getting in was a doddle – she was so frothing at the cleft. But from behind was especially nice. The round shape of her arse, when I'd docked liked a space satellite into Starship Enterprise, fitted snugly into the curve of my loins. We lay like spoons. I scratched her shoulder-blades in turn, then dragged my fingernails lightly down the furrow of her spine to the lovely dip of her lumbar region.

'Jeez, Leo. That is so rousing,' she said as I scratched her on the outside while stirring her inside, gently, slowly, doing a circular grind now and then. 'God, it is so lovely.'

When I passed my left arm under her side and my right arm around to the other breast and twirled both nipples, she went 'Mmm, mmm' and I started to feel

120

the walls of her innards tighten. The cash nexus was closing in, contracting, as if to kiss the lucky occupant. I must say: it was very good, secure, feeling her flesh gripping me like that. She might have been fifty-two, but she was alive and well in crucial ways. I found that the more I fondled Bobbie, the more her tissues squeezed me with an involuntary, unpremeditated tightening. I soon knew that if this internal massaging – these exquisitely erotic sensations – continued for any length of time *I* would be the one who'd be gushing forth the contents of their gonads.

'Yes!' she shouted again as I increased the tempo. 'Yes!' out loud, unrestrained, in a bedroom in a bungalow on the edge of Primrose Hill. 'Yes, yes, Leo – you lovely fucking boy!'

I didn't *have* one of those mutes at home; I wasn't a musician. But my mother and I weren't *that* poor. We did have towels in the bathroom and flannels too. Surely I could use one of the flannels, hold it in a kind, unmalicious way over Bobbie's mouth to shut her up?

I haven't written a memoir before so I don't know if one is allowed to leap forwards and backwards in time. What are the chronology rules of a memoir? Is a memoir supposed to be about one thing and one thing only, or can one deepen the story by sketching in the context too, the socio-political pandemonium raging outside someone's snug bedroom? I am a lawyer now, after all. The public realm is my bread and butter. Because jumping ahead a few years will help make better sense of what happened in 2002, bring out the full significance of the money I received from Bobbie Cullen by putting it in some sort of perspective, I'm going to do so, but only briefly.

Chapter 14

In this era which has seen businesses go bust left, right and centre for want of much-needed bank loans; millions thrown out of work in all sectors of the economy; Woolworth's 815 branches close for the last time in its 99th year; MFI disappear from the streets; pubs go out of business at the rate of about 35 a week; acres of unsold brand-new cars on disused airfields; people's houses repossessed remorselessly because they couldn't keep up their mortgage payments due to the breadwinners losing their jobs; middle-class families pawning their jewellery in growing desperation; parts of towns all over the country looking tawdry and desolate with rows of boarded-up shops spreading like a plague; and President Barack Obama's ambitious many-trillions spending programme to get the US economy working again frightening European leaders who believed that, if they followed his example, it might feed hyperinflation and leave their nations floundering as they tried to refinance astronomic levels of debt; when alliances of activists had protested angrily in capitals all over Europe against the bankers whose self-serving operations have made the world economy seize up and shrink; protestors demonstrating so vehemently that thousands of officers from police forces all over the UK had to be drafted in to support the Metropolitan Police as part of the security plan, costing an estimated £7.5 million, to protect the world leaders attending the G20 summit conference at the Excel Centre in London's Docklands from the rising waves of anger – at such a time, the last thing I wish to do is compare Bobbie Cullen's hungry heart to the destructive greed of bankers.

Bobbie wasn't greedy. She was hungry.

The worry in security circles was that the potentially chaotic protests – people's law-given right in a parliamentary democracy – might distract the attention of the police from a more enduring threat: an attack by al-Qaida on the leaders of the world's twenty most powerful economies, all gathered together under one roof, using chemical or biological weapons, or even a nuclear bomb.

Or was that just opportunistic pseudo-paranoia?

Just how much the bankers with their bonuses and huge pension pots, their secretive tax havens and offshore scams, had stoked the rage of ordinary citizens was demonstrated by the plethora of posters and placards with graphic imagery that began to appear in streets and squares everywhere. *Storm The Banks!* said one poster: *April 1st 12 Noon Bank of England. G20 Meltdown* proclaimed another. *Enough Is Enough*! commanded/pleaded a third. *Bash A Banker* with a scowling man wielding a baseball bat. *Bail Out The Workers Not The Bankers* and, outside the Royal Bank of Scotland building, *Eat The Bankers*.

The catastrophe of our times, threatening to spiral to depths lower even than the 1930s' Great Depression, was created, we kept being reminded, not by working people or poor people or uneducated people who didn't have a clue what they were doing, but by well heeled grandees and shady oligarchs whom politicians were always cosying up to, sucking up to, giving their investment banks and commercial banks all the deregulation they wanted, giving it willingly, merrily, encouraging blood-on-the-teeth capitalism to go rampaging on, while at the same time, as ever, wanting the votes of the wretched electorate whom they usually denigrated. The sudden grief and despair and deepening unemployment worldwide had been caused by individuals who considered themselves to be the best of

123

the best, the aristocracy of arrogance, the masters of capitalism's Anglo-Saxon model, as the French and Germans called it. They always wanted more, regardless of the suffering and squalor just out of their sight, and they believed it was in the nature of reality that they always *would* get more.

Bobbie Cullen also wanted more. But that's where the similarity ended. She'd wanted more of *me*. She wanted to *give me* money.

Immediately after the G20 summit meeting, the tension in my home town eased off, dissipated. Old Smoke breathed a sigh of relief. Well over one hundred protestors had been arrested for public-order offences and criminal damage. For all the world to see on television and the internet, a handful of militants dressed in black with scarves over their faces smashed through the windows of a bank opposite the Bank of England, clambered in and tried to set fire to the premises.

That changed the tone of the mainly peaceful protests to something more menacing. Television news kept showing a newspaper seller on his way home from work, not part of any protesting group, being hit with a truncheon from behind by a policeman in a black helmet who then shoved him forward so hard that he fell to the pavement. The poor man got up, wanting only to get home, walked a short distance, then collapsed and died on the way to hospital.

Heidi had brought bottles of Beck's beer in a wicker basket and six *Apfelstrudel* pastries flavoured with cinnamon. She, my mother and I ate and drank while we watched the TV news, the various groups of demonstrators converging on the City of London where the banks had their HQs. We glanced at one another as we watched the scuffles and skirmishes, chomping our pastries and swallowing beer.

124

The police that day and the next were a phenomenon rare in British life. They kept herding large groups of protestors on to the pavements and crushed them so closely together that many found it hard to breathe; they couldn't for endless hours escape from the tight police cordon to go for a drink of water to quench their parched throats or to relieve themselves decently. It was a frightening technique unseen before on television and known as 'kettling'. Wielding truncheons which they kept brandishing and occasionally swinging at the protestors, and wearing shiny helmets with protective visors and black, noticeably padded uniforms under lemon-coloured day-glo jackets, the police looked, chillingly, Heidi said, like platoons of state-sponsored bullies out of George Orwell.

The G20 meeting had agreed a massive shot in the arm to the world's economies. The leaders also agreed tight regulation of banks' operations and those of what France's President Nicolas Sarkozy called '*paradis fiscaux*' – tax havens. Heidi said Chancellor Angela Merkel and her German advisers referred to those corrupt institutions as *Steuerparadies*. Share values jumped in markets worldwide. Some people's hopes also rose, a tiny bit.

I thought there was something frantic about the resolute way the G20 leaders smiled and waved during the closing ceremony, even Brazil's white-bearded President Lula, the only leader there from a peasant background, even China's President Hu Jintao whose usually inscrutable expression seemed to say to us Londoners 'Your Olympics in 2012 are going to be shit compared to our Olympics in Beijing'. They all lauded unelected Prime Minister Gordon Brown and sang his praises for getting the gig to happen at all, especially Barack Obama, the new, black, highly literate President of the United States whose predecessor had left a huge pile of shit on *his* plate. India's Prime Minister Manmohan Singh in his blue turban put me in mind of footage I'd seen just weeks before of the two Sikh bodyguards who fired a hail of bullets into their boss Prime Minister Indira Gandhi as she walked in the garden of her residence in Delhi; it was in revenge for her attack on the Sikh temple at Amritsar.

Now they were all going home to save the world. President Obama was trying to 'press the *Re-Set* button' to start anew America's relations with countries his predecessor had so systematically antagonized with the 'war on terror'. One wondered how he was going to accomplish that. How would America's programme of 'extraordinary rendition' be explained away, in which individuals suspected of terrorist activities were kidnapped from their home towns and transferred 'extrajudicially' on secret flights to foreign countries where they became 'ghost prisoners' beyond the reach of due process and then subjected to extended periods of sleep deprivation, electric shocks, 'waterboarding' and other forms of 'enhanced interrogation' overseen by various intelligence agencies of the United States? Obama, a trained lawyer, one-time president of the Harvard Law Review, was going to need all his powers of intellect to undo the damage done to his country's reputation in the name of liberty before its sub-prime-loans malarkey burgeoned forth across the planet.

Economics as a serious discipline had been shown to be a fantasy, with little scientific credibility. No economists had foreseen the crash. None of their computer models had predicted it. Despite the reckless behaviour of their senior-most executives, the meltdown of the world's financial institutions took everyone by surprise. The mantra was heard repeatedly: 'What a surprise.' 'Who saw it coming?' 'How could we have known?' One wondered how economics could

126

be taken seriously as a science. No less a figure than Nobel-laureate economist and professor at Columbia University Joseph Stiglitz later confessed to *The New York Times* about the crisis gripping the world: 'It's just hard to see what will bring us out.'

Perhaps there still *is* a place for economics as an *arts* subject; its pie-charts with various colours can be quite pretty and its scattergrams are reminiscent of Jackson Pollock's paintings.

Unlike the outlook for the UK's economy, *my* prospects had *risen* a few years before.

Bobbie Cullen had agreed to give money *away*, not keep it for herself. My mother had said that Bobbie knew what she wanted and paid good money for it; she paid twenty-five grand for a single unaccompanied song. She seemed to know the adage that money is like manure: dig enough of it widely into the soil and, along with the input of other factors, good things grow. But keep it piled up in one place like a miser and it soon stinks to high heaven.

I hoped Bobbie would agree that I hadn't been a miser with my energy that first night. I hoped she would acknowledge that I supplied her with all the input she could contain, so much so that her ecstasy had frothed forth in such torrents that they clung to the skin of my thighs like slow-drying glue.

I've heard of *The Vagina Monologues*, of course, articulate expressions of puss experience including joy, masturbation, birth, rape and mutilation, but Bobbie's gushing had been a kind of wordless blather. It was gurgly, incoherent in comparison, except that it was saying one very precise thing emphatically over and over again: 'I love it! I love it! I love it!'

Chapter 15

The morning sun was beaming into the bedroom when I woke up. I looked at my watch on the bedside cabinet: 8:22. Above a chest-of-drawers between an armchair and a leather pouffe was a grid of shadows on the wall to my right cast by the sun against the window frames. Bobbie was fast asleep. I got out of bed carefully and stepped by a glass-topped dressing-table to the open curtains. The garden I saw under blue skies was a delight. It was surely looked after by someone who knew what they were doing, I thought, someone with time enough to care, probably a professional gardener.

There was a spacing of scarlet peonies in the bed along the perimeter. Among bluebells and purply crocuses, early daffodils were swaying yellow in the breeze. In one corner was a buddleia tree with a cloud of butterflies flitting around it, and, on the other side, a flowering cherry tree. Between two glass lanterns mounted on slim silver spikes rising from the well mown lawn was a large planter made from wooden slats; it boasted a billow of flowers I couldn't identify. There were separate curvy-shaped beds packed with clusters of low-growing polyanthus; their petals, red and white and purple and yellow, were so close together they seemed all to be part of one technicolor bush forming a base from which rose the stems of tulips whose buds weren't yet fully open. Two magpies were hopping about the lawn, their black-and-white feathers contrasting with the colour of the grass, their heads dipping as they pecked here and there for a bite.

The thin silvery beige branches of what I took to be a magnolia tree tangled upwards at the right-hand side of the window where I was standing; its broad pink-touched creamy petals were like upright fingers spaced apart, poised perhaps to capture any butterflies that might come their way. Positioned to face the buddleia was a recliner under a large matching sunshade. Beyond the wooden fence, orangey brown with what might have been creosote, was public land: unkempt weedy grass rising to the crest of what I supposed was Primrose Hill.

When Bobbie showed me around the house the night before, I saw in the other bedroom a framed oil painting of what she said was the Clifton Suspension Bridge in Bristol; she told me the bridge wasn't very far from the house where she grew up. I saw no sign that Bobbie did any work in *this* house. I saw no computer, laptop or otherwise, no filing cabinet, no desk with drawers which might have had folders with documents in them. I guessed she stayed in touch with her business life though her mobile phone. My mother had been impressed in the limousine when she saw Bobbie take the mobile from a sculpted bronze hand, key in messages and, smiling apologies, send them.

This house, Bobbie had said, was her London 'retreat'; she unwound here. For some reason, though, as I stood looking out at the garden, I thought it was something more specific than that, more than a vague 'retreat'. Last night's experience in bed made me think otherwise.

'Hello, Leo,' Bobbie's voice made me turn from the window.

Her head was still resting on the pillow. I noticed how the sunlight gave her blonde hair a bright sheen, and smiled. She smiled back. 'Did you sleep well?' she asked.

'Yes, I did, thank you. And you?'

'Best sleep I've had in yonks. I feel so good, Leo.'

'Do you?'

'Mmm,' she went. 'A bit sore down there, but

lovely. I had a nice dream too.'

'What was it about?'

'That's the thing. I don't remember much. I've been trying to remember, but can't. All I recall is me on a sandy beach somewhere on a hot day. There were other people on the beach too, also in swimwear. But the sun seemed to be shining only on me. I felt like a happy high-school girl.'

'Then what happened?'

She smiled and shook her head. 'Can't remember. The atmosphere was relaxed, friendly. It's so annoying, isn't it?' she added, 'when you can't get back into your dream, can't re-start it.'

'I know what you mean. Frustrating. You have a very attractive garden,' I said, motioning with my hand.

'It is. An old man, a pensioner, sees to it. Says it keeps him fit. He comes on a motorbike with his tools in a side-car,' she said with another smile. 'There's a tap outside. He doesn't have to come inside.'

'The blooms are beautifully laid out – they balance one another, somehow. Everything's so well kept. Has he been coming a long time?'

She pursed her lips and paused to think: 'Well over three years now – yes, getting on for four years. He wasn't the first gardener I tried after I bought this place.'

'There were others before him?'

'Three others. They didn't have his experience or his patience. He likes trying out different arrangements, testing to see if they work, but he always explains what he's after.'

'He keeps experimenting?'

'That's right,' Bobbie said, patting the bed. 'Come, Leo, lie beside me.'

I stepped to the bed, got back on and lay my head on the pillow beside hers. She pushed herself up, turned

130

and looked down. She glanced at my still-sleeping dick, at my abdomen, at the wisps of hair on my chest, made eye contact again, then traced a finger down each of the four parallel scars running vertical between my nipples.

'It must've been terrible,' she said, 'those metal prongs sticking in you.'

'It wasn't my best experience,' I replied. I hoped she wouldn't notice how conscious I was that an earlier lie, the one to my mother and Heidi night before last, had led straight to this further lie to back it up. My deceitfulness was making me into an ad-lib fibber: I didn't want anyone else to know about my activities with Drug Squad officers. 'It was such a freak accident,' I said, 'tripping in a field while running to keep fit. Who'd think there might be a rusty rake in the undergrowth waiting for muggins to fall on it? Luckily, it healed completely after the anti-tetanus injection. I prefer not to dwell on it.'

'Fair enough,' she said, sagging back down beside me. 'I was just testing to see if you still felt any pain.' With our faces close I felt again her light breath when she spoke and inhaled the last of her soapy mango fragrance. 'In fact, the word *experiment* actually means *to test*, in Latin,' she added, referring to her gardener's apparently random experiments with plants and shrubs and potted blooms. 'It's from the verb *experior*, I test – a deponent verb.'

'I know that verbs are active or passive, of course. But what's a *deponent* verb?'

'It's a verb whose ending *looks* as if it's passive,' she said and grinned, 'but has an active meaning.'

'Oh. So why's it called *deponent*? Why not, say, *pro-active*? A pro-active verb?'

I'd learnt from my reading of law books that it wasn't possible to avoid Latin phrases in my chosen profession – they were an integral part of legal language. I soon came across *in camera*, meaning in a room, i.e. behind closed doors; *prima facie*, on the face of it, at first glance; *post mortem* examinations which often reveal information to forensic pathologists which no one had suspected before the corpse was opened up and often suggest the kinds of things that might have happened before the person died. The warning to customers in Roman times, *Caveat emptor*, let the purchaser beware, still governs the exchange of money for goods and services today, viz the Trades Description Act 1968 which prevents manufacturers, retailers and service-industry providers from misleading customers as to what they are spending their money on.

'It does exactly what it says on the tin': that TV ad suddenly had me worrying that Bobbie might not agree that she'd got what she thought she was paying for. She'd made it clear in our living room that she expected 'a high ratio of bangs per buck'. She wanted 'customer satisfaction', 'proper fulfilment', 'deep renewal'. She definitely would *not* be content with 'in and out and Bob's your uncle'.

Another Latin phrase I'd discovered and explored was *habeas corpus* – You (shall) have the body. Why was I now thinking of the body I'd just had in this bed, when that most definitely was *not* the import of this Latin phrase? *Habeas corpus* was in fact a legal writ by means of which a person could seek relief from unlawful detention of himself or herself, or of another person. It was a crucial instrument for safeguarding individual freedom against arbitrary state action. A landmark development in the history of human liberty took place when the original 13 American colonies declared independence and became a constitutional republic in which *the people* were sovereign. Any person, in the name of the people, acquired the

132

authority thereby to initiate a writ of *habeas corpus*.

I knew some Latin phrases before I met Bobbie Cullen, but I'd never heard of a *deponent* verb.

Bobbie smiled and squeezed my thigh gently with her fingers.

'The word *deponent* means *put aside*,' she said. 'It's from the Latin *pono*, I put, and *de*, aside. In the case of *experior*, I test, the passive *meaning* is put aside, even though the passive *ending* of the word is retained. The verb has a passive *look* on the page, but an active import.'

'You still remember the Latin you learnt at school?'

'And at St Anne's College, Oxford,' she nodded. 'We had super teachers. We had to translate unseen passages from the poets and from Caesar's diary – excerpts we hadn't come across before. It tested our vocabulary and grasp of grammar. In Greek, I studied Homer's *Odyssey*, and *The History of Herodotus* written by him in 440 BC. Would you like to hear how Book One starts?'

'In English translation? Yes, I would.'

She threaded her fingers together and placed her hands behind her head on the pillow; there were threads of grey hair in her armpits. 'These are the researches of Herodotus of Halicarnassus,' she recited from memory, 'which he publishes in the hope of thereby preserving from decay the remembrance of what men have done, and of preventing the great and wonderful actions of the Greeks and the Barbarians from losing their due meed of glory...' She glanced at me and added: 'That was one of the happiest times of my life. There's no way I could've guessed that tragedy was about to hit me in the guts.'

'Tragedy?' I looked at her afresh. 'What tragedy?'

She shook her head. 'Never mind,' she said with a wan smile. 'I won't spoil this moment by troubling you

133

with details. You bring back a very happy time of my life. I'm grateful for that too.'

She moved her head closer on the pillow and kissed my cheek. It gave me a persuasive feeling after the Latin and Greek lesson, after learning about *pono* and *experior* and about Herodotus of Halicarnassus, that I was the teacher's pet, and I kissed her back.

Chapter 16

Bloody hell. What a hassle. How was I going to explain the money?

The saying goes that every cloud has a silver lining, but what about clouds brought by loads of silver? 'Silence is golden,' I'd been taught at primary school. 'Speech is silver.' But what colour is it when your pockets are suddenly bulging with bullion? What exactly is the tint of joy? Which part of the rainbow, which splash of the palette is it that infuses you with such vivid optimism?

So much very suddenly seems possible when you have the means to make it happen. The timid, shrunken self you used to be dissolves and disappears. The alter ego with such a wimpish, pale persona brought into being by indebtedness, by penny-pinching, by endless threadbare promises to pay the money back, to clear the slate, becomes, silently, quickly, inflated. You feel pumped up with what was all along your own potential. You fill out. You re-inherit the person your parents created. The person they shaped and, in some ways perhaps, fucked up, as Philip Larkin says, you rediscover and make anew. And you supervise this magical transformation with the enabler that has a wide repertoire of amicable names precisely because it is amenable and friendly to anyone in the world who would deploy its unfailing fruitfulness: bread, boodle, bucks, dosh, dinero, wonga, macha, the readies, lolly, geld, yen, yuan, rupees, spondulicks.

Money, money, money – it's a sexy thing.

Money, money, money – gives you such a zing.

'In the second drawer there,' Bobbie said, swinging her arm and pointing to the chest-of-drawers against the wall, 'you'll see a brown envelope, Leo. Fetch it, will

135

you? It's for you.'

Brown envelope. Brown envelope. Why did those bland words sound poetic? Why did they remind me of Ali Baba and the forty thieves and their stash of treasure in a secret cave? My heart started pounding. I felt the thudding in my chest. I also felt a turnover, from my left thigh to my right, my cock coming summarily awake as though summoned by a bugle call at dawn; it shrugged off sticky-eyed indolence, rose and stretched and would've yawned if it could. I pushed myself up, got off the bed and stepped by the leather pouffe to the chest-of-drawers.

I pulled out the second drawer and immediately saw an A5 brown envelope lying on what looked like a puff of two or three petticoats. I reached in, took out the envelope and brought it back to the bed. Bobbie twisted over to the other side, stretched an arm and brought up her handbag from the floor. It was the same bag from which she'd taken the wad of fifty-pound notes the day before, the bag my mother said Bobbie had told her cost £10,000.

She opened the bag, and, with her hands in it, peeled off four fifty-notes, then twisted my way and proffered them to me standing naked on a rug at the side of the bed.

'Add these to that envelope,' she said, making eye contact. 'I didn't know earlier what I know now.'

My fingers touched her palm as I took the four notes. I felt I'd never before seen such a kind, generously lovely face. I lifted the flap of the envelope and quickly counted the fifty-notes in it: there were six. I looked at her again, money in both my hands, nothing in my mouth, just dryness. She smiled when she saw my dick swing up in appreciation.

'It's five-hundred pounds, Bobbie,' I said when my lips came unstuck. 'Are you sure this is right?' I wondered if she could hear the pounding of my heart.

'Of course I'm sure.'

I sat on the edge of the bed, opened the envelope, took out the notes, spread them with the others on my left palm and counted them all again. Ten fifties. 'It's five-hundred pounds,' I mouthed, just audibly, so I could be triply sure: *hear* as well as see and feel my tremendous good fortune.

'Five-hundred, Bobbie. I didn't expect it.'

'What did you expect?'

'I don't know,' shaking my head, 'certainly not this much. It's very generous.'

'It's no more than you deserve. You've been here all night, Leo. How much is that per hour? You've pleased me terrifically, beyond *my* expectations. You're good company. Those fifties are yours because you're worth it.'

Five-hundred quid. I had to process the information to absorb its significance. Students like me usually had to work four or five weeks for this kind of money, if we were lucky enough to find the employment, competing with other minions with their backs to the wall – immigrants from Poland and Bosnia with names like Nowiski, Pawlak, Hadzipetrovic, people without papers from Asia and Africa, escapees from war zones and torturing regimes.

During holidays over several years I'd done whatever paid work I could get. I cleaned windows. I washed cars. I mowed lawns, tidied gardens and painted fences. For an extended period I changed tyres and balanced the wheels of cars at a pit-stop place, vans and lorries too; my hands kept getting filthy, my fingernails chipped and clogged with gunge, and every time I wiped the sweat from my brow with the back of my hand there was another smear of grime across my face.

At the frozen-food warehouse elsewhere in town, it was so cold despite the padded overalls and gloves we wore that the moisture in my nostrils would freeze and form tiny spikes that pricked whenever I lifted the chickens and turkeys wrapped in clingfilm. The spikes kept stabbing as I breathed while loading the goods into plastic crates and lugged the crates to the trolleys which my co-workers and I then had to push towards the exit doors. We had to get from the very coldest inner compartment across the vast expanse of the outer frozen area. Forcing the wheels over the lumps of ice that formed on the floor was a bugger. The wheels of the trolleys – rectangular metal affairs with two levels much more like hospital gurneys than supermarket trolleys – kept jamming, blocked by lumps of ice. We pushed and by sheer force of will and muscle power made headway between bags of frozen peas, frozen beans, frozen carrots, broccoli florets stacked in piles so high that they formed corridors along which we steered our stuff. Bags of boned chicken breasts, bags of oven chips, steak chips, mashed potato, boxes of potato waffles, king prawns, crispy potato croquettes, boxes of Yorkshire pudding, all frozen: such were the bricks in the walls we passed all day long. And every time we opened the doors to push the cargo out to the loading bay, a draught of warm air would hit the ceiling; the ice up there would melt again and drip to the floor, forming more irregular lumps which we had to negotiate in a state of growing disgruntlement – that was the hardest part of that particular job. The wheels often wouldn't budge for long moments of frustration. One consequence of our cumulative achievement: a floor knobbly with ice in new ways every thirty minutes or so.

Grafting in a tundra in the middle of town. Fingers stiff despite the gloves. Mouth hard and inflexible from the frozen moisture on our lips – yet uncomfortably sticky with sweat inside our overalls from all the pushing and forcing. That job couldn't compare either. It was a different kettle of fish altogether from luxuriating companionably in a bath full of hot fragrant water, then being fed appetizing *mezes,* then pleasuring a woman up for it with piles of money on a big wide bed in a house surrounded by a lovely garden.

And the measly money we made in those pursuits: we had to pay tax on it. No tax havens for us. We had bits chipped off as National Insurance contributions. Then there were the bus or tube fares getting to and from the job. Plus we had to ride the punches, put up with the scowls, the tones of voice, the swagger of the supervisors, guys who were superior to us because they had more experience of icicles in their nostrils. The bosses knew we were desperate. They knew there were hundreds ready to step into our place – more Kaminskis and Majewskis, more Haile Fikrus, more Ben-Hamids – if for whatever reason we baulked and walked out.

The thought that stayed with me when I left at knock-off time was chilling too. I wasn't a prisoner. I hadn't been found guilty of anything in any court of law. I was simply trying to earn enough to pay my way. Yet it seemed that I was heading for a life-style in which punishment was going to be the default mode. Despite my studies, despite all the books and documents I was poring over at home, it upset me to realize that I might be a minion forever, permanently broke and bitter.

So I knew very well the value of what I had.

I couldn't help smiling at the fifty-notes. I spread them out on my palms like playing cards. They seemed to be the best possible hand: four aces, four kings and two queens. They added up to a measure of independence, some little increment of integrity.

And I knew what I was going to do right away. Pay off some of my debts at last. And buy my mother something nice – a pair of quality shoes, perhaps, to wear when she sang at the Vortex gig. She could choose whatever make she wanted, whatever style. I was flush; I would pay. 'The eagle flies high,' that soul song says about the soaring power of a paypacket; 'Saturday night I go out to play.'

I wondered how I might use the money to express my love for Heidi, show my appreciation for everything she'd done for me. A smart restaurant wasn't a bad idea; some place upmarket for a change. In the West End perhaps, so we could head straight to one of the theatres in and around Shaftesbury Avenue after the last course of the meal. Heidi would like that. Maybe I should get seats for a play she'd been talking about. The two of us together in an auditorium full of other people: I'd always thought it emphasized our bonds, our being a couple, when we were in the midst of strangers, when neither of us knew anyone else in the crowd and were vivid in each other.

That's when the sabotaging thought exploded in my head. Heidi, ever sensible as she was, would want to know where I'd got the money to splash out so uncharacteristically. How could I afford it? What was the source of this sudden ostentation? It wouldn't be put in an accusing way, her question; it wouldn't be to pull me down or sneer. She'd just want to share the joy of my being flush, and thus deepen the joy, savour it thoroughly as the best way of congratulating me. Knowing how come I was one day flat broke and the next day rolling in it would make her love me even more.

Wouldn't it?

Like hell it would.

Rattled by the conundrum I was in, I suddenly got

an insight into why gangsters, racketeers, cocaine cartels in Latin America, the Calabrian 'Ndrangheta organization trading globally in drugs and weapons worth about $70 billion, approximately 3 per cent of Italy's GDP, as well as mobsters in Manhattan and New Jersey – why they all had to find ways of laundering their money.

Source of income: it was a basic starting-point in police enquiries. In Italy, they actually have 'tax police' whose primary purpose is tracking individuals whose flashy possessions indicate that they earn large amounts of money and ought therefore to have paid tax accordingly.

In the case of hypothetical Monsieur Ahmadou Conté, from a Muslim entrepreneurial family in Senegal, surveillance might reveal that: 'Your stall in Dakar market hasn't been doing very well, has it? The women traders alongside you selling tomatoes, onions, plantains and cassava have been more successful, haven't they? Your malachite statuettes simply aren't moving. Yet you want us to believe yams and pumpkins have paid for this gleaming Lamborghini and the gold-encrusted Rolex you're wearing? Please come with us, monsieur. You have to answer a few more questions.'

I was studying law at KCL because I wanted to be a lawyer with the Metropolitan Police; I'd be a in a good position then to bring grief to the illegal drugs industry that had brought so much grief to my mother for such a long time.

Yet here I was in a bungalow in Primrose Hill trying to think of an explanation for my new-found lolly, an explanation, no matter what the details turned out to be, that would amount to money laundering. I wouldn't be using banks, of course, or *bureaux de changes*, or kebab shops in Earls Court, but *words* with mendacious

141

meanings, verbal holograms, bullshit, fabrications, flannel. To get out of this fix I was going to have to be a politician to my girlfriend. I'd have to start practising a false smile because, no matter what I came up with, it would still amount to money laundering.

Jeez.

I felt soiled suddenly. My mind filled up with bits of Criminal Intelligence Service reports. How companies in various sectors of the economy all over the world, including the construction industry busy building skyscrapers at a rate of knots along the seafront in West Africa, had become entangled in money-laundering operations for cocaine cartels in South America. Huge sums, millions and millions, had to be 'cleaned'. The filthy lucre, ill-gotten gains, had to be made respectable. They had to be given a spotless, untraceable provenance by registered, legitimate, pukka corporations most of whose personnel probably never suspected that their jobs and incomes depended increasingly on the smarts of drug lords far away on another continent.

I can't eat meat in the morning; it's too serious nosh too soon. I prefer a pile of toast with honey, or some fried tomatoes on toast, plus cereal, a satsuma or some grapes, and coffee.

No worries on that score; Bobbie had it all in her fridge and larder.

'So when shall I see you again?' she asked in the kitchen. 'At the Vortex?' She put a grape into her mouth and watched me as I sipped my coffee.

I was respectable. I had my jeans and T-shirts on and knew where my zip jacket was. I'd had a shower to wash off the stickiness and get her dried-up juice out of my pubic hair. Bobbie was wearing her Japanese-looking robe and talking business on her phone when I came into the kitchen. She was giving orders, it sounded like, but in her equable, polite tone, having meetings arranged, insisting that someone be present at a particular venue, and someone else be back by a certain date. It didn't bother her that I was overhearing what she was saying; she made no attempt to turn away or to lower her voice when I passed her chair, opened the fridge and got stuff out to fix breakfast.

'I'll be with my mum,' I said, 'escorting her to the Vortex. I accompanied her to Ronnie Scott's in Soho too when she sang there.'

'Didn't she tell you?'

'Tell me what?'

'That the limo will pick her up and take her to the Vortex.'

'No,' I said, shaking my head, 'she didn't.'

'As far as I'm concerned, she's already a star,' Bobbie said. 'No one I've heard in recent years sings like your mother. And the songs she's been writing since your father died – her lyrics – they're extraordinary. Hers is can't-get material, Leo. I'm not taking any risks. Robin the chauffeur said she'd be chuffed to drive your mother.'

'The chauffeur is a woman?'

'Anything wrong with that?'

'No, nothing's *wrong* with it. But when I saw Robin the night you came to take my mother out…'

'Yes?'

'Well, Robin was wearing a grey suit and a driver's black hat with a shiny peak. Remember, when I pointed to where the council portaloo toilets were parked during Carnival?'

Bobbie's face broke into a grin. 'The chauffeur's kit made you assume she was a man – didn't it?'

'I supposed it did, come to think of it.'

'Only men can be chauffeurs? This is England, Leo,

not Saudi Arabia or Talibanland,' she said in an even voice. 'Robin's a good driver, experienced, reliable. She knows the streets of London – she has "the knowledge". She's driven clients of mine from Heathrow to Canary Wharf without a hitch, without satnav. It has no bearing that she likes to look like a man and prefers women in her private life.'

'Really? She's lesbian?'

'Yes, she's a lesbian and she works for me. Your mum will be in safe hands. Why don't you get in the car with her?'

'That would be good.' I couldn't help smiling as I saw myself in my mind's eye sitting beside my mother in a chauffeur-driven limousine moving through the busy streets to the Vortex club which in those years was still in Stoke Newington. I would be seeing London from a limo. I'd be tempted in my euphoria to wave at the pedestrians. Then I remembered. 'But I can't.'

'Why can't you?'

'My girlfriend – Heidi – we've agreed to go to the club together.'

'So? Go together in the limo.'

'Together in the limo?'

'With your mother. What's wrong with that?'

'There's nothing *wrong* with it.'

'Then why not? Listen, Leo. I'm not taking any chances with your mother's well-being. I care about her. I'm investing in her talent. We're going to make big money together.'

'Won't it bother you if my girlfriend rides in your limo?'

The penny dropped: I could see from the look in Bobbie's eyes. She had a good laugh, then chuckled on. 'It won't bother me at all,' she said. 'She's *your* girlfriend, Leo, not mine. And as you know, *I'm* no lesbian. It's *you* I want, not her. So when shall we be alone together again? The Vortex is one of a few warm-up gigs for your mother before her live recording at the Hi-Hat, but it's five days from now.'

She couldn't wait five days? She was in her fifties; my mother said she was fifty-two. I wondered what she was on. Skunk? Skunk nowadays was said to be much stronger than ever. I'd thought that people in their fifties were content to have sex once in fifty days. Perhaps it was something in the modern water supply. You never know: chemicals have been getting in everywhere. Pollution: it's the bane of the world: killing seabirds, poisoning the soil, filling the air with toxic particles, destroying the habitat of polar bears, and now, insidiously, making old women raunchy, making their memory fail, making them forget their decorum and that they're supposed to be demure, not gagging for it like teenage girls are said to do in the tabloid press.

'Is five days too far off?' I asked.

'Five days would be useless.'

'Why's that?'

'The Vortex is going to be full of people. We're going to be surrounded. Your mother will be there, happy and excited to be singing. Your Heidi will be there. The band has an international reputation, they're an all-star group – they and their instruments will be there. You call that a lovers' tryst?'

'It's a great night out at an awesome club, but no, of course not. It isn't a tryst.'

'Where's the secrecy in a club full of people?' she asked. 'We shook hands on secrecy. D'you remember, Leo?'

I nodded. 'Yes I do.'

'Don't you want us to stick to our agreement? Keep it a secret?'

145

'Of course I do.'

'So how would tomorrow night suit you?' she asked, her eyes locked on mine. 'Or the night after?'

'Where should we meet?'

'Here. It must be here, in this house. This is my retreat, my therapeutic pad. Here. Always.'

'Will I be staying overnight?'

'I'd like that very much. I'll make it worth your while. I love your style, Leo, your energy. You're my sherpa,' she grinned across the kitchen table. 'You've guided me up the mountain to the highest pinnacles of pleasure. I want you take me there again.'

It occurred to me that I might be sounding as though I wasn't keen, as though I was playing hard to get. I definitely wasn't playing hard to get. I wanted to get out of debt, that's what I wanted. I wanted to get ahead in my chosen profession, without having to rely so much on my mother and on interest-bearing loans and the feigned concern of faceless bureaucrats. This was a golden opportunity I'd stumbled on. I had in my pocket the beginnings of a nest egg and Bobbie was obviously willing to lay more golden eggs for me. She was right: it *was* incomparable. It was a welcoming, pleasantly accessible supply of the readies.

'Very well, then,' I said, mixing up in my eroto-fiscal excitement two separate personas and deploying my trainee-lawyer tone of voice instead of the concubine-man complaisance that was called for. I had to practise, I knew. I was too much of a novice at this game. I had to get my scenarios right. I had to keep my different selves out of one another's way and stop making the silly mistakes of an apprentice prostitute. 'Tomorrow night is fine, Bobbie. Same time again?'

'Yes,' she said. 'Always come after ten o'clock. My company's main office is in Islington – the house where I live is there too. Ten p.m. gives me plenty time.

There'll be food when you get here,' she smiled again, 'in case you're feeling hungry when you arrive.'

'Will you want to see my blood-donor barcode again?'

'No, Leo, not tomorrow But every time you receive a *new* letter detailing your next donor session, bring the letter and show me.'

Chapter 17

The traffic in Praed Street outside Paddington tube station was hectic as ever. Black taxis and delivery vans were vying with double-decker buses and private cars; some were honking impatiently as they waited for the obstruction in front to 'get a fucking move on', as one driver shouted through his window. Vehicles in the crawling congestion kept trying to overtake, worsening the snarl. Pedestrians in collar and tie dodging between the saloons and coupés risked life and limb as they crossed through the din from one side of the street to the other. Perhaps they were made reckless by the knowledge that St Mary's Hospital A&E department was only metres away around the next corner.

I knew where Maddox Eye Care was even though I hadn't been there for a while. The Paddington 24-hour Minicabs depot was along the opposite pavement, also a Burger King place. I passed a Snappy Snaps digital photo establishment and the Quality Crown Hotel and Fountain Abbey pub as I stepped towards Edgware Road. When he wasn't at college, my best friend Lester Maddox helped in his dad's shop which was somewhere on the other side further along from – I kept looking as I walked – the Chicken Spot, the BestLook hair and makeup studio, a Carphone Warehouse outlet, and, yes, there it was, just past a shop with a bright yellow front purveying gifts and novelties opposite the east side of the hospital. Up ahead was the sign of the Hilton Metropole Hotel at the junction with Edgware Road.

There were three people seated in the waiting area when I entered Mr Maddox's spacious shop. Although several of the seats were free, I didn't want to interfere with the business by taking any of them. Instead, I moved along slowly, looking at the rows of spectacle frames slotted into stands lining the panels on either side of the door. There were dozens of frames on display. Above or beside each stand was a printed caption: affordable frames, rimless frames, half-rim frames, super flexible super light frames, magnetic optical frames, classical frames for children, designer frames: Prada, Dior, Gucci, Bvlgari.

One sign in crisp lettering said: 'We only stock sunglasses that give 100% protection from UV light. We recommend polarized lenses because they are suitable for sports such as skiing, diving and on the beach. They block off reflected glare and maximize clarity and comfort.'

Alongside a large illustration of the cross-section of an eye with arrows indicating the outer choroid, the retina, rovia, sclera, macula, optic nerve, lense, iris, and cornea was a sign saying: 'Ask our qualified opticians about frame suitability for *your* lenses. We'll be pleased to adjust your frames so they are not too tight or too loose and fit comfortably.'

I heard voices behind me, turned and saw Mr Maddox emerge from a curtained-off area with a woman customer in a floral dress. Mr Maddox saw me, smiled, raised a with-you-in-a-minute palm and ushered the woman to the counter. He leaned over the counter and handed a sheet of paper to the young female assistant who'd just finished a telephone conversation and was putting the phone back on the cradle. Another assistant, also a woman, also in a white coat, but a bit older and with big ginger hair, was looking at the screen of a laptop computer.

Mr Maddox turned and smiled at the customer and told the younger assistant: 'Missus Freely wants to see whether contact lenses will suit her. I think they'll suit her very well.'

149

'So do I,' the assistant replied with a smile.

'They won't take too long to get used to, will they?' Mrs Freely asked.

'Not long, no. Give them a go and decide for yourself,' Mr Maddox said. 'You don't have any ocular problems, Missus Freely. No sign of glaucoma or macular degeneration. Your peripheral vision is excellent. We make sure our contact lenses meet the prescription requirements of each patient, including the oxygen requirements. We'll try a Cibavision pair, and a pair from Bausch and Lomb, then you choose.' He smiled and, nodding at the assistant, added: 'Jessie here will fix a convenient appointment for you.'

Then he stepped over, put a hand on my shoulder and steered me to another curtained-off room at the other end of the shop, and ushered me in. Lester was there, looking at his mobile and texting someone.

'Good to see you, Leo,' Mr Maddox said. 'Where've you been hiding?'

'At home,' I said, 'reading, writing essays.'

'How's it going? Still enjoying the law?'

'There's a lot to remember.'

'You still aiming to join the Met?'

'Nothing's happened to change my mind, Mister Maddox.'

'Stay with it, son,' he said. 'You won't regret studying. But don't make yourself so scarce, man,' he grinned and slapped my shoulder.

'Can you spare a minute?' I asked.

'For you, Leo – of course. What's up?'

'I have something for you, at last – and for Aunt Josie,' I said, bringing out a white foolscap envelope from my pocket and handing it to him.

'What's this?'

'The money you lent me – ages ago, one-hundred-and-twenty pounds. And thirty-five pounds for Aunt

150

Josie. Please remind her – she lent it to me in your kitchen nearly two years ago. She's probably forgotten,' I added. 'I'm sorry it's taken so long. But it's so cool, paying you back.'

He held my gaze. 'Really, Leo? You sure you can spare it?'

I nodded. 'Makes me feel good. You trusted me and now I've kept my word.'

'You're Leonard's son,' he smiled. 'I've known you since you were born. Of course I trusted you.'

'Then please take it. And tell Aunt Josie I'll see her at the Vortex Saturday evening.'

'All right, Leo,' he said, nodding thoughtfully and keeping eye contact, 'and thank you. It's going to be a good night for Arlene – the band has a high rep.' He put the envelope into a side pocket of his white coat. 'Stop by whenever you like.'

'Stop by whenever you like,' his son Lester repeated jokingly when his dad had turned and stepped back out through the curtain. Lester swung an open palm at me and we shook hands, as we did whenever we met, gripping first the heel of each other's hand, then clasping the palm. Lester wasn't as tall as his dad, who was about six foot three, and he wasn't as broad shouldered, but he was taller than me, by a bit, and darker skinned than me, having more of his father's black Caribbean complexion than his mother's Irish peaches-and-cream.

On one of the walls of this narrow room was an illuminated box with rows of letters of the alphabet arranged at random in decreasing sizes, letters smaller and smaller to check just how good one's eyesight was: X G M L Y and so on. I'd had my eyes tested in this same room years before by Mr Maddox when Lester and I were still at school. Now here he was, my best mate, wearing a white coat like a professional optician.

151

Facing the illuminated box was a leather upholstered chair, similar to the ones in a barber's shop, which the optician raised and lowered to the right level for each patient.

Lester motioned with his hand and I sat down on the chair. To my left, on a small table against the wall, was equipment like a double microscope for testing aspects of your eyes. For eye pressure, you had to keep each eye wide open in turn, focusing on a red dot, and a puff of air would suddenly hit the surface of your eyeball. Another measurement involved little lights blinking on and off on all sides of a screen, and you had to press a button in quick succession to show you'd seen every single blink no matter where it was.

A special piece of software took detailed digital photos of the interior back walls of your eyes and sent them straight to the screen of a laptop computer; in less than a minute you could see the pattern of veins at the backs of your eyes!

'It's to check whether the blood vessels have been damaged in any way, leaking a bit, perhaps,' Mr Maddox had told me. 'People with diabetes, for example, can't process all the sugar in their blood. Not all their sugar is converted to energy. So the remaining sugar goes round and round the bloodstream and could chafe and fray the surface of the blood vessels. If it isn't spotted early and dealt with, the person could go blind. If the blood vessels in their feet are seriously damaged, their feet could become gangrenous and might have to be amputated.'

Bloody hell, I thought. I hadn't guessed that opticians were medical investigators too. Luckily, Mr Maddox said my eyes were fine. I had 20–20 vision.

'So, Lester,' I asked, 'you've definitely made up your mind?'

'About what?'

'Being an optician.'

'The correct term is optometrist,' he said with a smile. 'Yeah, this is the game for me.'

'I once heard your dad talk about an ophthalmologist. What's the difference?'

'Let's see,' Lester said, touching his upper lip. 'I think I've got it right. Optometrists check people's eyes, usually once a year. They try to detect certain eye diseases and they prescribe eyeglasses for nearsightedness or farsightedness, or for something that's called astigmatism.'

'And ophthalmologists?'

'They're more deeply trained. They're full medical doctors whose speciality is the health of people's eyes. They diagnose eye diseases, and treat them, and sometimes perform eye surgery.'

'Eye surgery? Shit.'

Lester smiled and leaned back against the wall. 'Under anaesthetic, man. You aren't awake – not in the eyeball anyway.'

'So were your A-level subjects okay for a university course in optometry?'

'They were,' he said. 'My dad gave me good advice. I did biology, maths, physics and chemistry, and got three As and a B. They said I was an ideal applicant. That really amped me up.'

'Good to have a dad, hey – advising you.'

'It's a blast, brother,' he said. 'You don't waste time. You don't waste energy. You know what your target is.'

'Anyway,' I said, rising from the padded chair and taking four ten-pound notes from my back pocket, 'thanks for not hassling me for the dosh. It was a long time to wait, I know.' I proffered the cash. He kept looking at my face, but didn't move. I reached out, lifted his right hand and placed the notes on his palm.

'There. I've paid you back at last.'

'I don't want it back, Leo. You don't have to give me this money.'

'I know I don't have to, Lester, but I *want* to,' I said. 'When I needed it, you were there for me.' I took the notes from his palm, folded them and pushed them into the top pocket of his white coat.

'Where'd you get it – this dosh?'

'Small win on the lottery. Didn't come too soon. You still coming to the gig at the Vortex?'

His face broke into a smile. 'I can't help cheesing when I think of your mum on the stage there after the band's had a soundcheck. That place is awesome, always bumping – she belongs there.'

'Martha coming too? She hasn't changed her mind?'

'Why would she do that? That was her I was texting a minute ago. She heard your mum singing at Ronnie Scott's – she was with me all the time but I thought she was on X, she was so blowing up.'

I knew what he meant. I wasn't the only one whose heart was rapt when my mother sang. It was a kind of cardiac arrest. Her voice took over your inner life, gave your own memories deeper meaning, and, for the duration of the lyrics, somehow made you more vivid with the past happiness trying to hem in her pain.

I smiled at Lester. 'I have to go now,' looking at my watch, 'don't want to be late for an unusual lecture. See you and Martha Saturday night. Stay cool.'

'King's has for many decades been fortunate in attracting speakers from a wide range of backgrounds, professions and nationalities,' Professor John Naransamy-Judd said as he stood in his beige suit and polka-dot bow tie at the side of the lectern, a sheet of paper in one hand. Seated behind him at the back of the stage was a woman with brown hair cut into a bob and wearing a trouser suit whose colour was indeterminate, somewhere between light blue and purple.

'Among those who have kindly interrupted their busy schedules to come to Strand Campus and give us the benefit of their experience and understanding have been Archbishop Desmond Tutu, Lord Longford, and Sir Alec Douglas-Home, the only prime minister to have played first-class cricket, to name but three public figures. It gives me great pleasure today to continue the tradition,' the professor said, turning his smile from the left side of the audience to the right and nodding at particular faces he recognized here and there, 'by introducing a speaker who was at King's before – twenty-six years ago, to be exact, when she was an undergraduate on an LLB programme in the School of Law. You'll have seen her name on the roster of forthcoming speakers. She has come to give us insights into the legal difficulties and tensions, the anomalies and ambiguities which police officers encounter in the normal course of their work with the Clubs and Vice Squad unit of the Metropolitan Police. Her talk is entitled,' he added, glancing at the page in his hand, '*Policing Prostitution: More an Art than a Science.*'

The professor leaned forward and lowered his voice to a mock surreptitious tone that raised a few chuckles: 'It would be wrong to believe that reason reigns supreme in the relations between our country's legislature and those whose job is to enforce its enactments.'

He turned with extended arm to the woman and smiled at her. She grinned and rose from her chair and stepped to the lectern.

'Please give a warm welcome to King's College alumna Detective Chief Inspector Angelina Burdett.'

What a treat, I thought: a senior policewoman who'd studied at KCL. I couldn't have found better

155

confirmation that I was on the right track. A degree in law *could* lead to seniority at the Met. I'd always thought it could, been advised that it could, but here before us for all to see was living proof.

Professor Naransamy-Judd left the stage and sat in the only vacant seat in the front row. He was about eight rows down from me in the tiered auditorium, which was packed. DCI Angelina Burdett had a clear complexion; her posture was upright but not stiff. She acknowledged the applause with a few nods of her head, smiled and waited for the clapping to subside, then got straight to the point.

'I am very proud to have been invited back to my old college where I spent some of the happiest years of my life,' she said in a voice loud enough to be heard without a microphone. 'I learned something crucially important while I was at King's, something that has saved my sanity more than once. I learned not to believe that an intelligent person will *always* behave in intelligent ways, or that an organization staffed by rational individuals will *always* perform in a manner that is logical beyond argument.'

She paused briefly, making eye contact with members of the audience. 'I'd like you to consider the following facts and decide for yourselves whether they fit together coherently. Please do let me know what you think – this is going to be a talk, certainly not a one-way lecture.' She smiled and added: 'I wouldn't have come otherwise. The people in parliament do their best to pass laws that are logically consistent, laws which together show a unity of purpose, but on the ground, in the streets that make up the Vice Squad's turf, we sometimes feel that the right hand doesn't know what the left hand is doing. Anyway, here we go:

'It is legal in this country to provide sexual services in a private house or flat if you are the only person

156

doing so there. But if anyone else is doing there what you are doing, then you could be prosecuted under section thirty-three of the Street Offences Act 1959. The reason for this is that taking money for your erotic services ceases to be legally permissible as soon as someone else is known to be doing what is legal when you alone do it. It doesn't matter that the other person or persons selling sex do so at different times of the day or at different times of the week. You may not even know of their activities. What counts in law is that the house or flat is being used for "physical acts of indecency for sexual gratification,"' she leaned forward somewhat when she quoted the phrase, 'by more than one person. That is what transforms the premises into a brothel.'

She paused and smiled at us. I wondered if she was picking up the subtle change in the ambience. I wondered if it was only me who was conscious of the way the vibes were altering. I was secretly pleased to hear from the mouth of a Detective Chief Inspector that when I took £500 from Bobbie Cullen for bringing about her sexual gratification, several times, I didn't break the law of the land. I was still respectable. But somehow – was it my feeling of shame seeping out into the air around me? – I felt a certain judgmental starchiness begin to harden the atmosphere in the auditorium. Burdett was a senior cop. We were all staring at her. This was a renowned academic institution. So why did I feel that a certain seediness was spoiling the proceedings?

'Once a place meets the arcane criteria of a brothel,' DCI Burdett continued, 'arrests can be made. Incidentally,' she smiled again, 'when entering a house of ill repute, I've never heard any of my colleagues shout: "This is a bust!" Or "You are all nicked!"'

'Now consider this. Even if you *are* working as a

prostitute in a brothel you are not breaking the law. You are not committing an offence. The police have to find evidence to prove that you were in some way *managing* the brothel or *assisting in its management*. You can service twenty clients a day and still not be liable to prosecution if your behaviour is untainted by managerial duties.'

She had a way with words. I thought she was making a potentially uncomfortable topic sound palatable.

She nodded down to where Professor Naransamy-Judd was seated in the front row and said: 'The professor referred to the anomalies and ambiguities in the work which we in the Vice Squad do. I've been trying to illustrate what he meant. In this country it is not illegal to advertise sexual services in a public place with the intention of attracting customers. That is part of your freedom of speech. But if your ad is so effective that it is considered likely to' – she leaned forward slightly again – '"deprave and corrupt" persons likely to see it, then you could be taken to court under the Obscene Publications Act 1959.

'So you *can* advertise your availability for sex, but you *can't* do so too effectively.'

There was laughter in various parts of the hall; it didn't sound particularly mirthful, though.

'Here's another gem,' she said. 'Section forty-six of the Criminal Justice and Police Act 2001 prohibits, on pain of six months' imprisonment, anyone from placing, "on, or in the immediate vicinity of, a public telephone an advertisement relating to prostitution" if it is done "with the intention that the advertisement should come to the attention of any other person or persons". The catch is that this does *not* apply to telephones in places from which under-sixteens are barred.'

A student two rows in front of me put his hand up.

'Yes?' the speaker asked.

'What about sex between gay men?'

'What about it? I hear it's quite popular,' she said, and you could sense the atmosphere ease.

'Are there any, quote, anomalies, unquote, in the laws governing gay sex?'

'Let's see,' she answered, looking upwards for a moment. 'When the 1967 Act decriminalized some sexual acts between men, it specifically required that those acts had to be "in private" which was taken to mean between only *two* people, not involving any other individuals or being *seen* by any other person. But when several gay men were convicted for enjoying *consensual group sex* in violation of the 1967 Act, the European Court of Human Rights quashed the conviction in 2000, declaring in effect that such sex was legal.'

'So the laws governing sexual relationships change,' said the voice of a woman behind me. 'They aren't set in stone.'

'God, no, they aren't. About thirty years ago, in the early 1970s, an "alternative" newspaper called the *International Times* was convicted of conspiring to corrupt public morals by publishing ads for gay men. In a hair-splitting ruling, the House of Lords decided that, although sex between gay men was legal, *public encouragement* of gay-sex acts was not. The *International Times* had to close down as a result of that ruling. And yet, today, there are quite a few magazines that openly carry ads for male escorts who frequently display their erections as well as their prices.'

'If things have become so lax, so permissive,' a pink-skinned man with greying hair a few seats to my right asked, 'what is the point of the police? What do

159

they spend their time doing?'

'I assure you, sir,' DCI Burdett replied, 'we in the Vice Squad have our hands full. The Crown Prosecution Service decides which cases to take to court. Their personnel are guided by a document entitled *Offences Against Public Morals and Decency* which has a direct bearing on the operations of police officers. It's our job to keep prostitutes, male or female, off the streets, thereby preventing them from annoying members of the public. We are very busy trying to prevent gangsters, increasingly foreign gangsters from Albania and thereabouts, forcing women into prostitution. We believe on the basis of video surveillance that there have been set up in our cities what can only be called prisons for sex slaves. Servicing dozens of men against their will every day are young women who were enticed to leave their homes and families by the promise of good, well-paid jobs. Their initiation into a miserable life of unending prostitution takes the form of being raped by the men who have bought them – bought them for a sum of cash – from other men who've made money from smuggling them across Europe and into London.

'The scale of this problem only began to dawn on us when our people found evidence that gangs of traffickers were selling women into prostitution immediately they arrived on British soil. What are termed "slave auctions" attended by brothel keepers were taking place in airport precincts. One such auction was held in a coffee bar in a terminal where no one else realized what was going on. Some of the traffickers are also involved in fencing Class A drugs and guns.'

That was something that hadn't occurred to me. I hadn't thought that international drug dealers might be the same people selling women and guns. That was an avenue I was going to have to explore in more detail before I graduated. I suddenly felt grateful to whoever had invited this particular speaker to come and talk about her work.

I sensed the atmosphere in the auditorium change again. Everything the speaker in the purply blue trouser suit said rang true. She said it wasn't only places like Somalia and Sudan where respect for law and order were on the brink of collapsing and where people themselves were becoming tradeable commodities. There were women in England too under the control of organized gangs.

'It is part of our job,' she went on, 'to pursue, arrest and see penalized anyone who organizes prostitutes and makes a living from their earnings. The CPS document *Safeguarding Children Involved in Prostitution* reminds us that where under-age persons are concerned, our focus should be on those who coerce and exploit them. The penalties are up to fourteen years in jail.'

Perhaps it was because I realized that the Vice Squad were trying to track down the kind of people who'd killed my father that I felt my esteem for DCI Burdett go up and up as she spoke and answered questions for a full hour about the work she and her colleagues were doing. They had principles they abided by. They had operational guidelines. They had a strategy which, she said, was ever evolving in response to realities on the ground. No one was forced to join the police service, she reminded us. Coercion was psychologically counter-productive; it was the opposite of motivation. Our country, she said, despite the sleaze among politicians, the backhanders some of them have allegedly taken for smoothing the way for extra-parliamentary interests, for rich individuals wanting to buy ostentatious, la-di-da titles or a British passport quickly – our country still had justifiable pretensions to being a democracy.

There in the auditorium in the School of Law it occurred to me that whatever else I might want, I sure as hell didn't want to be associated in any way with deliberate coercion of anybody. I didn't ever want to make people cower, or shrink in fear, or brandish a pistol at their head. If I'd ever made anyone tremble, it could only have been unwittingly, in an unconscious way. I had witnessed my mother's misery too long, the repercussions in her endless lonely days of having seen my father murdered right in front of her eyes, to want to join the ranks of the cruel. I'd seen her weariness, which had nothing to do with being physically tired, too frequently. She often smiled at me, kissed me and held me close, but many times I fancied I saw cracks in her eyes. I heard her sighing as she forced herself, year in, year out, to trek across the terrain that was, without my father, her inner emptiness. Only singing had the power to save her.

Coercion wasn't for me. But taking money that was freely given, willingly given, for services rendered in a private house – whether the house met the criteria of a *fuckpad* or not – had nothing to do with coercion. It was much more like cooperation, I thought, like a physiotherapist being paid for restoring the balance between a patient's body and their mental well-being. It was an aspect of the Buddhist notion of *karma*, in that a fresh source of fulfilment was introduced where previously there had only been hungry longing. It was, as Bobbie Cullen said in the bath full of hot, foamy water, 'civilized'.

Chapter 18

My mother's gig at the Vortex went well – 'better than I dared to hope', she told me afterwards. The full-to-capacity audience rose to their feet and applauded her for minutes on end, after both sets. They clapped and whistled and called out 'More! More!' She looked cool standing at the mic, the members of the band behind her also clapping, the lights overhead reflected in the sheen of her full-length dress.

As I watched her, I recalled what Bobbie had said to me: 'As far as I'm concerned she's already a star. We're going to make a bundle together.'

When Arlene came down from the stage, I saw Bobbie kiss her, first on one cheek, then on the other. They were beaming at each other. Bobbie guided my mother to a table on the far side of the club from us where a bottle of champagne and two glasses were waiting. They sat down there and fell into a deep conversation.

Lester and his girlfriend Martha were seated at the table with Heidi and me. His father Mr Maddox and his mother Josie were at the next table along. Martha leaned over and told me she'd never seen Heidi looking so sexy.

'She's such a lovely girl, Leo.'

'So are you, Martha,' I replied.

'You don't have to be polite.'

'Who's being polite? I'm being honest. I wonder if Lester knows what a lucky bastard he is to have someone like you. He's a thoughtful guy, usually, so he probably does know.'

Martha grinned. 'You're sweet, Leo,' she said. 'What a singer your mother is.'

'I feel so proud of her tonight.'

163

'I'm not surprised.'

'Heidi and I heard her at Ronnie Scott's too – saw you there that night.'

'I was blown away.' Martha grinned, 'had no idea what was coming.'

Heidi was on my other side. She put an arm around my shoulders and pulled me closer. Her embraceable body was wrapped in a short ivory silk taffeta dress with open shoulders and deep neckline, its soft horizontal pleats clinging to her midriff and thighs. I loved the way she kept kissing me during that gig, looking at me with her large hazel-green eyes and smiling, her hand often resting on my thigh.

Lester for some reason was arsey that evening. At one point when he and I had stepped round to the men's lavatory and gone in, he gave me a funny look and asked: 'Why are you dressed all in white? What's your game? Trying to project an angelic image, are you?'

'What you talking about?'

'I know you're studying law,' he said as we stood side by side pissing at the shiny white surface streaming with water. 'I know you want to become a criminal lawyer with the Met and then,' pushing his lips into a pout and frowning, 'become the chief prosecutor at the Old Bailey, but that doesn't make you one of the angels, does it?'

'Angels? What you talking about, Lester?'

'You probably won't get the promotion you want.'

'Why not? How d'you know? I'm still at college, haven't graduated, haven't even joined the Met yet,' I said and went to wash my hands in one of the basins. There were guys around us pissing and others splashing their hands under the taps, still others entering or leaving the cubicles, but it didn't bother Lester that they could hear what he was saying.

'You're barking up the wrong tree,' he said, looking

down again as his arc of urine petered to a dribble. He shook himself dry, zipped up his fly, washed his hands and then pressed his fist against the silver button of the hot-air dryer; it filled the loo with a high-pitched humming. 'Your white kit won't help, even if you think it makes you look angelic. It's the wrong tree for you,' he said again.

The image broke me into a laugh. An angel with white wings leaning forward on its arms against the trunk of a tree, head tilted back to bark into the leaves above.

'You dissing me because I want to be a lawyer, or because I'm wearing white?'

'It's more than white, isn't it?'

'What is?'

'White suit, white shirt, white tie, white waistcoat, white shoes. It's a fucking whitewash, Leo. Who you trying to kid? You've never been decked out like this before – in the colour of angels.'

'Angels again. What's with you, Lester? Since when have you been religious?'

'Whose religious? I'm going to be an optometrist, not a vicar.' He looked at me as though *I* was the one who wasn't making sense.

Lester was my best friend. We were born in the same hospital ward within minutes of each other; that was when my dad first met *his* dad and they each agreed to be godfather to the other's infant. But we'd had our disagreements, Lester and I. He lived near us with his parents in a Victorian house in Powis Square off Colville Terrace. I was always with them over the years, when his older sister Samantha and brother Victor hadn't yet left home, especially after my father was shot and my mother sank into listlessness. Aunt Josie washed and dressed me and fed me. Lester and I played in the back garden of that house. When I was

165

six, they gave me and other kids at my birthday party bowls of rice soaked with the juice of my favourite fruit, mango. I used to do my homework in Lester's room. Nearly all my books and games when my mother wasn't well were given to me by Lester's parents or uncles. I often watched television with Mr Maddox and, with him, Samantha, Victor and Lester in their kitchen in winter, ate the scones made by Aunt Josie with strawberry jam and a dollop of cream on top.

I felt at home in their house. I felt they were my family. It was sometimes full of different accents, that place in Powis Square – the Jamaican lilt of the neighbours next door when they popped in; Samantha and Victor's rapping rhymes in London voices as they swayed and gestured to their inner beat; Aunt Josie's Irish brogue which tended to deepen when her brothers, Uncle Frank and Uncle Brendan Power, came visiting. They had the same light-brown hair as Aunt Josie, and the same greyish blue eyes. Both of them lived in London with their wives and children, Uncle Frank not far away in Kilburn, Uncle Brendan in Spitalfields in the East End where he worked with a company of architects who'd designed several of the new stations of the Jubilee Line Extension. The extension opened while I was still at school.

'Underground stations have unique requirements,' Uncle Brendan explained to Lester and me during one of his visits; we were drinking tea in the kitchen. 'We have to conjure up in those stations subterranean landcapes by means of, if you'll pardon the fancy phrase, topographical architecture. As you'll have noticed,' he said with a smile, 'people aren't moles. They weren't made to live in dark tunnels. So we have to design spaces that afford experiences which switch between confinement and openness, using artificial light and natural light accordingly.'

166

He told us about the unusually large underground station at Canary Wharf and about design elements in the ticket halls at Blackfriars Road and at Waterloo East, and the concourses at those places.

'I hope you don't mind my asking, Uncle Brendan, but I have a question about that,' Lester said. He and I were sixteen at the time.

'What's the question?'

'Is there good money in the work you do?'

'Don't be so cheeky,' his mother chipped in.

'No – it's a good question,' her brother told her. 'Who wants to work for peanuts?' Then he looked at his nephew again and asked: 'Do you know how much the Jubilee Line Extension cost?'

Lester shook his head. 'Naah, I don't. Millions probably.'

'You aren't even close. In the end it came to more than three and a half *billion* pounds. That breaks down to four million pounds per metre It was one of the most expensive projects in the world.'

'Per *metre*?' Lester was openly incredulous. 'So how many metres are there?'

Uncle Brendan smiled and said: 'You figure it out. The extension of the Jubilee Line called for the design and building by civil engineers of six brand-new underground stations between Stratford in the east and Westminster where the Houses of Parliament are, including Bermondsey, Canada Water and North Greenwich. Other stations also had to be upgraded. And get this: the extension crosses the River Thames four times. Someone had to dig those tunnels, boy – skilled workers with the most up-to-date equipment. Much of that work was done by Irishmen. Next time your Uncle Frank comes here, ask him who gouged out all the tons of mud under the river. Ask him who built the air vents and escape shafts, who fitted the thirty-four lifts in the stations and the hundred-and-eighteen escalators. Uncle Frank works for one of the contractors who actually did the work. Access to the platforms in the new stations is entirely free of steps. Buy a ticket to Bermondsey or Canning Town – you'll see for yourself. It's easy for the passengers – lifts or escalators.'

'I didn't mean to be rude, Uncle Brendan,' Lester said. 'I was just asking.'

'No, it's a good question. The new stations are the first to have doors that slide open and shut at the edge of the platforms.'

'Why's that?' I asked.

'For the convenience of passengers and to save money. The platform-edge doors stop the wind blowing through the stations whenever a train approaches – the so-called piston effect.'

From the time I was four years old I got from Lester's family, not only food and clothing and emotional bonds, but also interesting company. And years later when I was offered a place at KCL, the dark-blue suit I used to wear when I went to court to check out the proceedings – it was Lester's dad, Mr Maddox, who bought it for me.

'You've got to look the part, man,' he said at the time.

By then, leggy Samantha had graduated and was teaching English as a second language at a private college in Kent, and Victor had joined a dental practice in Hammersmith, not far from the flyover.

As we walked back from the loo to our table in the Vortex where my mother was such a big hit, I ignored Lester's question about my white outfit, which he'd said made me look like an angel. When a waiter brought the appetizing food after the first set which

168

Heidi and I had ordered, and laid out the plates and cutlery, the arsey moment with Lester melted away. Heidi and I tucked in. It was a double treat: watching her as she ate while I chewed my own mouthfuls.

I felt grateful to Bobbie Cullen that night. She never hinted in any way that she and I had any sort of interest in each other. To my knowledge, she never mentioned Primrose Hill to anyone that evening. She didn't once look at me the way she did when she opened the door of her bungalow and welcomed me in. She came across during working hours as an entirely different person. I was thankful for that, of course, thankful that she kept our liaison a tight secret, yet I wondered how she managed to do it so well. How did she suppress her feelings so thoroughly?

I know that *I* was nervous all the time, uncomfortable. Despite Heidi's soothing presence, or because of it, I was jittery; I expected the cat to be let out of the bag at any moment. Probably because I was unpractised in the arts of deception, never having been involved in a secret relationship before with anyone of any age, I was unsure how to keep my face looking calm, looking 'usual'. But nothing happened to give the game away. Heidi and I spent most of the time at our table, which was well away from Bobbie's.

The excellent response of the audience spurred Bobbie on. She lined up four more engagements which helped to establish Arlene Allen's reputation as a superb vocalist on the live-jazz scene. My mother sang with acclaimed bands at the Jazz Café in Camden Town, at Pizza on the Park in Knightsbridge, at Ronnie Scott's again (when I slipped and fell in the rain on the pavement outside, bruised my knees and ruined my white suit which had rubbed Lester up the wrong way; while I was down on my hands and knees with dirty water soaking into my trousers, it occurred to me that

Lester might have put a spell on my outfit, jinxed it). The fourth gig, in summer, was at the Café in the Crypt of St Martin-in-the Fields off Trafalgar Square. The acoustics at that venue were extraordinary. We in the audience sat on chairs under the 18th-century brick-vaulted ceiling and over the historic gravestones that lined the crypt floor.

Arlene Allen's performances became so well known in circles that mattered to her thanks to reviews in the press and cultural discussions on radio that Bobbie Cullen began negotiations for a week-long season at the Village Vanguard on 7th Avenue in Manhattan.

My mother could barely contain her excitement at the thought of going to New York towards the end of the year. Seeing her so upbeat and enthusiastic lifted my spirits. She seemed at last to be truly out of the shell of timidity and numbness where she'd been cowering since my father was murdered. With a bit of luck, I thought, her success would lay solid enough foundations on which she could build the rest of her life so that she could be happy *all* the time, not only when she was singing. Audiences loved her voice, her timing, the way she held notes, the way she enunciated and bent the lyrics. The future for her was looking better than it had been for twenty years.

Chapter 19

I'd never been sure of the differences between a woman's nightie, negligée, camisole and slip. I had assumed they were all bed-wear, each a subsection of lingerie which, until I was about ten and heard people saying it otherwise, I thought was pronounced linger-y. But these items of clothing weren't just for sleeping in, I began to realize. Each was meant to make the person wearing it look attractive to someone else, which seemed to imply that the wearer wasn't going to be in bed alone – unless she was so narcissistic that she had to see herself looking good even in her dreams. That's the other thing this kind of clobber possessed: some notional come-hither property.

By the time I was fourteen, I'd got the impression that a very short skirt and suspender-belt, in combination with fishnet stockings, high-heels, black bra and bare midriff, was supposed to be a sexually alluring *ensemble*. I kept seeing women in ads and mannequins in shop windows wearing that kit; it was supposed to make them look physically desirable, it dawned on me in my naivete, tempting, available for pleasure. The garb was designed to stir up the lust in male onlookers, make them long to get their own kit off and embark forthwith on a journey to sexual abandon. The models tended to stand with a hand on waist and one hip thrust out, when I was fourteen, their lower legs wrapped in long shiny leather boots.

The get-up seemed so pantomimey. I used to wonder if the items in it were acquired from a theatrical costumier, along with the bangles, earrings and the chain around one ankle. Then later I saw the hugely entertaining Bob Fosse film *Cabaret* starring Liza Minnelli as Sally Bowles performing risqué numbers introduced by '*Willkommen meine damen und herren, mesdames et messieurs, ladies und gentlemen*' in the Kit Kat Klub in decadent Berlin in the 1930s – before a fresh-faced young man standing in a beer garden in *his* shiny boots and Nazi uniform started singing *his* song, 'The future belongs to me', and a group of similarly clad young people joined him sonorously.

The rig worn by Bowles et al. was presented as rebellious, as an attempt to subvert suffocating convention. Given the times, it *was* daring, radical. But romantic? Sexually alluring? Only if you lived in that period, or were born during Queen Victoria's reign. Only if you were brought up to believe that flesh and blood per se were sinful. If your family had had it dinned into their heads, and had accepted and passed on to you uncritically, that all biological processes – hunger, thirst, digestion, feeling cold, feeling too hot, feeling tired, feeling ill, feeling the tug of appetites, feeling you've had enough to eat, feeling the need for a loo – were false sensations, baseless delusions, distractions from life's only true purpose which was to gain entry to a sanitized, ethereal realm beyond the clouds, then, probably, the flash of an upper thigh, a sudden glimpse of pubic hair, *would* very likely inflame your passions and bring you out in a cold sweat.

Negligée, slip, ooh-la-laa.

When I turned up for my second tryst at the bungalow in Primrose Hill I felt reassured. I hadn't taken anything for granted. Bobbie had said she'd make it worth my while, but still I hadn't considered the money to be in my pocket yet. I hadn't counted my chickens before they were hatched because caution was instilled in me by the saying my cautious mother had repeated over the years: 'Twixt the hand and the lip the morsel may slip'. Nevertheless, I felt that this was no trick. This was the real deal. More money was to be

172

mine, surely? More of the readies.

I went by tube again, of course. At that hour, there were only two other persons, seated far apart from each other and from me, but even so a whiff of stale sweat smudged the air in the carriage, left there by the dozens of passengers who'd been jammed together earlier in the day. The patterned moquette upholstery of some of the seats were indented from the weight of heavy backsides, ingrained no doubt with Londoners' body heat. I got off at Swiss Cottage and ambled through the cool breeze of the air-conditioning on the platform. From the station I walked down busy Avenue Road then left along Adelaide Road, past the bright-yellow Adelaide pub in a cube-shaped building where some of the people talking outside with pint glasses in their hands sounded like Australians. I passed the council tower blocks jutting up behind the rows of trees on the other side, glancing continually at my watch to make sure I didn't arrive before the specified time. Taking extra care not to be hit by any vehicle as I stepped between cars parked at the kerb and crossed the street from penury on my way to wealth, passing the orange-coloured hissing streetlamp and the gardens on either side and heading for the last door in my street of streets at ten-past-ten, I found when I got there that Bobbie Cullen wasn't leaving all the effort to me. She was helping me. She wanted me to do well. She had my interests at heart.

When she opened the door and welcomed me in, the house was just as it had been two nights previously. The love seat against the wall, the large colourful painting above it in the hall, the bare wooden floorboards covered with a rug here and there, even the mango fragrance hanging memory-jogging in the air – except that, I noticed a while later, where the vase of azaleas had been, there was now a froth of lilacs and

173

foliage. Spring wasn't just in the air, it was in all the rooms too. And the way Bobbie smiled; the way she embraced and kissed me lingeringly, it was in her spirit as well.

I felt a turnover, a penile perk-up, as her thigh pressed against me. She felt it too; I knew she did because she pressed against me a little harder and a look of approval came into her eyes. Her smile deepened, inducing me to rub against her thigh a bit more. She went 'Mmm', drew her head back and let out a sudden laugh, her mouth wide open, her lips shiny red.

'It's good to see you again, Leo,' she said.

'It's good to *be* here again, I assure you.'

'You had no difficulty getting here, I take it.'

'Difficulty? I know the way, don't I? I passed that pub again.'

'Which pub?'

'The Adelaide. There were people from Oz drinking outside.'

Bobbie nodded. 'It's not a bad place. The beer is good. They have live music and barbies in the back garden in summer.'

'You a regular there?'

'Been there twice. Two Texas executives finalizing details of a joint-venture contract wanted to experience a London pub.'

'What did they think of it?'

'They liked the music and the customers singing.'

'Did you bring them here afterwards?' I asked, keeping eye contact.

Bobbie shook her head. 'No way,' she said emphatically. 'I told you, I wind down here. This is my retreat. When necessary, I entertain guests in restaurants, or at my Georgian house in Islington. I have a chef on tap there, experienced staff. But not

174

here. No business here. This place is strictly private.'

I didn't know what to say, so I just smiled.

'What I meant was,' she added, 'you had no appointments you had to postpone to get here tonight? You didn't have to change your plans, put anyone off?'

'No, I didn't. Nothing like that.' I spied a little worry in her mind and thought it in my best interests to scotch it right away. 'Once I say I'll be here, you can depend on it.'

'That's good to hear,' she said. 'Would you like a bite now? I ordered different things to eat. Or shall we bathe first?'

Bathing again. I'd forgotten about that. Together. It occurred to me that if this relationship lasted any length of time, I was going to be cleaner than I'd ever been. I already showered every second day, at home. I used a loofah to reach my back and shoulder-blades. I would never risk meeting Heidi, or her parents, in a grimy, unwashed state.

'Let's eat afterwards. I can wait,' I replied, wondering what sort of nosh was on the table this time.

Bobbie was almost naked, except for open-toed low-heel shoes and a short, pale-pink satin garment embroidered with a spray of dark-pink blooms and a butterfly hovering near the petals. The upper edging of black lace highlighted the tops of her tits. The hem, way above her knees, was black lace too in a swirly wave which, when she turned to lead the way, barely covered her bum. Her bum did *not* look big in it; it just looked shapely, curvy, what I could see of it as she headed for the bathroom. That partial sight of her arse was redolent of the lolly I had come to collect. If she was togged out to get my juices flowing, to get my sexual equipment into gear, it was a redundant effort. She'd already succeeded. This sartorial ploy with satin was superfluous. The prospect of another bundle of money had aroused me already.

The towels folded on the rack against the wall were pink this time, but the large mirror was misted again with steam from the hot water in the bath. Mango fragrance was again everywhere. The tiles were opaque with humidity again, and again I undressed in that sensuous setting with a growing erection. Bobbie watched me as I pulled down my jeans, tossed aside my sweater and shirt and peeled off my pants.

Then she placed her left palm on my shoulder and folded the fingers of her other hand around my stiffy and squeezed it. Again, she didn't squeeze too hard. She kept eye contact as she squeezed, released, squeezed again. Once more, I didn't think there was anything overbearing or hostile in the gesture, or that she was showing who was boss. I simply took it that she was re-establishing friendly contact. Her squeezing pressures certainly had a good effect on *me*. I couldn't help smiling, couldn't help anticipating what was in store: pleasurable profit in one go, money's unrivalled sex appeal.

But *her* smile was gone, again. The more she felt my flesh with her fingers, the more the mirth disappeared from her expression. For some reason, when pleasure was imminent; when the prospect of joy was almost upon her, traces of delight disappeared from her face. I noticed that detail during all our get-togethers, twice a week for nearly six months. From the first time, in early spring, to the painful, drastically sudden last time in the blaze of summer a few nights before the Notting Hill Carnival in August: Bobbie Cullen's countenance always became intense when my flesh rose to the occasion and we were about to get into the bath of hot foamy water. Her smile faded for a while. Her eyes seemed suddenly to be looking inwards, to be focused in those moments wholly on a

176

vista or memory from which, for all I knew, I was entirely absent.

Then she let go of me and touched that hand to her cheek.

She lifted her arms, crossed them, grasped the pink satin and pulled it over her head. She kicked her shoes off.

'Shall I get in first?' she asked, her eyes focused on *me* again and smiling once more.

'Please do,' I replied.

She swung her right leg over the side of the bath and I did the same further along, and when she followed through with her other leg and I had done likewise, pretty much at the same time, that was the moment, I suppose, when this particular routine ceased being random, ad lib, and became another of our sex-business rituals.

They were pleasant, those rituals – no question. They led to luxury. Standing in the bath while getting used to the heat of the water, our arms around each other, her lips on mine, my stiffy pressed against her soft belly; then lying up to our necks in the spacious tub full of mango-flavoured foam – I made a mental note to tell Bobbie it didn't *always* have to be mango; she'd mentioned orange-and-cinnamon bath gel last time, and apple-and-aloe: I wasn't against trying them. All of this wasn't my idea of hard work. Feeling her slippery foot sliding frothy along my inner thighs, sliding back and forth, then pressing against my tackle expanding in the hot water – another of her ways of re-acquainting herself with me – was rather more stimulating than the strain of jacking up a stream of cars and removing worn tyres from their wheels at the pit-stop place where I'd worked, or pushing heavy trolleys over lumps of ice in a frozen-food warehouse.

I soaped her back again with one of the flannels.

Soaped her tits good and proper too. Got those knockers real clean, and the nipples. And I soaped her thick pubic hair directly, with my fingers.

'Mmm,' she went, 'that's nice, Leo. A nice prelude.'

And when we'd risen from the water and were standing in it again up to our calves and were about to step out to the shower cubicle, she soaped my tackle without the flannel, with *her* fingers. She made eye contact as the flesh got thicker and more rigid in her slippery hand, presumably so I'd know that personal hygiene wasn't her only concern. She was helping to ensure that I would again get way beyond the prelude and service her solidly. She wanted me to stay the night.

The food on the big table in the kitchen was again varied, plentiful and tasty. But this time Bobbie's spread wasn't all strange to me. My mother knew how to cook chicken curry and lamb curry. I'd long watched her doing so and had helped a bit. She had jars of spices on the work surface, and peppercorns, paprika, *elachi*. She kept green chillies in the fridge and gnarled lumps of ginger. She told me it was my father Leonard who'd introduced her to strong food. He showed her how to prepare the base for any curry: sliced onions, crushed garlic, green chillies cut fine, varying amounts of dry coriander, cumin and turmeric, plus, depending on the emphasis sought, grated ginger, cloves, cinnamon sticks.

Cooking wasn't just food for my mother. It was memory. The ingredients, the process and the bouquets gradually filling the kitchen reminded her of my father before that drug dealer shot him dead, how he used to slice cloves of garlic, salt them and crush them with the flat side of the knife, run water over a bunch of coriander and chop it rapidly on the slicing board, how he would savour a spoonful of the sauce and nod approval with a smile on his face.

Food didn't just keep my mother alive and healthy, it kept my father alive in her heart. It fed her recollections of when they were together, happy, hopeful. They weren't bothered by people's racial comments, unconcerned by emollient talk about opposites attracting, about black coffee and white milk mixing to a lovely caramel colour, he being black, she white, their little son in between.

I was proud of my mother Arlene Allen. She was brave, tenacious, soldiering on stoically. She was a cool, jazz-singing woman with her own style who always enhanced the musicians she was fronting and never sang a bum note. She needed the money, but chose her gigs carefully. She was a level-headed modern Englishwoman who'd brought me up alone.

Nevertheless, some of the dishes on Bobbie's table that second night *were* strange to me. I'd heard of onion bhajis, of course, and vegetable samosas, and lamb tikka and chicken pasanda, but what was *batak shaslik*? What was *lal mas tava*? *Nawabi laziz*? Just how was *peshwari* prawn different from prawns done in other ways?

I'm not complaining now, eight years later. I'm not picking holes in the appetizing refreshments Bobbie laid out for each of our trysts. One night it was sushi and sashimi, delivered, she said, from a high-quality place in Ealing that catered for the community of Japanese business people and their families who lived in that district. No, Bobbie was unfailingly generous. Those snacks, nibbles, *plats du jour* were always so ample they could easily each time have become a feeding frenzy, a blowout, because, really, each was a bacchanalian banquet whose overriding purpose was to ensure that my own meat and two veg had all the sustenance they needed to keep going until Bobbie was, as she said every morning after, 'well and truly fucked'.

So I wasn't surprised that the food did keep me going. It was nutritious stuff. Hardly any fat in it. There were glasses and bottles of Cobra beer on the table, a cold, not-so-gassy liquid contrast to the subtle curry flavours. But I took my responsibilities too seriously to succumb. Beer might undermine my staying power. Beer might make my willy wilt. Beer might cause me to disappoint my employer and blow my chances of making big bucks on that bed in Primrose Hill.

It was just high enough, that bed. When Bobbie knelt on it, presenting the cheeks of her arse to me, the sensuous furrow in her back sloping down between her shoulder-blades, I was standing in position to enter her from behind as she'd asked me to do while we were in the bathroom. She kept coming up with erotic requests, titillating wishes that sounded urgent. It made me wonder whether she was attempting to relive previous couplings, love-making with long-ago partners, or to do things which she'd never had time to try while hectically building her business career.

'Oh Leo,' she murmured as I got the rhythm going, back and forth with steadily faster strokes. 'Oh God, Leo. I love you up me.'

I know it might sound as though I'm currying favour with my former benefactor, boosting her image, when I say that they were gorgeous spheres, her arse, there at the edge of the bed. They were perfectly symmetrical, bisected beautifully by the curving cleft which I gazed at as I gripped her waist. I'd heard from Heidi's parents, Mrs Ilse and Mr Gregory Hathaway, that there was an ancient philosophical concept – *musica universalis* – according to which the movements of the sun, moon and planets formed

180

musica, the Latin word for music. The music wasn't actually audible, the Hathaways said, but consisted in a mathematical and religious harmony. One of the branches of that concept, they added, was *musica humana*, the internal music of the human body.

There at the side of the bed I understood what they meant as I increased the tempo of my thrusting. I soon had one reservation, though. The music *was* audible. It was a slurpy sound, a wet, sucking cadence. And when Bobbie's voice rose in pitch under the attentions of my slapping loins, and she started coming and shouting 'Yes, Leo. Yes, yes, you lovely fucking boy!' as though I were deaf and her arse began to judder, her flesh quiver, her torso jerk so rapidly that I had to hold her tight as I piled on more and more speed, I knew definitely that the *musica humana* was a gurgle. It was juice music, quim concerto. It was the sliding down my stiffy of a fifty-two-year-old woman's orgasmic ecstasy. It was her gush of joy, of come, again, again. Her arse kept vibrating. Her breathing into the duvet became a hoarse happy laugh when I responded with a few grinds and sudden deep jackhammer jolts. 'Oh!' she cried in delight after each plunge. 'Oh! Oh! Oh!'

Bobbie Cullen was young. I know that now. In certain respects, she was the same age as me. She was fresh, vividly alive. She liked trying new positions, and not only on the bed. One time we got going in the bathroom *before* getting into the water. She pulled me by my erection, stood naked with her back against the misted tiles and helped slot me in through her thick pubic hair. 'Aaaah' she sighed when I was home and adding our own moisture to the humidity around us. Another time she couldn't wait to finish eating and we were at it on the kitchen floor, one of her hands gripping a table leg, the other pressing down on my butt by way of encouragement, our breaths flowery from the mouthfuls we *had* managed to swallow.

What was driving her? Why was she so manic?

Chapter 20

She gave me five-hundred pounds the following morning. Five-hundred again, that second time. The money was again in a brown A5 envelope in the second drawer down. Ten crisp fifties. The cash was too serious for me to be blasé about. I counted it, several times, passing the notes from one hand to the other. I never took the lolly for granted. It always came as an uplifting treat, making my dick do a pendulum swing as I stood on the rug at the side of the bed.

Bobbie watched me standing naked staring at the money.

'You all right?' she asked.

'Very much so. Thank you for this,' I said with a grin, lifting and waving the wad.

'It's no more than you deserve, Leo. You're worth it. What else could I buy, what shopping could I do anywhere in the world, that would make me feel one-tenth as good as I'm feeling now?' She held my gaze with a benign expression for a long moment, her head on the pillow. 'I have something else for you.'

'Really? This is enough, Bobbie.'

'I'm feeling too good to get up,' she said, stretching her arms, yawning and turning on her side. 'Pop into the other bedroom, will you, Leo? There's a box on the table.'

We kept eye contact, but I couldn't guess what it was I was about to fetch. I put the money back in the envelope and the envelope in a zipped pocket of my sweater on the floor.

The other bedroom had a slightly different view of the garden. On my way across to the table I saw through the window two magpies hopping about on the lawn, their heads dipping in a rubbery way as they pecked in the grass for food; the black-and-white pattern of their feathers stood out in the sunlight, and the bit of blue down their fronts. I wondered if they were same two I'd seen from the other bedroom the last time I was here.

The box on the table was rectangular in shape, about the size of a shoe box, and wrapped in gold paper. I reached for it – it wasn't as heavy as a pair of shoes – and was about to head back to the door when I noticed a corner of paper sticking out of the table's drawer. I pulled the drawer right out to put the paper back in – it was a handwritten letter in faded ink – and saw near the back of the drawer a black-and-white photograph in a silver frame. There was a layer of dust on the glass.

I took the frame out of the drawer and looked at the photo. It was of a young, heavily pregnant woman, her cheeks smooth with puppy fat. Her swollen belly seemed to be the main focus of the shot. Her face had a pensive, wistful look. Something about her expression held me. The photo being black-and-white, I couldn't guess what colour her hair was, or the colour of her dress, but there might have been a breeze blowing at the time because the cloth was pressed against her full, round tummy and the hem against her thighs.

I wondered who she was, why the picture was in a drawer covered in dust, then put it back and shut the drawer.

Bobbie was still lying on her side when I got back to her with the box wrapped in gold paper. 'Is this it?' I asked.

'Yes. It's a gift from me to you.'

'What is it?'

'Why don't you open it and see?'

I sat down on the side of the bed, tore off the thick gold paper, lifted the lid off the box and looked inside. Fitted snugly into soft padding was a booklet with a silvery blue cover and on it a silvery blue piece of sleek technology with a little screen and keyboard. A wave of emotion swept through me when I recognized it.

'It's a mobile phone,' I said, glancing at Bobbie.

'It is,' she said.

'For me to use?'

'Yes, to keep and use.'

I looked into the box again. 'It's a Nokia.'

'An excellent make.'

'I've never had a mobile,' I told her. 'Lester has one. His girlfriend Martha has one. His dad has one, and his mother too.'

Bobbie smiled. 'They're spreading like wildfire,' she said. 'A young man like you, Leo – it'll be part of your identity.'

'It must've cost a packet.'

'Forget the price. It's a gift.'

'Bobbie, how can I thank you? I am *so* chuffed.'

'All I ask is that you respond when I call you.'

'I will, I will. But I've never used one.'

'Easy peasy. I'll show you how to make and receive calls, how to add new contacts, how to send text messages. Turn it over,' she said.

I put my hand in the box, pulled the phone from the padding and turned it over.

'It's a picture-messaging handset – a camera-phone,' she said. 'You can take photos and send them to your friends.'

'And to you,' I said.

'If you like. Come, lie by me,' she said, pushing herself up against the pillow, her nice tits in full view. 'I'll show you the functions. It'll take a few minutes and Bob's your uncle. It already has a SIM card.'

'I'm not really sure what a SIM card is.'

'It's your phone's unique ID. There's a battery charger in there too with the correct jack for this model.

185

Just stick the three-pin plug into the socket at home.'

'How often do I have to charge the batteries?'

'Depends. If you never switch the phone off, you'll be recharging the batteries quite often – and you'll probably be thrown out of theatres when your phone rings. As for costs, sending texts is much cheaper than making calls. Your top-ups will last longer that way.'

Before I left Bobbie's retreat that morning I knew how to use my new mobile. That was a few years before the BlackBerry came on the UK market with more features, and, later still, the iPhone from Apple with its touchscreen and seemingly endless array of apps, but *my* phone had all I needed at the time. I was going to add a load of contacts as soon as I got home. I'd be connected. I'd be in the loop. As far as Bobbie was concerned, she'd be more securely in contact with me.

That's when that particular penny dropped.

'This,' I said, raising my palm with the phone on it, 'means I'm your call girl, doesn't it?'

'Don't be silly,' she said with a grin. 'You're my call *boy*.'

'Call me what you like – I don't care,' I said happily.

I was about to go to the bathroom to have a shower, wash her dried-up quim juice off my skin and out of my pubic hair, when I remembered the photo in the drawer. I turned back to her.

'I wasn't prying, Bobbie,' I said. 'I didn't mean to be nosy, but when I opened the drawer in the table to put back a sheet of paper that was sticking out, I saw a photo of a pregnant woman.'

'What?'

'A pregnant woman. In a silver frame, with dust on the glass.'

'Where'd you see it?'

186

'In the drawer of the table. Who is she, if you don't mind my asking.'

The way Bobbie was looking at me, she obviously didn't know what I was talking about. 'It's in an old silver frame. Is she related to you, perhaps – your daughter?'

Bobbie sat up, leaned forward at the waist and pointed. 'It's in the drawer of the table in that room?'

I nodded.

'I haven't seen it in years. I thought I'd lost it.'

'Shall I bring it?'

'Would you?'

I was out of the door and back with the framed photo in two ticks. Bobbie took it from me and looked at it intently. She wiped the dust from the glass with the edge of her hand.

'Oh, you,' she said to the photo. 'Oh my darling.' She suddenly looked drawn and pallid. When she glanced up I saw that her eyes were glistening. A moment later tears slid from her lower lashes. She began to sob, then to cry and more and more tears flowed down her face. It made me very uncomfortable, the way her bosom was being racked by the sobs. The way her shoulders were quaking made me wonder in alarm what I'd done to destroy her composure like this.

'Is that your daughter?' I asked. 'What's her name?'

She threw her head back, caught her breath and inhaled deeply. It steadied her somewhat, though her tears kept flowing.

She smiled a strange, bitter smile and shook her head. 'No, Leo,' she said. 'It's me *and* my daughter.'

'Really? Where's your daughter?' I moved closer and looked at the photo again. I was sure there was only one person in the picture.

'Can't you see? She's in my womb. Three days before she was born.'

'That's *you*?' I looked at the photo again and looked at her afresh. There *was* something familiar in the features of the black-and-white image. 'When was that? How old were you, Bobbie? She looks quite young.'

'She *was* – *I* was – young. Twenty years old. I'd just graduated, had my honours degree in classics. I was a year younger than all the other students in my class.'

'Twenty,' I said. 'The same age as me. Where's she now? What's her name? – the baby.'

I guessed, the way she said it, slowly, bit by bit, that Bobbie was telling me a secret. 'Her name's Helen. She'd be thirty-two now. But I don't know where she is. Oh, how I've wanted to know all these years where she was and how she was.' Bobbie's reddened eyes were unfocused as she said that, or focused on some distant place.

'I'm so sorry,' I said; it sounded pathetic, gormless. 'I wish I hadn't started this.'

I felt callow, conscious of my inexperience. I had no knowledge that might be of use to her. In a way that I still haven't forgotten eight years later, I felt pointless, like a lifeguard at the beach who couldn't swim. She told me, on the strict condition that I never brought the subject up again, and never mentioned it to anyone else, how she became pregnant before her final exams at Oxford University. She'd won a scholarship there, called an 'exhibition'; she was an 'exhibitioner'. She studied Latin and Greek, the latter as a subsidiary.

'I wish I hadn't allowed myself to be manipulated,' she said in a dry, absent voice. 'I wish I hadn't given in to the pressure. They were so respectable, his parents, so pious. They forbade him to marry me – not that I particularly wanted him to – and he obeyed them. He said marrying me was out of the question. It was a class thing. I'd drag their name down. That was when I discovered they were from some branch or other of the

188

aristocracy. In my naivete I'd thought his accent was middle class of a different region. His speech had a practised weariness and was full of exaggerated politeness. I was at St Anne's College off the Woodstock Road. It was only about a mile down St Giles and beyond Broad Street to Brasenose College off the High Street, but what a social distance it was. The quads in Brasenose are all Gothic architecture, especially Chapel Quad, like the architecture of his mind,' she said with a weak smile.

'Brasenose?' I asked. 'As in fried nose, cooked nose? That's the name of a college?'

She smiled through her sad face. 'It's from "brazen nose," she explained. 'The college was founded at the beginning of the fifteen-hundreds. One of its original buildings had a brass knocker on the door in the shape of an animal's nose – hence brazen nose, and hence brase nose.'

'Oh – makes sense. I thought maybe they were gourmets.'

'Anyway,' she continued, 'I'd seen him around a few times, at classes we both attended. He was studying philosophy, politics and economics and had an interest in the ancient history lectures I also went to. We got talking. I don't know what he saw in me – a cheap grammar-school tart, I suppose. It was the only time I'd slept with him, my first time with *anyone*. His first time with a woman too – I'm sure of that. It was all self-conscious fumbling, pawing – he never looked at me while grappling, not once. Then it was over before I'd even got started. I'd heard sex could be pleasurable,' she shook her head. 'It was an ordeal, nothing else – ended in deep embarrassment.

'He and his friends were posh yobs, braying toffs. They'd been to expensive public schools. They referred to state-educated students as "stains". During my three

189

years at Oxford I heard bits and pieces about their drunken hell-raising. They'd get sozzled at their club dinners, trash restaurant as thoroughly as they could – smash the crockery, the mirrors, chairs, chandeliers, whatever – then, liquored up, completely pissed, they'd gleefully pay for the damage. Members of the Bullingdon club used to spend more on an evening's dinner, plus reparation, I heard, than my father earned in a year as manager of a hardware shop and my mother as a school teacher, put together.

'His parents wouldn't let me keep my baby. It was *his* child too, they said. He had just as much say as I. They made it clear that I was too down at heel to be given charge of blue blood. I wouldn't be able to feed it or clothe it to the proper standards. The child would grow up sounding common, like its mother. Better for all concerned, they browbeat me, to give the child a good start in life by giving it up for adoption to a family they knew and trusted. They made me feel selfish, hard-hearted, for wanting to keep my baby. It was 1970. He chose them over me without hesitation. Not surprising, really,' she frowned and turned her palm up, 'we scarcely knew each other.'

She paused in thought for a long moment, head tilted forward, then looked at me again. 'Before I went to his room that night I was an undergraduate virgin. I was keen on my studies and the music scene of the time. While I was doing my degree, the break up of the Beatles was under way. They'd played their last official concert at Candlestick Park in San Francisco in 1966. The following year their manager Brian Epstein died, of a drug overdose. *Sergeant Pepper's Lonely Hearts' Club Band* was released in June 1967. The *Abbey Road* album came out in 1969, and in my final year, while I was preparing for my Latin exams, Paul McCartney's first solo album, *McCartney*, was released.'

I was listening to her with different ears.

'Jimi Hendrix was making huge waves. He'd come back from being with the 101st Airborne Division of the US Army in Vietnam. His first hit with the Jimi Hendrix Experience was "Hey Joe", an immediate smash here in Britain. After that came "Purple haze" and "The wind cried Mary". He blew the socks off all his admirers while living and playing in London – Pete Townshend of The Who, the Rolling Stones, the Beatles, Eric Clapton. No one had ever seen or heard an electric guitar played the way Jimi Hendrix played it – you fancied it would burst into flames. And then, the year I graduated, the year my baby was born, Jimi Hendrix died,' she said, shaking her head in awe, on the brink of tears again. 'He was only twenty-seven. It was a crushing lesson – life's too short to waste on shit.

'Around that time, Phil Spector deployed his "wall of sound" technique and produced an enormous hit with Tina Turner performing "River deep mountain high". The excitement jolted my heart.

'Santana's album *Abraxas* was released in 1970. The track "Black magic woman"', she grinned, 'trying to make a devil out of me' was in my head for months. Two or three years after I graduated Roberta Flack's "Killing me softly with his song" reached the top of the US charts. I was smitten. I knew for sure I wanted to be in the music business, on the money, production, marketing side of things. My parents said I should go for it. They said I had the brains.

'Our class system here in England was a graveyard – pale ghosts pretending to be alive. They pretended they were modern people. That shit wasn't for me. It was slow poison. So in a way,' she smiled wanly, 'I was lucky. I just didn't know it at the time. The guy who knocked me up because he had no control of the workings of his cock – he was enamoured of social superiority, just like his parents. They like people to be deferential, to bow and scrape and tug their forelocks. They want the future to be the same as the past, with them still in control, but sounding and looking a bit different.'

I remained silent. What on earth could I say? She was remembering her young self, feeling sorry for her young self. She'd been coerced into doing what, under other circumstances, she would never have acquiesced in. I moved closer on the bed and put an arm around her shoulders. I wanted to soothe her any way I could. I was sorely aware, however, of being out of my depth. I had just discovered that my 'business partner' had a long-lost daughter who was now, wherever she might be, thirty-two years old. A daughter much older than me, a daughter who'd be a waif in the world, Bobbie was told, if she'd been allowed to bring her up.

I couldn't help wondering over the following weeks – right until the last time I saw Bobbie: it was a few nights before the Notting Hill Carnival that year – whether that dreadful experience had fed into her heart and become transmuted into sympathy and benevolence. I'd heard that people who knew hunger, who knew the pangs of privation, tended to share what food they had. I'd read that individuals who'd suffered at the hands of others, who'd been oppressed, misused, maligned for no reason they could understand, sometimes found that their moral compass was reset by the inner jolts and shocks they'd had to endure.

Was that partly why Bobbie was so open-handed and kind to my mother? Was I naïve to think that this might be the case? Was it too idealistic a notion in our grasping, rapacious world?

Bobbie had said that we all had our priorities. Might her priorities include more than self-aggrandisement, more than a puffed-up ego? Was that why she paid me so well and fed me so full?

Perhaps I was feeling guilty for the grief I'd churned up when I told her about the framed photo in the drawer and brought it to her. Or was it because her bitter sobs made me want to empathize with her, soothe her in any way I could? Whatever the reason, I moved my head closer to Bobbie's on the pillow and told her exactly what Seymour Allen, my grandfather, had told me about a newly married young woman from the West Country.

Chapter 21

Frances pushed a strand of her fair hair behind her right ear, leaned back against the wall at the bus stop and unzipped the bag hanging from her shoulder. She brought out the envelope, removed the letter and read it again. Alison was as thoughtful as ever, she mused as she read, planning ahead, hoping she wasn't going to be too much trouble. They hadn't seen each other since the wedding in May and it would be Ali's first visit to London, her first stay with Frances as a married woman and her husband Denton. What was it like being married? she asked in the letter. She was excited by the prospect of seeing her sister again and seeing the big-city sights, which she listed in detail in descending order of priority.

Frances had pale blue eyes and a clear, fresh complexion and in her heels, charcoal-grey pencil skirt and pink blouse with plunging neckline her shapely figure was conspicuous among the other people, mainly men in suit and tie, waiting for the bus. Several of them kept eyeing her surreptitiously.

Denton was leaning against the wall beside her, clutching his briefcase in his right hand. He looked at his watch.

'I hope it comes on time,' he said, glancing at the queue stretching along the pavement. 'I don't want to be late. Squadron Leader Drake went out of his way when he invited me to have a quiet word at his home. It's a privilege. I mustn't be late.'

Frances looked up from the letter and along busy Ladbroke Grove. The traffic was heavy, vans and lorries rumbling by; she noticed that all the vehicles' windscreens had a golden tint from the setting sun. 'The bus'll be here any minute,' she said, giving him a deep smile, then turning and kissing him on the lips. 'Relax, Denny. You said the meeting would take half an hour at most. It's his family home – less formal. So take it easy.'

'I suppose I should,' he said, returning her smile. 'You don't have to wait until the bus comes. I'll see you back at the flat.'

'Ali says she can't wait to get here,' Frances told him, putting the letter back into the envelope and holding it up in front of his eyes. 'Look, she's so excited about her visit that she addressed the envelope to Miss Frances Kendall instead of Missus Frances Barrow. She forgot that I'm married.'

'I hope she'll forget while she's here what a spacious room she left behind, in a comfortable, spacious house.'

'What d'you mean?'

'That's what she's leaving for the duration. It'll help if she doesn't dwell on how small her room is at out place. It's barely big enough for the bed.'

'It isn't *that* small. It has a bookcase and dressing-table. You've painted the ceiling and walls – that's all she wants, a clean place to crash. She's only going to be here for a week, and she'll be out and about, seeing London most of the time. So don't worry about it, Denny. Coming to us will be the longest trip she's made, and she's going to make the most of it, I'm sure. The furthest she's travelled to date was from our home in Hereford down to Bristol when she started university last year.'

'Did she go to Bristol because *you* studied there?'

'Partly, I expect. But she's keen on languages too and met the entrance requirements easily. I wonder if she knows how lucky she is. The professors in the classics department had a high reputation when I was there – the heads of Latin and Greek.'

'God,' Denton said, smiling, 'you girls are so clever. Latin, Greek and French too.'

'Don't forget English,' she smiled back, 'we were speaking it long before we'd heard of foreign languages.'

'Thank God for that. *Amo, amas, amat* is the full extent of my knowledge of the classics, thanks to your pillow talk.'

'Nice talk, isn't it? – I love, you love, he, she or it loves. It could easily have been I burn, I conquer, I pillage which the Roman legions did all over Europe with their swords and military formations.'

Denton let his briefcase fall to the pavement and took hold of her upper arms.

'I'm so happy, Franny,' he said, his eyes shining. 'I've never felt so light and optimistic. Your parents were kind and welcoming, not just Alison – the exact opposite of what I'd dreaded.'

Frances was about to respond when a rowdy group of young men came into view around the corner. They were talking at the tops of their voices, laughing, gesticulating and jostling one another. Denton reckoned there were ten or twelve of them, rough lads spoiling for a scrap. They hurled abuse at people they passed on the pavement, bumped them out of the way and brandished their weapons: knives, iron bars, heavily buckled belts and bottles sloshing with liquid that didn't look like milk.

Denton was taller than Frances and his immediate reaction was to enclose her in his arms and turn her away to the wall a few feet from the bus stop. The noisy throng swarmed by them and the other people in the queue, but just as Denton's tension began to ease and his muscles relax, the guy at the tail end of the mob stopped walking and turned to the wall.

His long dishevelled hair was ginger, his face

chubby and he was dressed in a striped jacket, stovepipe trousers and chunky black boots. In his right hand was a curved length of wood which looked to Denton like an axe handle.

'What the fuck have we here,' he exclaimed, glaring at Denton. 'Nigger,' he yelled. 'Get your hands off this white woman. You filthy swine.'

His friend nearest to him heard his voice and stepped back on the pavement, a cloth cap on his head, the downy beginnings of a beard on his face and a length of metal tubing in one hand.

This is what that kid Seymour Allen was talking about, Denton thought. These are the guys he saw in Talbot Road two days ago. They fire-bombed his neighbours' house and continued on their rampaging spree, he said. So help me, if they lay a finger on Franny —

'Are you deaf, nigger? I said get your fucking hands off this white woman!'

Denton turned his head away from Franny's. He could feel her arms trembling. His own limbs were shaking. There was a sudden hollowness in the pit of his stomach, a nauseous sensation. He didn't know if it was from the shock of the abuse, the humiliation in front of Franny, or the stark challenge to his sense of himself as a man. He'd heard about these mobs on the grapevine, not only from that kid Seymour in Talbot Road, and began to steel himself for an onslaught. He clenched his fists.

But he'd misinterpreted Franny's trembling arms. It wasn't the fear of a woman facing violent ruffians that had made her shake. It was fury.

'How dare you speak to my husband in that tone! Who do you think you are? Hitler?'

The force of *her* tone stunned the ginger-haired guy. His mouth fell open. Her outburst was the last thing

197

he'd expected.

Denton looked at Franny afresh. He too was surprised by the vigour of her voice despite the tremor in it. They'd only been married three months. How little he knew about her, he realized in an instant. At the reception her father had worn his full naval uniform – gold braid on the hat, on the cuffs of the sleeves and on the epaulettes – and, after dancing with his daughter in her bridal gown past the wedding cake on the long table amid the other guests doing the quick-step, and with a glass of wine in one hand, he'd thrown his other arm around Denton's shoulders and told him about life aboard his anti-submarine frigate in the Atlantic on very stale rations.

'Answer me!' Frances commanded. 'Who do you think you are raising your voice like that? The commissioner of police? In that case, show me some identification, some proof of your rank, your qualifications.'

She paused for a moment, turned her eyeballs fleetingly to Denton's in a signal of solidarity, then looked straight at the guy clutching his axe handle.

'I take it you do have qualifications,' she said in a rising, manic kind of pitch that held the thug fast, and his friend too. 'You *have* been to school, have you?'

'Yes,' he answered, barely audibly, nodding.

'Didn't you learn manners there?'

He didn't reply; something about him seemed to shrink under the force of her staring eyes. His pale face looked parched. Denton too was astonished by this display of his wife's inner strength, which he hadn't got an inkling of before.

'Did you ever finish school?' she asked the young hooligan. 'My husband here,' she gestured with her head, 'finished school years ago. He's an RAF navigator, off to see a squadron leader. His father was a

Lancaster pilot in the war – bombed the German bastards, he did. Flew missions to the Ruhr Valley, smashed Gelsenkirchen, smashed Düsseldorf and Aachen, then flattened Essen and its weapons factories. He bombed the fear of God into Jerry.' She paused for a second, then added: 'What did *you* do in the war, sonny? Do you know there *was* a war?'

Just then the red double-decker came into view. The impatient queue surged forward across the kerb on to the tarmac; Ginger-boy and his pal with the iron tubing were pushed along in the rush.

The bus pulled up, vibrating as the engine idled noisily, belching puffs of smoke from the exhaust as the passengers stepped aboard. Frances pushed Denton gripping his briefcase right past the two toughs and waited behind him until he was on the platform. He turned, leaned against the silver pole and grinned down at her.

'Will you be all right?' he asked, motioning with his head to the young guys. 'Shall I walk you back?'

'Don't be silly,' she said, smiling brightly at him and raising her voice as the engine of the bus began to rev. 'Have your chat. Remember, *he* invited *you*. Explain why the allocated quarters at RAF Northolt are perfectly adequate for us. We don't *need* to wait for Little Wings facilities. I'm not even pregnant yet, for God's sake. Impress on him we're ready to move in right away. Supper will be ready when you get back.'

It wasn't.

Once the bus disappeared and the pavement was clear again, the spell she seemed to have cast on the yobs wore off and they came to their senses. They remembered they had weapons and were part of a gang, and their courage returned. The guy with the wooden axe handle slapped it several times onto the palm of his

199

left hand; it made him feel virile again. His pal hit the wall with his length of metal piping; it vibrated in his grip and sent through him little waves of self-assurance that roused his dormant masculinity.

'Nigger-loving bitch!' he cried out, working himself up.

'Traitorous fucken tart!' the other yelled, affirming his Aryan credentials. 'They're the ones you have to watch, the enemies within – hate their own skin.'

'She's full of herself – hoity toity. Doesn't know her place.'

'She's only a woman – needs a lesson she won't forget.'

'It's up to us to sort her out.'

'Come on, then – before she disappears.'

They followed her pink blouse in the failing light under the railway bridge and drew closer when she turned left into Westbourne Park Road. They walked faster as she crossed Portobello Road, passing a few pedestrians heading home to their evening meal, glancing at each other nervously as they closed in on her. She was only a woman, and they were men armed with the necessary, but they needed each other's support to cross the remaining barrier holding them back from doing the righteous deed.

She was white, after all. She was supposed to be one of them. She *looked* like one of them; that was the confusing part. But she was the worst kind of enemy because she hated her own people so badly that she was doing her best to dilute their superior essence. She was born with a pure white skin, but she polluted her purity by sleeping with a nigger trying to be above himself, trying his best to be hoity toity too.

It was only fair: she had to be punished for doing the dirty on this green and pleasant land, this lovely English country of inventors and clever people.

England invented cricket and tennis and electricity. Who could deny that? True English men and women were sporting types. They were polite. They were civilized. They didn't live in trees. They didn't eat coconuts while sitting bollock naked in the mud.

When Frances Barrow turned into Basing Street, their fast walk became a run and they caught up with her between a car parked at the kerb and some concrete steps leading up to a porch. She turned her head to see who was so close behind her, recognized the guy with the cloth cap and baby beard; he was still wielding a length of metal pipe. But the first blow came from the other guy on the other side when he swung the axe handle with both hands and hit her across the spine. The force of the impact propelled her forwards so suddenly that she lost her balance and fell face down, cracking her forehead on the paving stone. Her cry was too weak to be heard, a single breathless gasp of pain. The thwack! thwack! of the blows that followed were more audible, each a distinct fleshy sound biting zealously into her back, ripping her pink blouse until it was so badly torn after six or seven blows that her bra strap began to show. Then he hit her hard on her arse too as she lay prostrate; it was such a fetching shape.

Blood spread out from her face on the cold stone about a hundred yards from where she and Denton lived in a flat on the second floor.

The chubby guy was breathing heavily, his dishevelled ginger hair more tangled than before. He wiped the spit from his lips with the back of his hand and glanced across the pavement at his pal. The look on his face was a mixture of triumph and pride, but once he noticed his friend's expression it became fouled by traces of what might have been shame. His friend with the cloth cap and metal pipe seemed about to be sick; his eyes were feverish in his failed attempt to convey approbation at the very moment when he'd discovered with absolute certainty that he didn't have it in himself after all to do what was necessary.

Frances Barrow didn't die, my grandfather Seymour told me.

When Denton returned from having tea with the squadron leader that evening in August 1958, he found her surrounded by an ambulance crew in the middle of the pavement. She was lying on a metal bed with fold-away wheels; a bandage wrapped round her forehead was seeping blood. Denton couldn't see the dressings or the welts all over her back, but the smell of iodine was strong, and it was that smell that frightened him most of all, more than the red smudge of gore on the ground where her skull had cracked when she fell from the first blow. It filled his nostrils, that sharp, fearful, purply fragrance, and made something inside him sag and die and muffle the talk around him of broken ribs and fractured vertebrae and the urgent need for X-rays.

Frances knew who Denton was when he spoke to her. His voice brought the glimmer of a smile to her stricken face, but she didn't reply. She couldn't. She wasn't able to say a single word for seventeen months. And when she started walking again, it wasn't properly, not really right ever again, because, a doctor said, the blows had damaged certain bones in her hips.

Chapter 22

My walk from Swiss Cottage tube station to Bobbie Cullen's retreat, and the train ride before it – from Notting Hill on the Circle Line to Baker Street; change on to the northbound Jubilee Line, pass St John's Wood, get off at the second stop, Swiss Cottage – became associated in my mind with lovely sums of money.

I found myself verifying a psychological theory which I'd heard other students discussing. It was Pavlov's theory of the conditioned reflex, and I was unwittingly showing it to be valid, much as the behaviour of dogs and rats in labs before me had done. As a rat, if you press the correct lever in a laboratory rat box, the theory goes, you get food. If you press the wrong lever, you don't get food. Press the correct lever again, receive your reward again. You get into the habit quickly of always pressing the correct lever. Pretty soon you start salivating as soon as you *see* the lever, because the lever in the past has been the prelude to food: your glands have been conditioned; spit dribbles from your mouth when the lever comes into view.

Catch a certain train in the evening and stroll a certain one-mile walk, and you get money. Do that trip again, you get money again. Next thing you know, just boarding the train gives you a penile turn-over, and strolling along Avenue Road and then left into Adelaide Road gives you no less than a full hard-on.

An old song I'd head in a compilation disc which my mother had bought at a car-boot sale – Helen Shapiro's strong-voiced 'Walking back to happiness, hooppa o yeh i yeh' – could have been *my* theme song, my signature tune. Nor would it have been as uncool as I initially thought. My mother said that despite making her name in pop music, Helen Shapiro had modelled herself on the likes of Sarah Vaughan whom my mother, for one, thought was more of a jazz singer, more dry and austere of tone in the manner of tenor saxophonist Lester Young, Billie Holiday's accompanist, than even Ella Fitzgerald.

'Listen to Miss Vaughan singing "Black coffee" or "How high the moon,"' my mother said, 'then come and tell me Helen Shapiro had the wrong role models.'

Jazz rivalries, voice tone and breath control aside, those pavements were *my* walk to happiness.

I noticed more and more details about the other pedestrians as each of my visits to Bobbie's retreat came and went. I registered the clothes they were wearing, their shoes, whether they were still wrapped in raincoats and carrying umbrellas, because the seasons gradually changed. The crocuses in the gardens I walked by in early spring were supplanted by daffodils and tulips a while later, and then, as people enjoyed the warm summer evenings in sandals, shorts and T-shirts and darkness only began to fall at about ten o'clock, pink and yellow roses began to appear. I started seeing clematis, bizzy-lizzies, and dark-red peonies, their massive heads bowed over their stems under the weight of their beauty. The lilacs were gone, the foliage a different hue. Along the edges of the beds in one of the gardens I passed were blue lobelia with their delicate little petals. Daylight was lasting longer, until an evening came when the sun still hadn't set as I approached Bobbie's bungalow at her stipulated time.

By then I felt I'd become a millionaire.

August of that year, 2002, while mainly hot and cloudless, *did* have the occasional overcast day which made it close and muggy and, in the trapped heat, feel a bit sticky. People out on the streets opted for skimpy clothes to catch whatever breeze there was. So did I. I was due to give blood in the evening at a hall near Oxford Circus hired for the purpose by the National Blood Service, but I had time to study for another two hours, which I did with the windows wide open.

There is so much to read and remember if you want to be a criminal lawyer. I knew what I was letting myself in for when I chose the law. I never regretted my decision to try to get back at people in the drugs racket who'd murdered my father; I was going to do so by deploying the full weight of the courts against them. It was going to be a long haul, however. It was going to be a slog and would take staying power. I would have to keep reading, reading, thinking, making notes, memorizing legal principles and precedents.

'Crime has always been regarded by the courts as a moral wrong and conduct demanding retribution,' I read in my copy of the Butterworths title *Criminal Law*. I'd had to scrape money together over long periods to pay for previous tomes, but for this one, and all the others now in my possession, I paid hard cash. No more interminable waiting for books to be returned to the library so that I could finally get hold of them. I could afford my own library. I also bought a secondhand bookcase.

'The law is based on the assumption that, in the absence of evidence to the contrary, people are able to choose whether to do criminal acts or not and that a person who chooses to commit a crime is responsible for the resulting evil and deserves punishment. The courts have generally seen their task as one of fitting the penalty to the particular degree of iniquity and dangerousness of the offender's conduct on this particular occasion. The sentence should adequately reflect the revulsion felt by citizens for the particular crime. Its purpose is seen not only as punishment but also as a public denunciation of the conduct in question. It may then satisfy the demand for retaliation by the public, or some members of the public, which serious crime sometimes arouses.'

I read that, in terms of the Criminal Justice Act 1991, a sentence, other than a fine, was either a custodial sentence or a community sentence. A custodial sentence meant, in relation to a person of or over 21, a sentence of imprisonment and, in relation to a younger person, a sentence of detention in a young offender institution under the Children and Young Persons Act 1933 or of custody for life under the Criminal Justice Act 1982.

I still don't know why it struck me as amusing when I first discovered that suicide was a crime in our country until 3 August 1961. From that date on, in terms of the Suicide Act 1961, it became perfectly lawful to kill oneself. On the other hand, in terms of an ancient, rarely well argued prejudice, homosexual acts committed in private by male persons who were 21 or over were offences until 27 July 1967. Such acts were then allowed in law by the Sexual Offences Act 1967. My textbook pointed out: 'The nature of the acts in question, their morality or immorality and their consequences do not change overnight; but their *legal* nature does.'

Among my books was a paperback edition of *Law in the Making* by Sir Carleton Allen, the Australian scholar who was appointed professor of jurisprudence at Oxford University in 1929, and who also wrote, among much else besides, *Bureaucracy Triumphant*, *Law and Orders* – 'I was only obeying my orders'– and *Aspects of Justice*. Concerning the wider significance of lawlessness and why it has to be dealt with resolutely and openly, Sir Carleton writes: 'Crime is crime because it consists in wrongdoing which directly and in serious degree threatens the security or well being of society, and because it is not safe to leave it redressable only by compensation of the party injured.'

I paused when I read that. It seemed to be referring to people in *my* position. *My mother and I* were the party injured, not only my father who died when that drug dealer shot him in front of an audience of jazz fans listening to my mother singing the blues in a London club. If I had ever thought of seeking compensation *directly* for the consequences which my mother had had to endure over the ensuing sixteen years; if I had tried to exact payment – what in olden times used to be called blood money – for the blood that poured down my father's face when my mother and club people piled him into a car and took him to Paddington Hospital, well, then *I* would have been just as guilty as the guy who'd killed my dad.

Awful, the law sometimes seems, so unjust.

But only when you're emotional.

When you calm down, as I eventually did, a deeper truth dawns on you. You stop to think of the mayhem, the murderous chaos that would envelop us if people in their separate gangs took the law into their own hands. It gives you pause, thinking along those lines.

If everyone started putting right the perceived wrongs done to them the way Jesse James and his brother Frank did in Missouri after the American Civil War, robbing banks and trains and killing innocent bystanders and relieving travellers of their valuables at gunpoint; if everyone armed themselves to the teeth the way the 1930s bank robbers Bonnie Parker and Clyde Barrow did, shooting dead any police officers they happened to see while 'doing their work'; if the gangster twins Ronnie and Reggie Kray were to be role models emulated for the brutal way they spread fear across London's East End in the 1950s and 1960s,

207

dominating their 'manor' so thoroughly that they sometimes eclipsed their South London rivals Charlie and Eddie Richardson who made *their* money from fraud, theft, protection, fencing stolen goods, steep interest rates on their loans secured by beatings, and whose name, the Torture Gang, sprang from their idiosyncrasy of hammering their victims to the floor with 6-inch nails and severing their toes with bolt cutters – if only ten per cent of us went down that route, taking revenge ourselves for our grievances, we would, soon enough, but too late, be on our knees begging for the mercy of any limit to personal freedom.

No. I knew what I was doing. I was playing a deeper game. I was planning to be a lawyer for the whole of my life. I was ambitious. I wanted to bust everybody in the business which had created my father's killer. I wanted to see everyone in jail, from the minions to the drug barons, from the dealers at school gates trying to spread their distribution networks *inside* the classrooms, to the 'chemists' in Turkey who processed the opium grown in Afghanistan and Pakistan into heroin, and the smugglers getting the stuff into western Europe and the UK where potential customers had the purchasing power.

The business was *demand-led*: that was the key understanding I had arrived at. The drug lords' transport routes when I was a student at KCL went through Bulgaria and Romania, then through Austria and Germany and the Benelux countries, and, via Dover, into England. Simultaneously, huge volumes of cocaine were being smuggled to the lands where rich people lived, from Latin America into the US via Mexico and Florida, and across the Atlantic by way of Jamaica or via West Africa and whatever route the smugglers decided had for the time being become more viable.

Just a little thinking made it clear that I would be a mug to leap angrily into this global network. I'd show myself to be a clueless git driven by emotion with no back-up from the vast store of knowledge and experience already available in the world. Like a typical upstart, I'd be carrying on as though I knew it all, as though I were inventing the wheel from scratch despite all the wheels already around me everywhere in the world. I'd be a conceited, dyed-in-the-wool Johnny-come-lately.

No, to get my revenge I had to rely on reason. I had to study, learn from what others before me had come to know. Mr Keith Hellawell, former Chief Constable of West Yorkshire who'd recently been appointed drugs coordinator by the government, had put a figure on the amount of crime the heroin addicts were involved in. A study showed that 700 heroin addicts had, within a three-month period, committed 70,000 crimes to raise money to pay for their drug purchases. Mr Hellawell said at the time: 'If the performance indicator for a police force is to reduce burglary by, say, X per cent then, as 50 to 60 per cent of house burglaries are to feed the drug habit, it makes sense to deal with the root cause of those burglaries. This may be by getting the burglars into arrest referral schemes, by dealing with them through drug testing and treatment orders, or by treating them in prison.'

Mr Dick Kellaway, chief of the Customs and Excise national investigation service, pointed out that seizures of heroin had rocketed in the past year from £59 million worth of the drug to £145 million worth, an increase of 135 per cent. That was the volume that had been *seized*. He and his colleagues could only guess at the much larger quantities that had eluded agents on the look-out and got through.

'In considering whether conduct is intentional, it is

unnecessary to ascertain whether the party knew of the rule of law.' This guideline expressed by Granville Williams in *Criminal Law*, 1961, underlay every legal response to felonious activity, whether organized or not.

In my very first year as a law student it became obvious that I wouldn't be able to remember everything I read, the date of every statute – there were simply too many of them. The history of law making was much too long. Instead, I would study my prescribed texts and recommended reading to grasp the drift of things. I began to build an index of significant rulings and precedents on my laptop as I went along. I would look up details on a need-to-know basis. I wanted to savour the spirit of the law, not just understand the letter.

Section 36 (1) of the Criminal Justice Act 1988, for example, gave the Attorney-General the right to apply to the Court of Appeal for a review of a sentence in a case where it seemed that the trial judge at the Crown Court had erred on the side of leniency. I found it instructive that trial judges could be considered to be either too lenient or too harsh when passing sentence. On closer inspection, however, this wasn't very surprising. The *range* of sentences available to them seemed to me to be too wide. But then, my reasons for becoming a lawyer weren't entirely dispassionate.

Sentencing in relation to drug offences was one of my main interests. According to Section 24 of the Drug Trafficking Offences Act 1986, the sentence for *possession with intent to supply* depended on which class of drug was involved. For Class A and Class B it was life imprisonment, which I considered to be wholly appropriate. For Class C drugs it was five years.

As for *producing or supplying* Class A and Class B: Life sentence.

Class C: five years.
Possession: Class A: seven years.
Class B: five years.
Class C: two years.
Permitting the use of drugs on premises Class A and B:
14 years.
Class C: five years.
Assisting in drug trafficking: 14 years.

These were the sorts of penalties that had attracted me to the legal profession in the first place and made me feel that I would be honouring the memory of my father seriously if I devoted my working life to the law. It wouldn't be a dead-end street or a blind alley that I was going down. Rather, all along my road would be helpings of revenge, each one a cold dish and all the more satisfying for that. Members of the Howard League for Penal Reform probably had a different slant on things.

My trouble was that there were so many mitigating circumstances. Possession of Class A drugs was what was called an either-way offence. If the police decided to charge the offender, the case could be dealt with either by a magistrates' court or by a crown court. If the offender was found guilty at a magistrates' court (so-called summary conviction), the maximum sentence was lower than it would have been in a crown court. The magistrates' bench book says: 'Possession: should be committed for trial unless the amount is consistent only with personal use.'

That's what rubbed me up the wrong way: the mitigating factors. The variety of possible factors were so many that the *range* of sentences handed down was bound to be wide. Is the prisoner a first-time offender? A persistent offender? How pure was the heroin? 44 per cent pure? 33 per cent pure? How many wraps was the offender caught with? Was he caught in the act of selling the drugs? It didn't surprise me that a document on relevant sentencing case law pointed out: 'The possible variety of considerations is so wide, including those of a medical nature, that we feel it impossible to lay down any practical guidelines.'

A drug dealer caught bombed out of his head on the backseat of his car with 35 bags of heroin, as well as his weighing scales, was found guilty of intent to supply and sentenced to only nine months in prison. Yet someone caught with 'only' ten bags was sent down for three years.

It wasn't a particular accomplishment to notice that the common factor in all drugs cases, despite the range of other circumstances, was money. Money alone was what the drugs barons cared about. They paid no heed to the lives they warped and destroyed. The family relationships they ruined; the human potential they conjured away in puffs of smoke or with hypodermic needles meant nothing to them. What interested them was addicts' praise for the stuff, the quality of the hit: it meant that they'd find the money somehow and be back for more.

Another document in my possession was a report by a journalist called Stuart Millar which reduced to its essentials the process of getting hooked on drugs. It was a little monograph detailing the experience of an intelligent, professional man in his early twenties a few years before I started my legal studies. 'In the past my friends and I had tried all the usual drugs – hash, E, coke. I knew one or two of my mates had tried harder stuff, but I was never really interested because I just wanted to take stuff to go out and bounce about on.'

Then one of his mates offered him some smack. He had no idea where his mate had got it and he refused because he'd heard that smack was the hardest gear as far as drugs were concerned. But his mate said they could smoke a bit of it and there'd be no problem as the trouble only started when you injected. So he did smoke some. 'It was a great hit, completely different from anything I'd tried before.' He'd been having a bad time at work, struggling, but those difficulties just slipped away while he was under the influence. Smack wasn't a sociable drug, he said. 'When you take it you go into your own world. You don't care a toss about anybody else.' Just like the dealers, certainly, who didn't care a toss about anything but the money.

This young professional only used gear twice over the following four weeks, but smoked a little bit more each time. He reckoned he became addicted after the first two months, but felt cool and in control. 'I know now that I have a serious problem and I'm going to go through detox. I've managed to just about hold everything together but I don't want to get to the stage where I'm stealing to pay for gear.'

He was amazed, he said, how much more available heroin was now. And how cheap it was in some places. Just one year previously no one he knew would use it because it was expensive and had bad connotations. Now loads of his friends used it.

That was the big difference, he said, from when he was at school and being shown films about kids dropping dead the moment they went near drugs. It was part of the culture now, he declared. If cocaine and ecstasy were the drugs of the 1980s and early 1990s, then heroin was the drug for the millennium.

Yes it was, as long as you had the money to pay for it. Because money, after all, was what made everything the same. That's what I had found in one item on my recommended reading list: its title was 'The metropolis and mental life' and it was by Georg Simmel, the German sociologist who died aged 60 in 1918.

'Money,' Simmel writes in that paper, 'is concerned only with what is common to all: it asks for the exchange value; it reduces all quality and individuality to the question: How much? All intimate emotional relations between persons are founded in their individuality, whereas in rational relations man is reckoned with like a number, like an element which is in itself indifferent....Money, with all its colourlessness and indifference, becomes the common denominator of all values; irreparably it hollows out the core of things, their individuality, their specific value, and their incomparability. All things float with equal specific gravity in the constantly moving stream of money. All things lie on the same level and differ from one another only in the size of the area which they cover....That is why cities are also the genuine locale of the blasé attitude.'

In that same paper, first published in 1903 under the title, according to my girlfriend Heidi Hathaway, '*Die Großstadt und das Geistesleben*', Simmel writes that 'throughout the whole course of English history, London has never acted as England's heart but often as England's intellect and always as her money-bag!'

Chapter 23

When I arrived at the community hall near Oxford Circus, there were two huge vehicles bigger than fire engines parked in the courtyard with the National Blood Service logo on them. Bloodmobiles they were called, and there were queues of men and women waiting to enter the side door of each vehicle.

It was a muggy day, sticky, with lots of low, grey cloud. The women were in short skirts and chiffon blouses, or loose dresses, breezy culottes; several men were keeping cool in three-quarter cargo trousers, baggy shorts, T-shirts and baseball caps. Their skin shone with perspiration; they looked as though they would welcome a cooling breeze. They were waiting to enter the bloodmobiles, take their turn to lie down inside and donate their blood.

The letter informing me of the date and location of the donor session hadn't mentioned anything about bloodmobile sessions, so I walked by the queues and went into the building, as I'd done the previous time. August was usually a sparse month for blood because many donors tended to be away on holiday, yet here were two queues of them.

While waiting to have my barcode scanned at the reception desk, I saw that there were again three rows of about ten metal-framed collapsible beds with donors lying on them. One sleeve of each donor's shirt was rolled up and a sterile hypodermic needle connected to a bag by a thin tube was inserted into a vein in their inner elbow. A nurse was seated by their side, chatting as they supervised the donation and the silently filling blood bag.

Doctors in white coats sauntered along the rows of beds, stopping to inspect, exchange comments and give the go-ahead for those not yet connected. Those who'd already donated when I arrived were lying back, resting briefly, a bit of cottonwool taped over the insertion point. There were other individuals seated at tables at the far end of the hall, enjoying a cup of tea to restore their liquid levels and a biscuit or bag of crisps. Chairs and tables were stacked against the wall until the session was over and normal community business returned to the hall.

I noticed the same subdued purposeful activity which I'd perceived at all my previous donor sessions. It was a calm, good-natured, smiley atmosphere with a dead-serious objective. The people in the hall, most of them strangers to one another, having arrived from different directions and due to disperse to all points of the compass, were for this short spell, less than an hour altogether, integrated into the same crucial project.

The feeling reminded me of the atmosphere in a couple of old World War Two films I'd seen, one of them starring Jack Hawkins called *The Cruel Sea*. The other was about the Blitz, when London had its back to the wall and bombs were raining down from the sky full of Luftwaffe planes, Messerschmitts and Focke-Wulfs, Dornier and Heinkel bombers and Stuka dive-bombers. Frantic people below were scurrying past the blazing fires and over the rubble of smashed walls and collapsed roofs to the refuge of Underground stations and the company of other Londoners, many of them suddenly destitute. All that stood between Britain and German enslavement were the brave and selfless RAF pilots in their Spitfire planes and Hawker Hurricanes. Germany's losses in the sky were more than Hitler could bear; he turned his forces instead to an invasion of Russia.

I was much too young to be sentimental about the Second World War, but still, there was a sense that all of us here with our National Blood Service barcodes were in this together. We were standing up for people who'd been injured in accidents, burned in fires, and wounded in fights, stabbings, shootings. We'd come forward for them because they were *our* strangers, *our* women giving birth, *our* patients having operations and needing blood transfusions in the dead of night. They drank the same London water we drank and travelled on the same crowded tube trains twice a day. We'd come forward because *our* blood could boost *their* blood, top it up, make it viable once more. Without our platelets, their blood wouldn't congeal; they'd bleed profusely from the slightest cut and quite possibly die.

When the barcode on my letter was scanned and I was asked by the receptionist how I felt and I'd responded to a sequence of questions about my health, and had handed in my pre-completed questionnaire signed to give my consent and declare that my donation would be safe, a drop of blood was taken from my finger. This was dropped in front of me into a coloured fluid in a test tube; it was to test whether I was anaemic. If the drop of blood sank in the test tube, that was proof that it had enough iron in it.

I glanced at the posters on the walls while waiting to be called to a free bed. One publicized a local Eating Disorders Support Group, another praised the healthy attractions of the countryside; next to that was one seeking new members to Help the Aged. The brightest poster I saw there that day was advertising a hiphop competition.

The guy sitting next to me in a T-shirt and worn-out jeans had a blue-and-red tattoo of a big butterfly on the back of his neck and of an open-winged bird on his left forearm; his trainers, gleaming white, looked brand new. The woman on my other side was a middle-aged brunette with a bird-like nose, a beak; she was reading a hardback book. I peeped as she turned a page: there was dialogue on both sides, so it could've been a novel.

My name was called out and a male nurse in track-suit bottoms led me to a bed between two large windows. I could see the dark clouds outside, and traffic passing by the side of the building.

'You feeling all right today?' the nurse asked me.

'Yes, I am.'

'Lie down,' he said with a smile, motioning with a hand. 'Someone will be along in a tick.'

It was more like half a tick.

A blonde nurse with brown eyes and a watch clipped to her bosom went through the double-checking routine.

'Please confirm your name,' she said, glancing at the sheet on a clipboard.

'Leo Allen,' I said.

'Your date of birth?'

I told her.

'Address.'

I gave it.

'Have you been ill, or feverish, or had a cold in recent weeks?'

'No. I've been fine.'

'Roll up your sleeve, please,' she said with a smile, and when I did she dabbed my inner elbow with damp cottonwool.

'If you clench and unclench your fist,' she said, 'we'll find a vein more easily.'

I complied, and just as she was saying, 'That's good, that'll do,' an Asian man in a white coat and horn-rimmed glasses stepped up to the bed. His shiny dark-brown face was like polished teak, contrasting with his head of white hair. The name-badge on his lapel said *Dr Adam Iqbal*. I'd seen him several times before.

'How are you, Mister Allen?' he asked.

'I'm fine, Doctor.'

He smiled big teeth and said: 'Thank you for coming.'

I nodded and smiled back. 'Those two bloodmobiles outside,' I said, 'I've never seen them here before.'

'It's to meet the overflow,' he said.

'More donors than usual?'

'Many more.'

'Why? What happened?'

'We put out an urgent appeal to our regulars on behalf of our soldiers abroad.'

'Yeah? Where abroad?'

He smiled again. 'It doesn't matter, does it – where?'

'Naah, it doesn't matter.'

He turned to the nurse, took the hypodermic needle from her hand, pressed a thumb down on a vein in my inner elbow and began to insert the point. I looked away, as I always did, psyching myself up for the moment, but the needle was so sharp I didn't feel the piercing pressure.

'What a light touch you have, Doctor,' I said.

'It's not me,' he replied, pointing to the needle, the lights overhead shining in his glasses. 'It's this excellent technology.'

I clenched and unclenched my fist from time to time, to keep the blood flowing through the tube into the bag on the nurse's lap.

I was having my cup of tea at one of the tables and a bag of salt-and-vinegar crisps – I preferred them to the other choice, cheese-and-onion flavour – when my mobile rang. *My* mobile. I'd forgotten for a while that I had one. I pushed my chair back so suddenly to pull the phone from a pocket in my jeans that the small boy

219

standing next to his mother burst out laughing. My tea sloshed into the saucer. I rose from the chair and turned away, the way I'd seen other people doing with a phone to their ear. I reached out my other arm and leaned against the stack of chairs against the wall.

'Hello, Bobbie.'

'How are you, Leo?'

'You're the fifth person to ask me that.'

'Yeah? Who else asked you?'

'A receptionist, a male nurse, a blonde nurse and a doctor. I'm at a blood-donor session.'

'Oh. Sorry to interrupt.'

'You aren't interrupting. I'm done here – just having a cuppa.'

'I wanted to remind you, Leo. Robin and I will be at your mother's place in the limo to pick you all up at eight.'

'She's very excited, as you know. Very happy about being recorded live at the Hi-Hat.'

'Yes, she is. So am I. It should go well. I've made all the arrangements. We have the best technicians.'

'I'm sure you have. Heidi's excited too – so am I. I've never knowingly been at a live recording.'

'If you applaud loud enough,' she said with a chuckle, 'we might hear the sounds of your clapping and cheering on the CD. You can tell people: those are *my* hands, baby, pulling out the stops.'

'Fame at last,' I said. 'I owe you so much, Bobbie.'

She laughed again and said: 'See you all at eight. It looks a bit overcast, but so what?'

'Yeah. So what?'

Chapter 24

A fine drizzle was falling, one of several brief downpours that evening, when the gleaming white limousine drew up in front of my mother's house in Colville Terrace. In one smooth move the vehicle with a long expanse of dark windows on either side parked at the kerb. I saw the wipers sweeping slowly across the windscreen. The driver's door opened and Robin the chauffeur got out. She was wearing a light grey suit and had a black hat with a shiny peak on her head and an umbrella in her hand. She opened the umbrella, raised it overhead, looked up at our front door and stepped across the pavement.

I turned from the window and smiled at my mother and Heidi sitting on the couch. I wouldn't say they were dressed to the nines, just that they looked particularly good for this special gig. It was going to be recorded live and form the basis of Arlene Allen's first album. Bobbie was overseeing the production personally and had been talking about her marketing strategy. My mother's pale gold dress and matching headband chimed in with the lemon-coloured shoes I'd bought her. She also chose from the same shop in Bond Street the clutch-bag now resting on her lap.

Heidi was a knock-out in a black silk dress with little silver streaks that matched her silver shoes. I'd paid for those too. I thought it wiser, more sexually controlled, not to keep embracing her. As for my own kit, I'd bought another white three-piece suit, and white shoes, after ruining my outfit when I fell down in Soho in front of the entrance to Ronnie Scott's. I didn't want Lester to think his silly talk had put me off white as a suitable celebratory colour. Having received so much money in brown A5 envelopes – £500 twice a week for

24 weeks and lots of free delicious food whose fat-making carbohydrates and sugar I then lost forthwith through sexual exertions in that bungalow in Primrose Hill, staying as lean as I was before I'd met Bobbie – I was feeling light, almost light-*headed*, my feet off the ground, and I wanted to *look* it on my mother's special day.

I'd asked Heidi earlier that evening what she thought of white clothes for a man. She was checking her hair in the mirror in my wardrobe; I was sitting on the side of the bed.

'D'you think white is poncy, effeminate? That's what Lester seemed to be implying. Or angelic? That's what he said – angelic.'

Heidi shook her head. 'Of course it isn't, Leo,' she said. 'With one proviso.'

'Which is?'

'That it doesn't make you start *behaving* like an angel.'

'What d'you mean?'

'You know, as though you were pure.'

'Pure what?'

'Just pure. That's what white symbolizes in church – purity. A bride in white wants everyone to believe she still hasn't had sex, no matter how old she is, and she wants to broadcast it to the world.'

'What about her sex drive, her natural feelings?'

'She's supposed to deny them, pretend she doesn't have them.'

'Really? Why must she do that?'

'God, Leo,' Heidi turned from the mirror. 'You sound as though you haven't heard of religion.'

'Don't be sarkie – of course I have. My mother said she used to go to church occasionally – she liked singing the hymns – until my dad was shot dead in front of God's eyes. God let it happen, she said.'

'Your poor mother,' Heidi replied, shaking her head.

'Right out of the blue, she lost her man.'

'So did you, Leo,' Heidi added. She came and sat by my side on the bed and kissed me on the cheek.

'Yeah. So did I. But I was four when it happened. It doesn't kill me the way it still kills her. She once told me that Bob Marley's song "No woman no cry" seemed to have been written about her. My mother is English, as you know. She isn't *half*-English and half-something else.'

'Like me, you mean – half-German,' Heidi said with a smile.

'Yes – no, not like you, not like me. All her grandparents were English. Both her parents are English. She was born right here in London. She's never been to Jamaica, but that song, and the voice singing it – No woman no cry – somehow became her anthem.'

I kissed Heidi lightly on her lips and kept eye contact. 'What was I saying – before I got side-tracked? I've lost my thread.'

'A woman's sex drive – her natural feelings. You asked why she was supposed to deny them.'

'Yeah. So she can wear a white wedding dress?'

'It's supposed to be the proof of her purity – the colour white. It's a symbol of celibacy and innocence – proof that she hasn't succumbed to the evil that is her flesh. White says she hasn't been sinful. She hasn't explored the pleasures of her body before her father gives her away in church to a man who also knows nothing about his body.'

Heidi's words took on a slight German accent whenever she felt strongly about something. It must have been her mother's influence.

'Those of us who start having sex before marriage,'

223

she said at the side of the bed, 'are impure. Full stop. No matter how good sex makes us feel. White means you belong to heaven's host – as though you have no physical desire in your loins, Leo, no genitals, or you have no urge to satisfy the longing pounding in your blood.' She kept eye contact. 'If that's the image you want to put across, who are you trying to kid?'

'I'm not trying to kid anyone,' I said and rose from the bed.

She rose too, moved her hand to my crotch and took hold of my tackle through my trousers.

'You won't kid *me*, Leo,' she said with a serious look on her face, 'no matter what colour you wear. That's where I disagree with Shakespeare.'

'Shakespeare? What's *he* got to do with it?'

'"The apparel doth proclaim the man," he said. 'Remember? So even *he*, our great bard, could be shallow. Deceiving people with clothes is such an old con. Paedophiles in church do it all the time. Prisoners escaping the lock-up sometimes wear priestly garb. People wear black at funerals to pretend they're sad because of the death of someone they actually loathed. Men shine their shoes and wear a suit and tie when they go to the bank for a loan, even though they hate grovelling.'

While Heidi was talking, it occurred to me, not for the first time, that I might one day, in some way, have to pay for betraying her trust. What a lovely, bright woman she was. What a traitor *I* was. All the cash I was depositing, in two different banks and a building society, didn't change that. How would *I* feel, I wondered, if I found out that Heidi was fucking some other guy in a place I'd never heard of? If she said she was doing it for the money, for pressing economic reasons, to buy food, pay her way, would that make *me* feel any better? Because bills had to be paid?

It amazed me that Heidi didn't sense my unease whenever she spoke about trust or honesty or being up front.

Probably because her trust was as deep as my deceitfulness, it never occurred to her to suspect that anything between us might be out of kilter. I loved her. I adored her, and not just in bed. Bed wasn't the only place where we devoured each other in between the times we were apart for days on end. She read novels and non-fiction, biographies, history at her parents' house, and played the piano at least an hour every day. Her course at UCL was comparative literature, discerning, I presumed, the similarities and differences between certain German and English-language authors, while I was poring over law books and Home Office reports in Notting Hill and making notes on my laptop computer.

I had shown Heidi, and my mother, a Lottery ticket I'd bought to explain the source of my new-found cash. It was a small win, I said, nothing spectacular like the huge bonanzas announced on television every week. It was more like a little windfall that came the way of dozens of disappointed hopefuls whose winning numbers were shared by too many others.

Is it a law of dishonesty, that one lie leads inexorably to another lie to back up, validate, the first lie?

If you lie to someone you love, does that mean you *don't* love them? Why didn't I feel that to be true in my heart? Was truth straightforward, always narrow, simple, unlayered? Was it entirely unaffected by experiences in one's past life, by traumas in childhood, perhaps? Was truth painted only in primary colours?

Was that why I'd long been feeling that I was one day going to pay for my betrayal, in some heavy way? Was it my guilty conscience acting up, 'pricking me', as people said?

The only reservation *I* had about my white suit, a very ironic one, certainly, was that some people at the Hi-Hat Club might take me for an upmarket drug dealer. They might associate my flash with ill-gotten gains. At least I wasn't glittering with gold medallions hanging from my neck. There were no jewel-encrusted rings on my fingers or bracelets on my wrists. Bling wasn't my thing. Bling was the hoi-polloi demonstrating that they'd made good; it was ghetto guys proving they hadn't succumbed, hadn't knuckled under, proving it mainly to *themselves*. They weren't yet accustomed to the high life. Nor would I be arriving at the club in Camden Town in a blood-red Ferrari with bodyguards who looked as tough as Mike Tyson.

No. *Our* transport was a shiny white limousine. And *our* chauffeur was a tallish lesbian who, according to Bobbie, had never been late in the last six years for any of Bobbie's appointments. Whether it was up the M1 to the 1853 Gallery in a 19th-century textile mill at Saltaire north of Bradford where David Hockney's paintings were on display, or to Gatwick Airport down the M23 and from there, with an overseas client, to Brighton on the Sussex coast to roam around the Royal Pavilion, Bobbie said Robin never let her down.

'She has a good sense of routes. It's always a smooth drive with her at the wheel. The car never jerks or stops with a jolt – unless some idiot in front makes it necessary.'

When the bell rang and I went to open the front door, Robin was there, smiling. 'Hi,' she said, umbrella in one hand. She took her hat off with the other and as she inspected it I noticed how short her hair was; it was almost severe, like a soldier's. 'You all ready?' she asked, putting her hat back on. 'Bobbie's in the car, but she said to tell you there's no great hurry.'

Robin's voice wasn't deep, not as low as my mother's; it was more like Heidi's. The paleness of her face was emphasized by her dark eyebrows and dark-brown eyes and by her lips that were painted a glossy red. I wondered if that meant she was a 'lipstick lesbian'. I didn't know how to ask her if she *was* a lesbian. I didn't think I should. I didn't want her to think I was anti-gay or judgemental or that it bothered me how people got their kicks. I valued diversity and couldn't stand conformity, the idea of people being indistinguishable from one another, like bread rolls in a baker's oven. Variety, after all, was said to be the spice of life. Live and let live, I believed. To each his own. But I could see: despite a long, old scar down her left cheek that was unlikely to fade any more, she'd have had a lot of boyfriends, if boys had been her thing. She probably did have lots of women admirers. There was something compelling, charismatic about the beauty of her face. It was Heidi's guess when we first met Robin a few months previously, the night she drove us to the Vortex gig in Stoke Newington, that the scar on her cheek had been caused by jealousy, by some rival who'd tried to spoil her looks with a blade.

I wondered if Robin was in a steady, long-term relationship. Or was she slipping and sliding around between partners, trying to 'discover' her sexuality or inhabit it in a new way? I couldn't guess or figure it out. The biology/psychodynamics of same-sex desire was beyond my ken; whether it was fixed forever, or altered from time to time under the control of feelings way below conscious thought, I couldn't say. My lecturers at law school never offered any insights into such matters.

'Yes,' I answered, 'we *are* ready. Quite excited too.' I stepped back into the hall and called out: 'Mum, Heidi – it's time to go.'

We left the house and went down the steps to the limo. A few drops of rain fell on Heidi and me as Robin held the umbrella over my mother's head. Bobbie was waiting on the horseshoe-shaped back seat talking on her mobile; my mother got in and sat beside her. Heidi and I sat on the spacious middle seat behind the chauffeur's. What with the tinted side and back windows and the sound insulation built in to the bodywork, that car was like a cocoon on wheels as it swished along the streets. The pedestrians on the pavements, the neon signs pulsing above them, the vehicles ahead of us: it all seemed like a clip from a silent movie.

In the back of the seat in front of me was a TV screen. In the door on Heidi's side was a selection of drinks: malt whisky, cognac, real ale, small bottles of shandy. On my side was a fridge. I opened it and had a quick look inside: *mille-feuille* pastries, de-luxe ice-cream, Thorntons chocolates. The sight of those goodies conjured in me a fantasy: playing the part of an Ethiopian emperor by opening the electric window and throwing to the grateful rabble in the dust outside pastries and chocolates and bottles of drink.

I should have indulged that fantasy, perhaps, while I had the chance. Strike, the saying goes, while the iron is hot. Little did I know that the trip to the Hi-Hat Club was to be my last ride in a limousine, the last time I would see London from a limo.

I had no inkling that there was going to be a bad scene at the Hi-Hat. I didn't know something was going to happen there that would lead to the end of my visits to Primrose Hill. I didn't have a clue that I had already received my last £500 in a brown envelope.

How could I have known?

I don't think I ever made a false move, or said anything that unwittingly upset Bobbie, in all my visits

228

to her retreat.

She was never irritable with me. She had never shown any sign that she was tiring of me. Nor had there been any hint that she was bored with luxuriating with me in her bath of steaming water or of closing her fist on my stiffy and squeezing it. She'd read two more letters from the National Blood Service informing me of upcoming donor sessions; she regarded those letters as continuing confirmation that I was in good health, safe to be intimate with. Nothing about my sessions with her had made her stop smiling at me or stop telling me about her life each morning after, about the different sectors of the economy in which her company's various divisions operated, the places her overseas clients asked to see after hours. She'd told me that she and her colleagues still hadn't secured the contract to make television programmes to promote London's Tate Modern art gallery.

There hadn't been anything for me to fret about, surely?

Bobbie Cullen had always been relaxed with me, confidential.

She pulled down the zip of my jeans impatiently each time in the lecherous bathroom. She was keen on my energy in bed, raving with pleasure each time in a noisy, gasping way. Only three nights before the Hi-Hat gig she'd shouted again at the top of her voice right into my ear: 'Yes! Yes! Keep going, Leo, you lovely fucking boy!'

Chapter 25

We were welcomed into the Hi-Hat club by two doormen in white dinner jackets and black bow ties. They smiled and greeted my mother and Bobbie warmly, and nodded at Heidi and me.

On a wall as we passed the box office just inside the front entrance were photographs of Courtney Pine and of the bass guitarist/bandleader Kyle Eastwood who looked just like his tall, lean father, the actor/director Clint Eastwood. Between the pix was a large framed sign impossible to miss with a printed message: *This is a jazz club. If you came to talk while the musicians are playing, please go elsewhere before the gig begins.*

Other club staff were showing other patrons to their places. They too looked sophisticated in their evening wear, but, burly and with faces like professional boxers, they also looked capable of throwing anyone out who might want to make trouble. Aggro was the last thing on my mind, but they reminded me of a recent research paper in the Home Office *Crime Detection and Prevention* series which I'd read entitled *Clubs, Drugs and Doormen*. It laid bare in detail the connections between door supervision and drug dealing, how a minority of door staff turned a blind eye to the dealing in exchange for pay-offs.

The Hi-Hat was full. Arrivals were making their way in the lamplight to their tables arranged in about five rows in front of the stage and partway down either side. The drums were already set up. The double-bass was leaning at an angle. The grand piano was open. A brass-coloured alto saxophone was on its stand and, next to it on an open case, a gleaming red amplified Gibson guitar. To the left of the stage was a long bar with illuminated bottles on the shelves. On a counter beyond that I saw what looked like a selection of CDs and associated ads. The club's rear entrance was somewhere behind the stage and probably led out to a service street. There were menus on the tables and jugs of water and glasses.

Covering almost every centimetre of three of the club's four walls were framed photos of renowned singers and jazzmen who'd done their stuff at the club over the years, performers from America, from Europe, Brazil, South Africa. The lamps on the tables with their retro, orange-coloured tassled lampshades were reflected in the glass of the framed photos everywhere, creating an intimate, softly-lit atmosphere. There was a humming air of expectation by the time Heidi and I sat down.

One of the doormen guided my mother and Bobbie round to their reserved table. I saw Bobbie kiss my mother on each cheek, say something to her and then watch her step to the back of the stage where the band members were beginning to assemble. My mother's long-awaited moment was about to commence.

One of the waiters came to our table and asked if we'd like to order food to eat after the first set, and perhaps a drink before. We ordered a bottle of lager each, and Heidi went for a fish dish – lemon sole with vegetables and caramelized onions. I chose the chicken kiev with grilled peppers and tomatoes.

I looked around and saw in the lamplight Lester and Martha way over on our right-hand side. Mr Maddox and Aunt Josie were at the next table along. They waved to us and we waved back. What a good vibe there was in the place; you could sense how amped up everyone was. And when the band had taken their positions, the bassist had plucked two strings as a final check that they were in tune, and the MC came on stage, I felt his words wind up the audience's

231

expectation even more. He was tall, chubby faced, had a noticeable paunch and a voice incongruously high pitched.

'Ladies and gentlemen,' he said, 'it gives me great pleasure to welcome you to the Hi-Hat Club tonight where our policy has always been to bring you the best musical talent. Top of our bill as you know from our website and the talk of the town is London's very own rising star, a superb blues singer, crooner, chanteuse,' he grinned and raised a hand, 'describe her as you will, recording live here where *your* pleasure too will be captured on the disc for posterity,' he beamed again and paused for effect. 'From down the road in Notting Hill, home of the Westway flyover…ladies and gentlemen,' turning at the waist and indicating with an outstretched arm, 'Arlene Allen!'

Waves of applause brought my mother to the front of the stage where the mic was. The guys in the band too were clapping. Couples behind us were cheering. Heidi was rapt. I thought it a bit weird; it made me uncomfortable that people should be applauding *before* my mother had even started singing. I wondered if it might put a spell on her, jinx her performance. It didn't seem to bother her, though. She smiled and nodded this way and that and looked, I thought, cool in her pale-gold gown.

The MC grinned and pushed his palms downwards several times to get the audience to ease off the applause so he could be heard.

'It gratifies me to be able to tell you,' he said, 'that Missus Allen's reputation has already travelled beyond these shores and that in December she starts a weeklong season at the Village Vanguard on Seventh Avenue in Manhattan.'

The clapping and cheering surged again and I wondered if it might be raising expectations about *tonight's* gig a bit too high. My mother hadn't even opened her mouth yet. Wouldn't the adulation affect her performance in some negative way, or was it just *me* being jumpy?

I needn't have worried. She combined with the band and delivered again to the highest standards. Sitting next to Heidi, I felt more proud of my mother than ever. Every song she sang – mainly her own ones, which she began writing after emerging from her postmortem depression, ballads, blues, up-tempo rollercoasters – every breath control and curving, bended note was a distillation of rapture from melancholy and heartache, her voice tapping the dregs of happiness.

When the first set ended and my mother and the band left the stage, Heidi said she felt lucky to be in the audience. She wouldn't forget this gig for a long time, she said. She couldn't wait, she added, for the album to be released so she could buy a copy and play it to her parents, Ilse and Gregory Hathaway.

Then she said: 'I have to go to the loo.'

'Me too,' I replied.

'Must be the lager,' she grinned, taking hold of her bottle and tilting it to check that it *was* empty.

'I think the loos are across that way,' I said, indicating beyond where Lester and Martha were seated. 'Come,' I took her arm and we rose from the table.

People behind us and on either side were checking the menus in the subdued light or trying to catch the attention of the waiters bringing from the kitchen trays of the food ordered earlier; others were chatting and laughing. I noticed again on the walls the orange-coloured lampshades reflected in the panes of glass of the framed photos. It was a distinctive ambience.

We stepped away from our table towards the stage

233

and followed it round to the back till we came to an area out of everyone's sight. It was a well-lit space with a bench against a wall. On one side were two doors facing us, one marked *Men,* the other *Women* under male and female metal silhouettes. On the other side of the space, a few metres away, was a cubicle marked *Private No Entry.*

'Wait for me on that bench,' I suggested.

'You'll probably have to wait for *me*,' Heidi said.

'Okay, I'll be here,' I said, and we pushed the doors open and stepped into our adjacent loos.

Guys were standing all along the stall pissing shoulder to shoulder. Others were splashing their hands in the basins or drying them on paper towels. The four cubicles on the opposite side were all engaged. I waited briefly for a place in front of the sanitary wall streaming with water, then stepped up and relieved myself.

And that should have been that.

My freelance source of income should have remained intact.

Bobbie Cullen had specified the date of our next meeting: I had no reason to think that my services would suddenly no longer be wanted on Primrose Hill.

But when I'd pulled my zip up, washed and dried my hands and stepped back out, and saw that Heidi was still in the women's, I paced the floor while waiting for her to appear. I walked from the toilets and the bench on one side of that secluded area to the other, and that was when I smelled something burning.

The smell was coming from the cubicle marked *Private No Entry* on the far side from the toilets. It smelled like cloth burning. I thought I saw flickering shadows on the ceiling above the cubicle. A fire could be starting, it occurred to me, flames, which could grow and spread. There were dozens of people in the club.

234

I went closer and realized that the cubicle's door wasn't quite shut, so I stepped right up to it and pushed it open to have a look.

Slumped back on the lavatory seat in the narrow room was a woman about Heidi's age with thick brown hair. Her makeup and eye shadow contrasted with her crimson sleeveless dress whose hem had ridden halfway up her thighs. Sticking vertically out of her left forearm was a needle affixed to a syringe. She was breathing heavily, struggling for air, as though having an asthma attack. Even as I took in the spectacle, a tinge of blue began to discolour the skin of her face and spasms made her stomach quake.

The man standing beside her didn't seem concerned. He was calm. Wearing a shiny silver-grey striped suit and bright-green tie and green hat, he was counting a bundle of ten-pound notes in his hands. On the window ledge above the woman's head the flames of three candles were flickering. Beside them on a strip of cardboard was a ball of soggy wool, several tin-foil wraps and teaspoons, and two syringes. That was when I twigged that I'd stepped into a makeshift heroin den. The heroin had been heated in a spoon on the candles to increase its viscosity. It was filtered through the wool, which gave off the peculiar burning smell, then drawn up into the syringe and injected into the woman's arm. Or maybe she'd injected it herself.

Her difficult breathing changed to a mixture of noisy delirium and heaving as I stood staring at her. She tried to catch her breath, control her gasping, while crying out bits of disjointed speech – 'My job! What am I going to do! I'll lose my flat!' Her lips too became blue and, when her right hand jerked up in sympathy with her stomach spasms, I caught a glimpse of her fingernails. They were also turning blue.

Was I witnessing the effects of an overdose? How

pure was the stuff?

This young woman on the brink of death by suffocation in a drug delirium didn't look like my father; not at all. She was white, like my mother. My father was black. She was young. My father was quite a bit older. But in a moment of angry derangement I saw in her face *his* face, saw my dead dad dying all over again at the hands of a drug dealer – and in London again, in a jazz club again.

I lost my rag. I saw red and went ballistic.

I stepped into the narrow room, clenched my fist and thumped down hard on the guy's hands; the pile of notes fell from his grasp, scattering on the woman's thighs and on to the floor. As he gawped at me with gaping mouth, I grabbed his lapels and dragged him out of that small enclosure. He tried to resist. He jerked back to pull free. He scowled and squealed 'Hey man!', but I kicked his feet out from under him and he went tumbling to the deck, his bright-green hat flying off. I bent down and grasped his ankles and, as I proceeded to drag him across the space towards the bench, I started shouting at the top of my voice.

'Help! Doctor!' I yelled. 'Help!'

'Leo!' Heidi called out as she emerged from the women's loo. 'What are you doing?'

'Go for help. There's a woman in there,' I motioned with my head. 'I think she's dying from an overdose. She's going blue.'

'What?'

'In there. Go'n fetch someone, Heidi. Quickly.'

'Who's that?' she asked, pointing down to the guy wriggling and kicking to loosen my grip on his ankles. He pulled one foot free.

'A dealer shit full of confidence. He supplied the woman in there.' I turned my head and looked to see if anyone had come yet, and shouted again. 'Help! Call a

236

doctor! A woman's dying!'

One of the doormen in a bow tie and another man with a black bag appeared from around the stage.

'In there!' I yelled, pointing. 'She's going blue!'

They hurried across to the *Private* cubicle. Heidi followed them. Other men and women emerged from the toilets.

The scum on the floor kicked me in the knee with the boot of his free foot. The pain zinged into my bone, but it made me furious and I grabbed his raised leg with my other hand too and began to turn and swing the bastard around on the floor. His shoulders and head kept thumping the carpet. More people appeared, some holding drinks, one woman with a bare midriff. Next thing I knew, another bouncer grabbed me from behind with both arms around my waist and yanked me away so hard that the guy's foot fell from my hands straight to the floor.

'What's going on here?' the bouncer said into my ear, then turned me around roughly by the shoulders. His blue eyes glared down at me. 'Just what are you trying to do? This is a fucking *jazz* club, not a fight club. You trying to spoil the evening for everyone else?'

'There's a woman can't breathe in that room,' I told him. 'Her skin's turning blue. This guy gave her an overdose.'

'That's what *he* says,' Silver-suit hissed as he pushed himself up and rose from the floor. 'You know, me, Jimmy – wouldn't harm a fly.'

'You believe this shit? I *saw* him in there.'

'He tried to rob me,' Silver-suit countered. 'Tried to take my money – it's all over the floor in there. It isn't dignified, Jimmy. You understand? This isn't right.'

'He's a dealer. There's candles in there, syringes. The woman was struggling for air and he couldn't be arsed.'

'I suggest you calm down, sir,' the bouncer said to me. 'Take a deep breath. You hear me? Take a deep breath...Good. Hold it in.' And when I'd held it in, because there was no other way to deal with his burly, menacing presence, he said in a more conciliatory tone: 'I saw you earlier. You're Arlene Allen's son, aren't you?'

'And you're Jimmy – right? What's that got to do with anything?'

'You should be proud of your mother. She's made a big hit here tonight.'

'This guy's hit has already killed the woman in there, for all I know. Why don't you call the police? This is a crime scene.'

'No, it's not,' he said. 'It's the Hi-Hat Club, and your mother's top of our bill tonight. I saw you arrive with her and Miss Cullen.'

I couldn't believe this guy. 'So?' I asked him. '*So*?'

'Don't make trouble,' he replied, menacing again with a wagging finger, his cold blue eyes holding mine. 'That's the best advice I can give you.' He looked at the dealer, told him to turn around, then dusted off his jacket with a few flicks of his fingertips.

'If you go in there,' I told him, 'you'll see the needles and the wraps. It's this guy's gear.'

'Don't malign the man, sir. Don't cast aspersions. We have a medical doctor in the house. He's resident. He'll do whatever's necessary. People sometimes faint here. Emotions overcome them, you know? – feelings. Qualified medics know what to do – she'll be all right. You shouldn't interfere. Everyone knows you and your mother live in Notting Hill. She's going to be good for business here at the Hi-Hat and we'd like you to come again and enjoy yourself.'

'Not me,' the dealer said, slimy in his shiny silver-grey suit and green tie. 'That's not what *I'd* like. This fucker owes me,' he said, pointing at me with daggers in his eyes. 'You're gonna be sorry for what you did, bruv, trespassing like that.'

Jimmy the bouncer began to usher me away forcibly, a hand pressed to my back, pushing. I turned to look again at the dealer and saw Heidi behind him coming towards us.

'Leo!' she called out.

I stopped. 'That's my girlfriend,' I told Jimmy.

'Leo,' Heidi said again as she approached, 'the doctor gave her an injection. He said she's going to be all right. She stopped panting, and she stopped babbling.'

'What did I tell you?' Jimmy said with the hard semblance of a smile. 'Don't be so overwrought, kid. Mind your own business and we'll take care of ours.'

'I'm looking forward to that fish dish,' Heidi said into my ear and kissed me on the cheek. 'It's lemon sole. Come, let's get back to our table.'

Chapter 26

The Notting Hill Carnival had of course been attracting revellers to the Royal Borough of Kensington and Chelsea, not only from other parts of England and the UK, but also from as far away as Hungary and Hong Kong and, in recent years, Brazil and California. One year a group of teenagers from Latvia with knapsacks on their backs stopped me in Portobello Road opposite the Electric Cinema and asked for directions to the Tabernacle Arts Centre; they said they'd heard that the food at the tables in the courtyard there was good and affordable. I happily showed them the way. The two guys in their group were blonds, the two girls had darker hair. Their spoken English wasn't bad, not too much searching for words, and their smiles and conviviality confirmed to me that the word about Europe's biggest street party had spread far and wide.

The pavements became packed during the August Bank Holiday with up to two million people letting their hair down in a small number of streets along which the carnival parade swayed to beat music.

Despite the revelry and high spirits among the happy crowds, there have nevertheless always been, as far back as I can remember, some residents who can't stand what they call 'the aggro and the noise' of the festivities.

Even staid locals have their rights, of course, but every year these glum bums become more tight arsed than ever and make it known that Carnival ruins their 'peace and quiet'. I've heard individuals mumbling in pubs that the music and the gloriously decorated floats, the stunningly colourful costumes and amazing headgear of the Mas dancers divided into seventy-odd competing teams called 'camps' – their outfits put together with scissors, needle and thread over many painstaking months with such verve and panache succeed only, as far as certain individuals are concerned, in 'lowering the tone of the borough'.

These uptight gits hate the sight of people boogie-ing in the streets – or maybe they're just jaded from having witnessed Carnival so many times before. It unhinges them to see merry-makers tottering about in tipsy joyfulness. Women in the summer sun clad only in bras and hotpants gyrating their butts to the beat in front of guys with beads of sweat on their brows from all the booze they've been drinking – such gay abandon is frowned upon every August by householders who don't necessarily live in the parts of the borough that have the highest property prices in the whole of the UK.

The implication, even if not spelled out in so many words, is that Carnival isn't tasteful. Carnival isn't as demure and decorous as another of the borough's big annual attractions: the Chelsea Flower Show. My mother and I have been to that show three times, once with Heidi, always in May. The blooms on display, the extraordinary floral arrangements and creative ideas have never failed to impress us, even on the occasion when it rained. We were bowled over each time. The spectacles were awesome. There was so much to take in: water gardens, mosaic gardens, patio gardens, garden fountains, the endless range of colours and foliage and lovely scents. The resourcefulness of the gardeners involved, their patience and artistic originality, stay in one's mind long after one has left SW3. The enthusiasm of those competing for the coveted Royal Horticultural Society Gold Medal in various categories keep raising the show's high standards.

What disturbed me for some reason each time we

walked from Sloane Square tube station and entered the eleven-acre site through the London Gate in Royal Hospital Road was how many elderly people there were among the visitors. Was London ageing so rapidly? Were these codgers, old fogeys, senescent citizens all from within the city's limits, or were at least some of them from beyond the M25?

The site seemed to be a Mecca of men and women on their last legs wearing straw hats and blazers, nodding appreciatively and muttering approval as they leaned on their walking-sticks and went slowly along the pathways between the displays in the Great Pavilion. It was a congregation of discerning veterans and old ducks, many of them octogenarians, surely, preparing themselves, perhaps, for their imminent journey to a far superior garden high up in the sky where the season never changes, where it is always summer, the petals never fade, and where plants never die.

'It beats me how anyone can compare the Notting Hill Carnival to the Chelsea Flower Show,' I said to Heidi as we lay side by side on her bed in her parents' house. We'd had a bite to eat and she had played the piano in the living room for a while. 'It simply isn't comparing like with like.'

'I know,' Heidi said. 'It's like me saying I love Rachmaninov, I love Chopin's pieces, and therefore I can't also love John Coltrane's "A Love Supreme" or Chet Baker blowing "Let's get lost".'

'Daft, isn't it?'

'It's narrow-minded. That's what happens sometimes when money and ignorance mix,' she said, gazing at the ceiling. 'Money is supposed to elevate your taste. It's meant to make you prefer stuff that is supposedly exalted over stuff that is earthy. It can make you such a snob, money can – especially if you don't

242

have loads of it and are only trying to project an image.'

Heidi had had money all her life. She had deeper insights into it than I would ever guess at.

The Royal Borough of Kensington and Chelsea was a bit like that, I thought, a mixture of money and ignorance. Being home to the Science Museum, the Natural History Museum, the Victoria and Albert Museum and the Royal Court Theatre, as well as a slew of fashionable, high-end retail outlets where celebrities liked to shop and flaunt their purchases, and flats and houses costing £2 million and more in Holland Park and in and around Cheyne Walk along the Thames, the borough was a mixture of super-wealthy homes and wretched dumps, rather like Islington. Very rich people breathed the same air as very poor folk, multi-millionaires and families existing on benefits. Sleazy politicians in exquisite apartments on the take from tycoons and Russian oligarchs did their thing nor far from emaciated drug addicts sweating in rehab a stone's throw from upmarket saunas where pretty things went for their twice-a-week massage.

Notting Hill, on the north side of Bayswater Road, away from Kensington Palace and its gardens and surrounding parkland, had come a long way from what it was in 1949 when immigrants from the Caribbean arrived on the SS *Empire Windrush* to meet the demand for labour after the war. They brought with them their music, bright clothes and cultural exuberance. Their traditional Masquerade processions – in which their slave ancestors had been allowed once a year to copy and mock their masters' extraordinarily fine garments – gradually began to brighten the grey, northerly parts of the borough where they'd found derelict accommodation rented out by slum landlords which they might just be able to afford.

In 2002, the town's tight arses/prudes/spoilsports who could never abide a street party were still behaving predictably. When the August Bank Holiday came around that year, they, the borough's few disgruntled dwellers, drew their curtains, shut their windows, locked their doors and went to a suitably dull place elsewhere for the duration.

Two days after my mother's gig at the Hi-Hat Club, it had rained several times on the Sunday of Carnival weekend, but the Monday was bright with the sun blazing from a clear blue sky. Heidi and I spent that morning dancing in the sunshine. We started off at the Rampage soundsystem outside Number 1 Colville Square a short distance from my mother's front door along Colville Terrace. We then moved through the shimmying crowds to the Studio One System on the east side of Powis Square. The beat music there was bouncing off the houses as people around us jigged and jived, swaying, snogging, laughing and calling out to one another. Food stalls were taking money hand over fist: there was Cajun salmon, jerk chicken, fried snapper and, simmering in large metal pots beside stacks of paper plates, curried goat. Bowls of rum punch were strategically located. There were empty beer bottles and cans everywhere, already.

The echoes of the Funbunch soundsystem at Sutherland Place seemed to our ears to merge in the warm air with the vibes of the Jah Observer system off Talbot Road, creating the sensation that the huge loudspeakers stacked on top of one another were really *inside* our heads; they only *seemed* to be out on the pavements. I felt my chest vibrating with the rhythmic sounds and couldn't hear what Heidi was saying – just saw her lips moving, her eyes smiling.

We gradually made our way through the pulsating

streets to Westbourne Grove where, after trying for half an hour, had to give up the struggle to buy a drink at the bar in the Duke of Norfolk pub. That pub was so full of people crushed together trying to buy booze that I couldn't even put my hand into my pocket to get money out. So we squeezed our way interminably between the bodies of perfumed and skimpily clad women and men waving paper money overhead back to the door and outside again. Then we tried to get to the edge of the pavement to have a better view of the troupes of Mas dancers in their dazzling costumes swaying between the flower-bedecked floats on which bands of steel drummers were beating out their rhythms.

Perhaps if Heidi and I had gone to the Walmer Castle pub instead in nearby Ledbury Road, or to the Earl of Lonsdale further along Westbourne Grove, I might have escaped a lot of grief. Who knows? I might have avoided hospital and might still have all my own teeth today and a face without scars or stitch-marks across my forehead. The Duke of Norfolk pub is no longer in business; it closed for the last time a few years later when the credit crunch was biting so badly that something like 35 pubs a week were going bust. I'm sure nobody who was in that over-crowded boozer that day would have believed it would ever run out of customers.

I had my arm around Heidi's waist. The crowd of onlookers enjoying the music and the colourful spectacle in the immediate vicinity were pretty much jamming us together. The only clear space was overhead: a huge blue sky. Some individuals high up were clinging to the streetlamps to get an unobstructed view; others were sitting in upstairs windows, still others leaning over balconies, swigging beer as they clocked the procession passing by below. One man with a baby strapped to his back was standing fast at the kerb, aiming his camera and taking shots, turning and taking more shots.

I didn't link Bobbie Cullen in any way with what was about to happen – not then, anyway. Bobbie gave me *money*, not grief. She enabled me to pay off my debts, pay my college fees upfront, buy for cash the books and journals I had to read. The money I got from her made it possible to study with a mind undistracted by worries about how to afford things, how to pay for meals, how to keep up the pretence that I was too busy to have a night out with friends, or an occasional drink with them, and not too broke to do so.

I'm convinced that Bobby's largesse was one of the principal reasons why I did become a lawyer, even though I was suddenly not as easy on the eye as I used to be. When people say I'm a forbidding presence in court, they are referring to my face, my bent nose especially and lopsided eyebrows, not my cross-examining skills or the contents of my legal mind. The contents of one's mind are invisible, whereas the landscape of one's face is permanently in view, unfortunately, especially the promontory of one's nose. The first thing Heidi said when she visited me in hospital after the bandages and dressings had been removed was that I reminded her of a character in *Henderson The Rain King* whose face, she said, was described by the author as 'an unfinished cathedral'.

I'm sure, however, that Bobbie Cullen had nothing directly to do with the systematic rearrangement of my features.

The first hint I got that everything wasn't peace and goodwill to all Carnival lovers was when I felt Heidi being wrenched away from me; she was pulled bodily from my arm around her in front of the Duke of Norfolk pub. I turned and saw two guys in black T-

246

shirts push her out into the path of the dancing procession. Then they turned to me, grabbed my arms and started dragging me through the crush of people on the pavement. I wriggled and writhed, tried to shake them off, but couldn't manage it.

'Heidi!' I shouted. 'Go home! Wait there! Tell Arlene!'

I saw her face fleetingly once more against the background of the brightly coloured costumes and gleaming headgear. I wasn't sure she'd heard me in the din. My mother's house in Colville Terrace was only two streets away up Colville Road, but the dense crowds and the groups of people boogie-ing in front of the soundsystems stacked high along the thoroughfares and in front of the stalls selling tasty bites guaranteed that she'd have a struggle to get there quickly.

'What d'you want?' I shouted at the two big guys pulling me along. 'Let go of me, man!' They pretended not to hear. They didn't look like cops in their jeans and T-shirts; cops were the people I was hoping to *join* one day, not escape from. I kept yelling as they dragged me and forced their way forward through the press of torsos and limbs: 'What's your fucking problem?'

I was a law student with several years at college still to go, but I knew it was a mark of professionalism to use language appropriate to the context. They ignored my query. I wondered where they were taking me in such a determined way. Their fingers in my armpits, hands gripping my wrists, they kept pulling me through the crowds on the pavement. If anyone noticed my predicament, they probably thought I'd been drinking like everyone else and was being helped on my way by a couple of friends.

One of my abductors was a white guy with dark-brown eyes and a mop of hair which was, I now recall eight years later, not unlike the hair of 27-year-old

247

Andrey 'Shava' Arshavin, the Russian goal-scoring talent and master of the precise pass who'd recently come to Arsenal's Emirates Stadium from Zenit St Petersburg in a £12 million transfer deal swung by Arsène Wenger. Except that, unlike Arshavin, this guy had heavy rings on his fingers, a stud in the lobe of one ear and a five o'clock shadow on his face, even though it was only about eleven in the morning.

His buddy in brutality, a black guy, was wearing a pair of those fingerless driving gloves with little holes in them. He was black, not '*half* black', or '*political* black' as some people have described it, like President Barack Obama or Arsenal's impressively fast 20-year-old winger Theo Walcott – both of whom had a white mother – but *black* black, like Everton's French striker Louis Saha who scored the fastest goal in FA Cup Final history within 25 seconds at Wembley Stadium – a cracking left-footer against Chelsea from way, way out.

A black-and-white minstrel show these two guys comprised. They pulled me through the crowds to the first side street they came to, Ledbury Road; it was wide enough in normal times for two lanes of traffic, but was now chock-a-block with revellers gawping at the bare flesh of the Mas dancers swaying along the procession's main drag with shiny tiaras on their heads, their nipples barely concealed by golden cones perched on their tits. Once they'd dragged me out of Westbourne Grove, I discovered quickly what these guys wanted.

Beat the shit out of me, that's what. Which they proceeded to do straight away, no preamble, no explanation, and paying no attention to the people around us pretending for the sake of their own well-being that there was nothing untoward in this rather different Bank Holiday side-show.

The white guy hit me in the face and forehead with

248

the rings on his fingers, shearing my skin and drawing blood almost immediately. The black guy's holey gloves did nothing to cushion the impact of his punches. They took turns, a few blows from each of them, one dancing forward to let loose a two-fisted barrage then side-stepping so the other had the whole target to himself again. They switched their shots from my head to my body. The black guy knocked the wind out of me with a punch to the solar-plexus that had me gasping doubled up; the white guy then kneed me in the face. The pain in my nose was excruciating. I'd been quite fit, exercising regularly, nor was I exactly tiny at five foot eleven, but my attempts to block or to smother their punches by staying in close succeeded only partially. When I raised my arms to protect my head I was hit in the ribs with a solid whack; when I dropped my guard to cover my stomach, I'd get a one-two on the temple and jaw.

Whoever they were, these guys weren't in a hurry. They paused and exchanged ironic comments about me not being as wimpish as I looked. The white guy put a cigarette in his mouth and got a light from a passer-by in between belting and hooking me hard. The black guy snorted and ducked and weaved as though to avoid punches that never came from me.

They beat me in such a coordinated, almost choreographed, way that it occurred to me as my head jolted back that they had probably done this sort of thing before. Even when two of my teeth left my mouth on a copious spurt of blood and I wondered when my misery might come to an end, I fancied, for some reason, despite the pain they were inflicting and my difficulty breathing, that they weren't thrashing me quite as thoroughly as they easily could have done. They weren't wild, out of control. They were measured, systematic. I sensed they were deliberately holding back. At one point I thought I heard one of my ribs cracking under a body shot but the sound was drowned out by the loud zinging in my ears from a blow to my head.

I think I resigned myself after a while to the beckoning appeal of unconsciousness. Falling senseless, into coma, had a seductive pull even if, for all I knew, it might be the prelude to my death right there in the celebratory atmosphere of the Notting Hill Carnival. Where were the police? The old complaint was suddenly plain true: they were never around when you needed them. Was I about to die very near to where I was born? A rhythmic counterpoint to each combination of punches was a short blast of saxophone-and-drum music coming from the floats passing by on Westbourne Grove.

My mouth sticky with the puke-making taste of blood, my lips a dribbly swollen sensation, my nose somehow not right, I felt warm piss pouring down my legs as I fell to the cobblestones. That was when the white guy's ringed fists ceased coming at me. The black guy's gloves with holes also desisted. I stopped hearing the words of a song about raindrops falling on my head when boots started coming down instead, on to my chest and arms, and, as I tried to bunch up into a protective coil to make myself a smaller target, on to my thighs and backside and shoulder-blades. I squirmed with my back on the cobbles, reached up and grabbed one of the boots as it rose in its staccato stomping.

'Fucking cunt! He loves it! Wants to hold it!' the good Samaritan said to his philanthropic partner. 'Try this one, cunt! It's even better!'

He stamped down on the fingers of my left hand which had been lying limp on the ground, sticky and warm with my unstinting haemoglobin, my red cells, white cells, my platelets and plasma which I would much rather have donated at a blood-donor session where you get to help yourself to a cup of tea afterwards and a biscuit or a packet of salt-and-vinegar crisps.

I suddenly saw two of my teeth in front of me and wondered, in the cacophony of music and the duet of passionate cursing, what they were doing in such an unhygienic milieu. All around my two teeth, close to them, threatening bacteria, infection, were kebab wrappers, ketchup-smeared chips, chicken bones with gleaming gristle, empty beer cans crushed out of shape, the left-overs of what might have been curried goat, but I couldn't be sure: the congealing blood in my nose was interfering with my sense of smell.

'This is your first and last warning,' Holey Gloves hissed at me. 'Don't ever mess with our business again.'

'Stay the fuck out of our way,' the guy who wasn't Arshavin followed up, pointing down at me. I glimpsed smears of blood on his rings and knuckles. The stud in his ear flashed in the light. 'You come anywhere near our transactions one more time and you're dead, bruv. You hear? It won't be fists that do for you.'

What business are you in? I wanted to ask. What is your vocation, your career path? But I wasn't able to coordinate my swollen lips with my smudged-down tongue or get enough of a puff out of my voice-box to articulate what I considered to be a reasonable question.

When had I come anywhere near their transactions? In what way had I 'messed' with their business? I had no rings on my fingers for slicing people's skin. I had no holey gloves. I clearly didn't have the means to make my way on their patch or to mix with men who had their kind of venom. I had no clue what I was supposed to have done.

Where, I wondered, were their business premises?

Where, I tried to think when they left me at last to groan and ache and seep blood in peace and shimmied away to grind their hips to the beat elsewhere, might I have unwittingly stumbled on their enterprise?

The rhythmic drumming and the blasts of horns coming from behind my head on the cobblestones and bouncing off the walls of the surrounding buildings didn't exactly make cogitation easy. I found it hard to think joined-up thoughts. I found myself stitching together images, memories and non-sequiturs into a kaleidoscope of brilliantly coloured nonsense. The mental mishmash was vivid.

Was this, I wondered as I lay damaged, the way men like Bolton's Amir Khan felt when pounded mercilessly in the ring where he went on to become world king? Was this what Manchester's Ricky Hatton suffered when Manny Pacquiao knocked him down twice in the first round of their world title fight in Las Vegas then knocked him stone cold in the last minute of the second round? 'I didn't have to count,' the referee said.

At least those pros know in advance the time and venue of their bouts. They train. They do roadwork. They spar and skip and do shadow-boxing. I had no training at all. No tickets were sold, no TV rights. Out of the blue I was dragged away and set upon by a couple of incognito combatants, without the benefit even of a referee or timekeeper. And there was no purse at the end of the beating, no hard-earned cash. Just the lumps and the gashes and the missing teeth.

No wonder I couldn't think clearly. Heidi and I had been having such a good time moments before, dancing and hugging and kissing in the streets, that bad vibes, bad scenes, were completely forgotten.

Poor Heidi. What had *she* done to be manhandled

like that?

Who had *she* upset or antagonized?

Who would have a grudge against *her*? Be jealous of *her*?

I touched my fingers gingerly to my lips, prised them carefully apart and, after spitting out sticky red saliva that hung like long wires from my mouth down to the cobblestones, found the gap in my upper teeth. I felt the cold keening as I sucked in air; a nerve was surely exposed. I twisted at the waist and tried to push myself up into a sitting position. It took a while, a few agonizing goes. Finally, my back was sagged against the wall.

And that was when I twigged. Sagged against that wall, I suddenly understood this visitation of grief.

The *transaction* had been in that cubicle of the Hi-Hat Club. The one marked *Private No Entry* across from the men's and women's lavatories where I saw a young woman slumped backwards on a toilet seat with a needle and syringe sticking out of her arm.

The smell. I suddenly recalled the smell, like cloth burning; I remembered thinking it might be a stocking burning. The smell, rising above the cubicle, was from the wool that junkies use to filter the heated heroin; that's what gave off the smell of burning fibre. And on the ceiling I'd seen what looked like the flickering shadows of flames.

The dealer in his silver-grey suit and green tie standing beside the woman was counting a fat wad of notes. It didn't bother him at all in his matching green hat that she was struggling to breathe or that her skin was turning blue right next to him. She had thick brown hair and looked to be the same age as Heidi; she was slumped back on the seat, her torso quaking with spasms.

That was it, for sure, the transactions those two guys

were on about. That was the business I'd supposedly messed with. That slimy dealer in his shiny suit had glared at me with daggers in his eyes and said: 'That's not what *I'd* like. This fucker owes me.' He wagged his finger at me and fumed: 'You're gonna be sorry for what you did, bruv.'

That was the link, no doubt. That was the explanation. Bobbie Cullen wasn't involved at all. The only connection Bobbie had with it was that she'd arranged the gig at the Hi-Hat Club where my mother was such a big hit and where the MC told everyone in the audience that she was going to be doing her stuff fairly soon at the Village Vanguard in Manhattan.

And yet.

Why didn't it satisfy me, that explanation?

Why did I feel that there was something *justified* about the way they beat me up? Something poetic, as in poetic justice.

I'd long had a strange, sinister feeling that I would have to pay one day for betraying Heidi, for making money behind her back.

I hated those bastards for what they'd done to me. And yet somewhere in my heart I didn't really hate them: not with any rancour. To hate them felt as though it would be continuing my betrayal of Heidi. It would be denying my culpability, which did deserve punishment.

That was the thought that made me feel perhaps they had damaged my brain with their fists and not just my face. They'd hit me on the temple, forehead, nose and cheekbones so many times. Was I going the way of Muhammad Ali, slurred of speech and unsteady of step from all the poundings to the head he'd taken in the ring, especially from Smokin' Joe Frazier?

Would *I* be slurring next time I saw Heidi? Slurring at the age of 20?

Would Heidi want to look at my face any more, I wondered. Would she want to be seen with me in public again? How long before she'd be able to hug me without making my ribs scream in pain?

The revellers in Ledbury Road paused for a moment and gazed at the bloody spectacle I presented: my shirt and jeans a mess of gore, my trainers splattered red. The way they looked at me, I felt like an animal in a cage, an animal with an aching torso, a somewhat stiff, funny feeling in its face, and rising and receding noises in its ears. Despite my discomfort, I clocked the pity – or was it just pseudo fellow feeling? – in their eyes when they glanced my way.

Not one of them, for a long while, came forward to ask if I needed any help. Fucking tourists.

Then, when I was beginning to wonder how I was going to get up and get home to check if Heidi was all right, a guy and his girlfriend came over. They squatted on the cobbles in front of me. They both had freckles. He had a green tartan tam-o'-shanter on his head with a white pom-pom on top. She was wearing a green tartan skirt. They looked closely at my face.

'These contusions are serious,' she said in an accent that reminded me of how Sir Alex Ferguson sounded when he commented on camera after a Man U match. 'Your nose under the blood looks bent. It might be broken. With all these gashes you need an anti-tetanus shot. Your eyes are bloody. D'you understand what I'm saying? You need medical attention right away.'

'She's a trainee doctor,' her companion said, also in an accent which reminded me that Sir Alex played for Dunfermline, Rangers and Aberdeen before he started his management career. 'She knows what she's talking about – works in a hospital. You aren't looking good, feller,' he said, shaking his head. 'Been fighting, haven't you?' He turned his head to her and said:

'Doesn't smell drunk.'

'D'you know where you are?' she asked me and I felt her breath on my face. 'What's your name?'

'It's,' it was as though my mouth wasn't used to shaping words, or my lips were out of synch, 'it's…'

'Can you remember your name?' she asked again, and when I failed to reply, not because I'd forgotten, I don't think, but because my speaking apparatus was messed up, for the time being anyway, she said to her boyfriend or husband: 'Come, let's lift him up,' and to me: 'We'll get you to a taxi. Okay? We'll take you to hospital.'

While they were helping me to get up off the ground surrounded by rubbish, one of them on either side of me, a hand each in an armpit, a sharp pain shrilled along my arm. Then it shrilled again, hurting like a bugger. I looked at it; it seemed skew, sticking out at a daft angle. But my *eyes* might have been skew.

Her eyes were blue. They met my bleary ones. 'It's probably broken,' she said, then added in her Scottish accent and with a smile that was friendly and phlegmatic at the same time, 'but that isn't the end of the world. They'll re-set it, put it in plaster.'

I hoped this couple would make a phone-call for me. I wanted to be sure Heidi was all right. I hoped she'd got through the crowds safely.

As I shuffled along between those Celtic Samaritans, one arm over the man's shoulder, my ribcage burning, blood seeping from my mouth in which my tongue felt much larger than usual, making me choke and want to retch, Lester's face flashed into my mind's eye. Where were the police, the enforcers of law and order I was aspiring to join, when I needed them so badly? Was Lester really against the Met, I wondered, or just against white three-piece suits.

My aching, burning ribs; my mashed lips; all the

slashes and cuts in my face and forehead making my skin feel that it was sizzling, my broken arm and flattened fingers; my two gone teeth, swollen tongue and inability to speak, to utter anything at all, as though I'd been stripped of my higher faculties: twinges and pangs and stinging sensations overlaying the crushed feeling in my nose – it all gradually congealed as I shuffled to where there might be a taxi into a crystal realization.

You've seen the last of Primrose Hill and Bobbie Cullen. That's for sure. No more hot baths with her foot along your thighs. No more meals sitting naked at the table under the gaze of her dark pink nipples. No more exotic fifty-two-year-old gushing her pleasure voluminously, then asking straight out after a doze to be taken from behind. It's the end for you also of ad lib lessons in Latin syntax and grammar, and of brown A5 envelopes loaded with lolly.

Count your blessings, Leo Allen. Some of them are already in the bank. You have the money to fork out for all your fees – in cash, upfront, no interest to pay, no debts piling up.

I tried to console myself, tried to assuage the pain in my face and ribs and lift my spirits as I shuffled along between my two helpers. Go to all the lectures, I urged myself. Research and write the essays well in time. Stay with it and complete the course. You'll be a lawyer yet; your time will come. You'll blast the bastards for what they did to Arlene for so many years. With carefully planned stings, you'll bust the drug dealers and their suppliers, and, steadily, in due course, in collaboration with other cops, the barons in overall control too – one by one.

But your time of seeing London from a limo, and paying cash for everything, has ended. This is the end of selling yourself, of acting on the advice of careers advisers and business gurus. Your nights of pleasuring an older woman for good pay, of making money as a freelance prostitute, are over.

Acknowledgements

Ruth Florence is a trained classicist who at one time taught Latin and Greek and now proofreads books for publishers. Her ears are attuned to metre and cadence. She listened patiently when I read aloud various passages in the course of writing this novel. (Bum notes do spoil sentences, even though, curiously, they *can* re-grab your attention, the way Thelonious Monk's dissonances do in compositions such as 'Well you needn't' and 'Epistrophy'.)

It was my wife Ruth who introduced me to the love poems of Catullus, in Latin, for which I have long been indebted to her. This book is a token of my gratitude for her companionship and many insightful intimations.

Enver Carim, Greater London, February 2014
envercarim@yahoo.co.uk